FACES IN THE FOG

19 Intriguing Short Stories

STEVEN HAGY

WingSpan Press

Printed in the United States of America

Published by WingSpan Press, Livermore, CA
www.wingspanpress.com

The WingSpan name, logo and colophon are the trademarks of WingSpan Publishing.

ISBN 978-1-59594-229-6

First edition 2008

Library of Congress Control Number 2008921014

Cover Artist: Clay Butler
Cover Photograph: Steven Hagy
Cover Model: Wendy Bruce
Story Consultant: Craig Barnett
Proofreader: Linda Weller
Doce Robles Winery: Wonderful friends, great wine, heavenly vineyards, and an inspiring place to write.

Contents

Fog: uncertain or confused state of mind.

To my sons,
GARY, KEVIN, AND JEFFREY

THE DROP ZONE

TODD BUNDT CROUCHED in jump position on the landing gear strut of the single-prop plane. He clutched the wing support bar as the wind whipped around him at 70 mph. His face was gaunt and etched with despair as he stared down at the landscape. Mother Earth looked heavenly with her sparkling canals, and patchwork of fields, vineyards, and orchards. Regardless of her splendor, Todd contemplated jumping without opening his chute.

Earlier that morning, after a long, hot shower, Todd had dressed and made a strong pot of coffee. He grabbed a cup, then stepped out to the porch, where he picked up the Sunday paper and sat in a plastic deck chair. Exhausted and troubled, he leaned back, heaved a heavy sigh, and watched the sunrise.

His century-old farmhouse and weathered barn sat on a two-acre parcel surrounded by forty acres of pistachio trees. Lawn and flowerbeds embraced the home. Dirt, weeds, and tractor marks surrounded the barn. A gravel driveway parted the short distance between the two structures. The single-story Queen Anne house was of simple design, with a covered porch that hugged its front and sides.

Todd had completely remodeled the interior of the house with new carpet and tile, plumbing and lighting fixtures, ceiling fans, and a skylight. He looked over at a drop cloth and a can of yellow paint in the corner of the porch. With just a few more brushstrokes, he would finish painting the bright yellow lap siding of the house. He could then move on to the semi-gloss white trim. The old place looked quite cheerful with its new paint, despite the unhappiness that dwelled within.

He glanced at the orchard and noticed the morning sunbeams filtering through the leaves, shining on the pinkish clusters of nuts. He hung his head, closing his eyes. His farm had produced a bumper crop, but in the current surplus market, he stood to lose money. He had worked so hard—for nothing.

He finished his coffee and headed to the kitchen for a refill, finding his wife Jadee pouring a cup.

"Good morning," said Todd without enthusiasm.

"It would be good, if I wasn't so tired and buried with work," she complained, setting the coffeepot down.

As Todd picked up the pot and began to pour, he shot back, "Maybe it would help if you didn't stay up so late, giggling on your cell phone with Anthony, Mr. BMW."

"Please Todd, it's too early for an argument, okay, but for your information, tomorrow's the final day of the case and he was helping me with my closing statement, so quit jumping to conclusions." She took a sip of her hot coffee.

"Well, where there's smoke, there's fire," Todd snapped. "And the smoke is thick, babe, so the fire must be hot!"

"That's silly Todd, and I refuse to argue about it!" She walked a few steps into the dining room, set her coffee on the table, and said, "Though there is something else I'd like to ask you about. Are you planning to fix that skylight anytime soon? Every time it rains—it leaks. You've been promising me for two months, and it still isn't done, and it's supposed to rain next week."

"Cut me some slack, please! I've been painting this damn house for the last two months so the weather doesn't destroy it!"

"I know Todd, but during the last storm it dripped so much water it stained our bedspread and ruined the carpet. Please, just fix it!"

2

"I'll fix it, all right? But one last thing: With all I've been going through—my dad, my mother, the store, and this farm—why can't you show me a little affection? Why don't you laugh with me like you do with Anthony?"

"How can you possibly expect me to laugh when I'm so unhappy? We've discussed this a million times: I want to leave this farm town and move to Sacramento. I'm tired of the forty-mile commute. And, I need to be closer to my clients and associates."

"You mean Anthony, don't you?"

"Again Todd, please don't go there. Anthony and I are just friends!"

"Well, what about kids? We've waited for six years. When are we going to start a fam…?"

"I'm not ready yet!" Jadee yelled, cutting him off. "You know that! I'm doing really well as a junior partner, and I can't slow my momentum to birth babies and wash diapers. My father sacrificed as well as you and I to get me through law school. I'm not going to throw my career away!"

"Well, okay then, Jadee, let's just say that I'm unhappy too, and that good ol' Todd has had enough!"

"And what do you mean by that?" she questioned, as if she were cross-examining a witness.

"Well…" Todd took a deep breath, trying to calm down.

"What are you going to do, Todd?" she pressed.

Todd wanted to talk to her about his anguish, but doubted she would listen—or even care. "I guess," he spat, turning to leave, "I'm going to fix the leaky skylight!"

"Oh—okay," she said, surprised by his answer. "Are you still going skydiving?"

He stopped, turned, and shot her a smoldering look. Todd knew exactly why she was asking. She noticed a darkness creep over the features of his face, like the sudden dimming of daylight when a rain cloud drifts in front of the sun. She took a step back.

"Yes Jadee," he replied in a voice of disdain, clenching his teeth, "of course I am." As he turned to leave, a slight smirk slinked from the corner of his mouth. He then ambled out to the barn for his extension ladder.

Jadee felt uneasy about his response, but dismissed it, and sashayed off to the shower.

As Todd sealed the leak around the see-through, Sun & Stars skylight, he looked down at their bed directly beneath it. He caulked a bit more, then looked again, seeing Jadee, naked, and entering the bedroom.

She peered up through the skylight at him, frowned, and said, "Why don't you grow up, Todd?"

"Is it wrong," he shouted, so she could hear him through the skylight, "that I cherish my beautiful wife?"

She ignored him.

He continued to gaze down at her as she dressed. He adored her Oriental features: long, lustrous, black hair, almond shaped eyes, and soft flawless skin. Her aerobic classes had perfected her body into firm sensuous curves.

He recalled a trip they had taken to Mendocino two years earlier—before she had started practicing at the firm. They had spent a week wine tasting amidst picturesque vineyards in Anderson Valley, hiked among gigantic redwoods, and dined in restaurants overlooking the jagged rocks and whitecapped waves of the northern coast. They had held hands, cuddled, kissed, and laughed. Every night they made love with great passion and pleasure. They were happy. He still burned with desire for her, but she shunned him.

Once dressed, she left the bedroom, and sat at the dining table to review trial documents.

Within an hour, Todd had repaired the skylight, climbed down the ladder, and, without a goodbye to his wife, sped off to the airfield a mile or so from his house.

Jadee watched out the window as Todd drove his pick-up truck down and out of the driveway. She pushed speed dial and then the send button on her cell phone.

The tiny airfield had two drab buildings and a pitted landing strip just long enough for small planes and ultralights. One building housed the modest tower, the other, "SkyFly," a skydiving club and jump school.

To the west of the asphalt runway was a sixty-acre clearing with a thirty-foot yellow circle painted on the ground. From any jump altitude, parachutists could clearly target the yellow ringed drop zone.

In the chute room, Todd rigged, and then packed his parachute. He stretched his tight, free-fly jumpsuit over his six-foot muscular body, pulled on his gloves, and strapped an altimeter around his wrist. He brushed back his dark hair, then put on his helmet and goggles. He let them rest on his helmet, just above the despair in his listless blue eyes. Skydiving had become second nature to him. He wasn't a "newbie," because he had earned his basic license and owned his equipment, but he wasn't a "skygod" either since he had only made twenty-nine jumps.

Zack, one of the two jumpmasters, already wearing his rig with harness and pack, popped in, and said, "Dude, are you like ready to fly? I mean like, totally ready to soar?"

"Uh—sure Zack. Yeah—ready to fly," Todd replied in a monotone.

"Oh, dude, what's the matter? You seem like, mega-bummed, man."

"I just have a lot on my mind Zack. I'll be ready in a couple of minutes."

Zack glanced out the door at Wade, the pilot, and Reno, the other jump instructor, who were climbing into the plane. He turned back to Todd and hollered, "Bro, let's do it! It's boogie time! And remember, leave your woes on the ground and focus on slicing sky!"

As the high-wing, Cessna U206 lifted off and gained altitude, Todd peered expressionless out the right rear window. The pilot sat in the plane's only seat, while the three jumpers sat on the floor facing each other.

From the lofty altitude, Todd could see the breadth of the small city and the farming community that surrounded it. His eyes followed Main Street to the railroad tracks, where he located the gray roof of his family's store, Bundt's Hardware. It had survived sixty years in business, beginning with his grandfather, then his father, and now him. His grandfather had been gone for a decade, but his father's recent heart failure had caused Todd unbearable grief. He remembered the days when business was slow, and his dad's cousin Frank would run the store, permitting Todd and his dad to go fishing at the Delta, or duck hunting at the bogs of Los Banos. His dad had always listened, and shared his wisdom, but now, he was gone.

Not far from Bundt's, the plane flew over the gigantic roof and vast parking lot of a national chain store that had lured his customers away, forcing him into bankruptcy. The closing of the family's store saddened him. He had worked there since he was ten years old. He would miss helping the customers, the sound of nails dropping in a paper bag, and the flying sparks when making keys. He looked away from the window, cradling his helmeted head in his gloved hands.

As the plane banked, he looked out again to see the roofs of homes, along with their yards and pools. He spotted the city park with its fountain, and its entire block of treetops. Across from the park was the nursing home where his mother—suffering from Alzheimer's— lived. He missed how she used to talk excitedly, describing in detail about anyone or anything that she deemed meaningful. When he had last seen her, a few days before, she had no longer recognized him. She just lay in bed watching TV, ignoring him, and not speaking a word. He leaned his helmet against the plane's window, feeling overwhelmed.

As the airplane buzzed beyond the city limits and over farmland, and reached jump altitude, Reno popped open the door, allowing the loud and turbulent wind to rush in. The door rolled overhead on its tracks and locked. Todd maneuvered on his knees to the open door. He fastened the chinstrap on his helmet, and pulled his goggles over his eyes. He stepped out, gripping the wing support bar, while crouching on the peg of the landing gear strut.

Undaunted, Todd peered down at the ground. The plane's line of flight was approaching the airspace over his farm. He spotted his forty acres of trees, his house, and, as he expected, he saw Anthony's BMW parked in the driveway. Beyond his land, he spied the airfield and the prominent yellow circle of the drop zone. The thought of Anthony alone with his wife made his mind sting with jealousy.

Anthony looked up into the enchanting eyes of Jadee. The sun's rays from the skylight glinted off her glossy black hair, and her perfect skin was softer than he had ever known. An affair with an Asian woman was something new for him. He closed his eyes in ecstasy, as she leaned down and kissed his shoulder, then sighed a warm breath into his ear. Breathing heavily, he opened his eyes, and gazed up at the blue sky through the skylight. He felt as though he were drifting among the clouds.

Jadee admired Anthony; he was a top gun attorney with highly publicized cases. Who knew how far he would go: judge, senator, or governor? He had it all: talent, class, wealth, good looks, and contacts. She realized their relationship was shallow, and mostly sexual, but she was confident, overtime it would grow deeper.

Todd, ready to bail, turned and glanced into the plane at

Reno and Zack. Both were grinning, with their thumbs up. All they lived for was the thrill of their next jump, cutting through altitude at a hundred miles an hour. They didn't have a clue about Todd's intentions.

Todd nodded his head, popped a thumbs up, then turned back to the aerial view of the drop zone—the big yellow circle. For a fleeting moment, he stared down at the landing mark while his mind raced, and then, with a wry smile, he dove into naked sky.

Once in freefall, Todd moved into the basic arch position making an "L" with each arm, and then curved his back to create drag. He then relaxed into a box position with his face, chest, stomach, and thighs parallel to the ground. From his jump altitude, he had calculated about 45 seconds of freefall, and to live another day, he needed to pull the ripcord at 4,000 feet.

After Todd jumped, Reno stepped out into floater position on the strut, flashed a wide grin at Zack, and then bailed into the wind.

"You go dude!" Zack hollered, then he stepped out to stand on the strut. His mind was psyched, his body pumped, and he was set to fly. He glanced down to see Reno soaring like a bird, but to his alarm, he saw that Todd's chute had not opened, and he was dangerously close to the ground. He waited a few seconds, stepped back in from the blue, leaned toward the cockpit, and yelled, "Wade! Wade!"

The startled pilot turned; surprised that Zack was still onboard.

"Wade, get on the radio! Get on the radio now man and take us down!"

As Todd hurtled down at a blurring speed, he checked his altimeter. It flashed a "dirt alert," a blinking red light warning that the ground was rapidly approaching. He had just passed below 4,000 feet without deploying his parachute. As sky dashed by, and the earth swelled, his mind screamed: *Pull the ripcord! There's always hope! Pull it before it's too late!*

His will to die over-powered his desire to live. He stared without blinking, and maneuvered his plummeting body into a delta position, pointing his head toward the ground, with his arms slanted back like the wings of a jet, and his legs stretched out in a "V." As his incredible fall rate increased, he steered precisely over the fast expanding yellow circle. He thought: *Nail it man, nail it in the center.*

At Zack's beckoning, Wade, radioed the tower, who dispatched emergency vehicles to the drop zone.

Seconds from death, the ground zooming in, Todd had positioned himself to hammer dead center into the yellow circle of the drop zone.

As the earth became huge, and the ground consumed his total field of vision, the reality of his fate hit him. His protective mind talked fast: *What am I doing? I can overcome all my hardships. It's not worth dying over a cheating wife. Maybe, just maybe, there is hope for me. There's always hope!*

Hope and the instinct to live changed his mind. With all of his might, he jerked the ripcord. The pilot chute popped out dragging with it the main canopy. The canopy needed time to fill with air. He was too late. Unopened, the parachute streamed out above him without reducing his force of impact. Todd crashed into the earth at over 200 miles an hour.

Detective Tom Lockman pulled into the driveway of the quaint farmhouse surrounded by pistachio trees. He walked around a fire truck and the two ambulances, and stepped into the house. Ricky, one of the ambulance drivers said, "Hey Tom, we've got a really strange scene in the bedroom. There's three victims, all DOA. There was nothing we could do."

Without a reply, he squeezed Ricky's arm, then entered the bedroom. With twenty-three years of experience, he had never seen the like. Amidst the debris were three bodies: two naked—a man and a woman—and a dead skydiver. The parachute's rigging stretched out of the skydiver's pack up through the hole in the ceiling, where the nylon canopy blocked out the sunlight. It was as though there had been an explosion in the room. Strewn about were pieces of the shattered skylight, splintered wood, and shingles. The headboard of the bed had smashed through the exterior wall. The footboard had shot across the room, crashing into a dresser and bursting a large mirror into small reflective pieces. Like a hen house after a fox raid, scattered pillow feathers littered the room.

As he surveyed the odd accident, his partner Dave walked in, and exclaimed, "Tom, you're not going to believe this!"

"Try me Dave, what is it?"

"Well, first of all, one of the fire department paramedics knows the couple who own the house. He confirmed that the woman is Jadee Bundt and the skydiver is her husband, Todd Bundt. The other victim, apparently, was her lover. But this is the part you're not going to believe: When I checked the perimeter, I noticed an extension ladder reaching up to the roof, so I climbed up to take a look. Once I shifted the parachute out of the way, I noticed something weird." He shook his head, looked directly at Tom, and said, "Up on the roof, where the skylight used to be—someone has painted a big yellow circle!"

Poison Goro

"S AKE!" YELLED THE old beggar. "And sushi!"

"No more sake!" snapped the inflamed chef. "And no more sushi! You shout outside my restaurant door every night and scare away my customers. Soon I will have none. Go away, before I call the police again."

The beggar, Goro Shiga, stood next to a rusty, banged up dumpster, in the dingy alley, at the back door of the restaurant. Fog, slipping under the Golden Gate Bridge, and drifting down the San Francisco streets, rolled past him like trolley cars made of mist. The downcast glow of a grimy, bare light bulb exposed him, a pitiful figure, hunched in the night, with the creases of old age and the gutters of suffering evident upon his face. He was, as he appeared, homeless and destitute: gray tousled hair and unkempt beard stiff with dirt; suit coat, shirt, and slacks soiled and wrinkled; dress shoes scuffed without a glint of shine; his tie lost—like his dignity.

"Sake!" And sushi!" Goro screamed again, ignoring the chef's warning, knowing all too well that the police would simply escort him to the shelter, and then he'd return.

"No sake, nor sushi from me!" growled the chef, Hiroshi Eto. He stood inside the back doorway of Eto's, his small sushi bar located in the heart of the city, just up a hill from the Golden Gate Park and the Japanese Tea Gardens. He wore the traditional white smock and baggy pants of a sushi chef, a red neckerchief, and a white *taffeta toque*: a round, brimless, satin hat. His face, glowing in the stark light, bared shadows of disdain.

"For over three months, Goro, I have tried to show you kindness, but with the recent passing of my dear wife from cancer, and with my daughter, running away with her low-life boyfriend, I am overwhelmed with grief, plus I am overburdened, preparing the food, serving customers, cleaning tables, and washing dishes. I am barely surviving, let alone dealing with you. Go away and beg at another door. I am sorry, but I will not collect the leftover sake or sushi for you any longer."

"But if not you," replied Goro with a raspy voice from yelling, "then who will show me kindness? If my own wife Momo, had not been murdered in the robbery, I would not have drank myself into bankruptcy, and I would still have my jewelry store, and I would still be an esteemed businessman in this neighborhood, and I would not be begging at your door. During the war at the internment camp—I had my wife. She had me. When our daughter Momoto, overdosed and died down on Haight-Ashbury in 1967—I had my wife. She had me. We helped each other survive. Like you, without my wife and daughter, I cannot survive. I am alone—I am penniless—and I am a drunk, so please," he whispered, then demanded loudly, "Sake! And sushi!"

"I will not! I must get back to my customers. Please, go away!"

"I will not! I will shout at your door until your kindness is awakened."

As Hiroshi slammed the door shut, locked it, and went back to waiting on his diners, he heard Goro yell, "Sake! And sushi!"

Mr. Matsuo, a wealthy businessman, and a rotund, enthusiastic eater, shifted his sumo-size buttocks on his bar stool, and grumbled, "Mr. Eto, why do you ignore me, your best customer, who is waiting for his green tea ice cream, and instead mess with that worthless bum?" He drew in a quick breath, pounded his chest twice with his fist, belched, and then continued, "He is an old, drunken fool. It is heartbreaking what happened to his wife, unfortunate that he lost his business, and pitiful that he has no family to care for him. He would be better off dead. Nevertheless, he is not, because we hear him shouting. I must inform you, that there is much talk from your regular customers about dining at Yakamoto's instead of here. He doesn't have the skills of a master chef like you, nor does he have a license to prepare *fugu*, but, nor does he have a beggar yelling incessantly at his back door every night."

"I am so sorry Mr. Matsuo. Even when I refuse him, he will not go away. I have called the police, social services, and the temple, but there is no help for him."

A middle-aged couple sitting at a table, two University of San Francisco students sitting at another, and a traveling businessman at the bar interjected that the noisy man disturbed them also.

Hiroshi bowed and apologized to them as well, and feeling flustered, he abruptly changed the subject, asking Mr. Matsuo, "How was the *tora-fugu-sashi*?"

"Ohhh, it was delightful, Mr. Eto," praised Mr. Matsuo. "The slices so thinly delicate, I could see the plate's colorful design through them. And the *ponzu* dipping sauce—very delicious!"

"Thank you. You honor me."

"Who would of thought," remarked Mr. Matsuo, as he glanced over at the six fishes swimming in the saltwater aquarium, "that those *tora-fugu*, when frightened, swell into a spiky ball, and that their neurotoxin is twelve-hundred times deadlier than cyanide. Just one tiger-pufferfish has enough poison to kill over thirty people, and yet—I crave the *fugu's* subtle flavor, the tingling on my tongue, and the fearful thrill that maybe the chef slipped up."

"As happened in the case of one of Japan's famous Kabuki actors," said Hiroshi. "The chef unwittingly served him *fugu* liver. The actor ingested a lethal amount of toxin, followed immediately with numbness in his mouth, stomach pain, nausea, paralysis, and with no antidote, he died within twenty-four hours. Though the thrill of possible death is part of the dining experience Mr. Matsuo, I assure you, that I, with experience and skill, know exactly how to prepare the deadly fish. You will enjoy it, and live to taste it again."

"Ahhh yes, indeed, Mr. Eto." said Mr. Matsuo. "Thank you for the reassurance. As they say in Japan—I want to eat *fugu*, but I don't want to die."

Hiroshi served Mr. Matsuo his *matcha* ice: green tea ice cream, and then thanked the other diners, bidding them goodnight as all of them left.

Mr. Matsuo ate the frozen dessert with pleasure, and then set down his napkin, paid for his meal, and strolled toward the door to leave. With his hand on the doorknob, he stopped, turned, and warned Hiroshi, "Mr. Eto, I would hate to see you lose your customers, thus lose your restaurant, all because of a screaming tramp, and I would miss my *tora-fugu*, so please—do something about it."

"Thank you for your concern Mr. Matsuo," said Hiroshi as he bowed to the large man. "You are my most valued customer. I will think of a solution."

Mr. Matsuo returned the bow, and spouted, "Please do. Goodnight," and then disappeared into the foggy night.

Hiroshi locked the door behind the beefy man, finished cleaning up the tables, the sushi bar, and the kitchen, removed his neckerchief and his hat, and then loosened his smock. He sat down in a chair at a table next to the fish tank. In the stillness, with only the sound of the gurgling air bubbles, he sipped a small cup of hot sake, while mesmerized by the pear-shaped *tora-fugu*.

"Sake! And sushi!" screamed Goro, disturbing the peacefulness.

Frustrated with Goro, Hiroshi tapped on the aquarium with

his knuckles, frightening the swimming delicacies to expand into prickly globes. He watched them floating, fluttering, until he bowed his head, his face in both hands, and wept. He missed his dear wife Natsuko. How unfair it was, that at forty-one, she would die so young, suffering such an agonizing death, and he, at only forty-three, a widower. He needed her by his side, at the restaurant, in the city, and in their bed. He missed and worried about his little girl, Kiku, seventeen, petite, pretty, and a missing run-away somewhere out in the menacing city with a troubled young man.

Hiroshi knew, that the quarrel with her the night she had left, was not so much about her spending less time with her boyfriend and helping more hours at the sushi bar, but it was about her anger and sadness over losing her loving mother, and his anger and sadness over losing his beloved wife. If only they could have reached out to each other in their grief.

"Sake! And sushi!" Goro yelled again.

Hiroshi stopped weeping, as his grief altered into fury. Oh, how he hated Goro for tormenting him at a time of so much grief. With a scowl upon his face, he stared at the poisonous puffers, now deflating back to their usual size, and realized that, right in front of him swam the solution. It was simple: Poison Goro.

After a few more minutes of watching the fish, and pondering murderous thoughts, he finished sipping his sake, shut off the lights, and trudged up the stairs to his apartment above the restaurant. Exhausted, he nodded off to sleep even as Goro shouted, "Sake! And sushi!"

The night was darker and the fog thicker as Goro, hoarse, weary, and cold, finally gave up yelling, and left the alley. As he walked the half-mile back to his cardboard box under an onramp to the 101 freeway, he shuffled past his jewelry store, now a pawnshop. He peered at the deadbolt lock, the same lock, now re-keyed, that he had twisted open and shut countless times for over thirty-five years. It now, not only locked him out of his store and small apartment in the rear, but it locked him out of the honorable life he once lived. He peered in through the window, as his thoughts lurched back to the day of the robbery—he, changing a light bulb in the jewelry case; his wife Momo, preparing the bank deposit. Suddenly, the loud door buzzer, two men, black ski masks—terror, guns, threats, crashing glass, grabbing, stealing, and then—crazed power, cocked pistols, pleading, and wild eyes. Boom! Boom! A fatal gunshot to Momo's chest. A bullet grazes his skull. Momo's funeral. Days and nights, weeks, and months of grief, sake, despair, and more sake. Past due, bankruptcy, IRS, locked doors, homeless, hopeless, hungry, and begging at Eto's alley door, screaming, "Sake! And sushi!"

Goro dropped to his knees next to the pawnshop's door, and sobbed over the loss of his daughter, his wife, and his life. As a police car slowly approached, he stood up, tramped the rest of the way to the overpass, and crawled inside his cardboard box—a discarded refrigerator box. He slept fitfully, waking up from the pangs of his indigence, and the roars of cars accelerating up the ramp overhead.

Weeks passed, and Goro yelled at Eto's back door every evening hoping to awaken Hiroshi's kindness. Because of the nuisance of Goro, diners stopped coming into Eto's, except for Mr. Matsuo, who craved his *tora-fugu*.

One night, as Goro hollered, "Sake! And sushi!" out in the alley, Mr. Matsuo sat on his usual barstool and spoke with a grave tone to Hiroshi. "Mr. Eto, I see that it will be another night with me as your only patron, and I still hear the beggar at your back door."

"I am grateful that you have come," said Hiroshi. "As you know, I have filed for a restraining order, but I receive little or no support from the police. Goro always returns."

"Well, regardless of my voracity for your *fugu*, I wanted to inform you, that I will not be dining here again. Your sushi is pleasing, but the beggar is annoying. As for tonight, I will order *fugu*, and enjoy it."

"Again, I am so sorry," said Hiroshi, as he served Mr. Matsuo a bowl of *miso* soup, and then walked over to the *fugu* tank. "Goro is very distressing for me, and I fear that I will become as crazy as he is." Using a small net with a handle, he caught one of the fish, which immediately puffed up into a ball. He then returned to the sushi preparation table behind the bar. "And I apologize that I have to apologize to you every time you come in."

"Hiroshi, stop apologizing," said Mr. Matsuo. "You have the answer to your loud panhandler problem right before your eyes, on your table, and very close to the edge of your sharp knife." He then pursed his lips to the rim of the soup bowl, sipped, swallowed, and exhaled, "Ahhh," then continued, expressing his thoughts. "A few bites of *tora-fugu* prepared the *wrong* way for him, will surely relieve you of your distress. Give the bum his sake and sushi."

"No. What you are suggesting, I could never do," said Hiroshi, as he nonchalantly killed the fish with a quick slice from his *fugu-hiki*: a special razor-sharp knife for slicing *fugu*.

"Ah, but Hiroshi, think about it. It would be merciful to put him out of his misery. If he could get his hands on enough sake, he would drink himself to death. He wants to die. No one cares about the old man, except that he is an embarrassing eyesore to our fine neighborhood. Besides, the way he rummages through all the dumpsters, who'll know how he died, or more so, who'll even care? It would surely be ruled a natural death, without an inquiry or an autopsy."

"But what if there were? I am the only chef with a license to prepare *fugu*, they will suspect me of murder." He cautiously sliced the fish, but as he cut away the poisonous liver and ovaries from the delicate meat, his hand trembled for the first time.

"Ah, it was, but an accident; a slip of the knife. You might lose your license temporarily, but they would most likely suspect that he had climbed into your dumpster and ate rotten garbage. Plus, how could they even suspect such a distinguished businessman as yourself, grieving for his wife and run away daughter?"

Hiroshi became quiet, as he contemplated Mr. Matsuo's words.

Mr. Matsuo stopped talking, because he wanted Hiroshi to concentrate on the preparation of the *fugu*, so there would be no err of the knife.

Hiroshi arranged the slices of *fugu-sashi* on a plate, in the intricate pattern of a crane about to take flight: a symbol of longevity in Japan. He then poured into a small ceramic bowl, a dipping sauce, made with soy, scallions, radish, red pepper, lemon and other spices. He served the dish to Mr. Matsuo, and then prepared the *fugu-kara-age*: thin slices floured and fried. He placed this before Mr. Matsuo, along with *fugu-hire-zake*: a cup of hot sake drink with a grilled *fugu* fin.

Mr. Matsuo moaned with pleasure with each bite and sip. Upon finishing his meal after a dessert of *taiyaki*: a fish shaped cake filled with sweet *azuki* bean paste, he burst out, "Mr. Eto, thank you again for the delicious food, and the beautiful presentation of it. You are not only a superb chef, but a splendid artist as well."

"Thank you, Mr. Matsuo."

"I am happy and sad. Happy that I am alive to eat *fugu* again, but sad that I will not return here until you have taken care of your problem. Once there is no more noisy beggar, and we can dine in peace—myself, and the rest of your customers will return."

"I understand, Mr. Matsuo. I will seriously consider our conversation."

Mr. Matsuo walked out and Hiroshi closed the door and locked it. Unnerved, he marched back to the sushi preparation table behind the bar, and stared down at the *tora-fugu's* liver saturated with deadly toxins.

"Sake! And sushi!" Goro howled, unnerving Hiroshi further.

Hiroshi's eyes narrowed, as he swallowed hard, brooding over Mr. Matsuo's words. A bead of sweat escaped from under the rim of his cap, drizzled down his temple, over his cheek, and dripped off his jaw. He squeezed his grip on the handle of his sharp sushi knife.

"Sake! And sushi!" bellowed Goro louder than ever.

Hiroshi winced. He couldn't stand it anymore. He dabbed his sweaty forehead with the end of his neckerchief, and clenched his teeth with resolve. Tonight, after closing—sake and sushi for Goro!

Kiku Eto, Hiroshi's teenage daughter, awoke to the sound of nearby wailing sirens. She glanced at the clock—9:40 p.m. Tired from boredom, and weak from hunger, she had fallen asleep early, just after nine-o-clock. She slid out of bed, and shuffled over to the open window. She wore panties and one of her boyfriends T-shirts. Her black hair, cropped short and spiked, looked the same in bed or out. From her boyfriend's scant one bedroom apartment on the second floor of the shabby tenement, she peered out at the downtown street, and saw a flattened big drink cup, cartwheeling down the street in a rushing wind. A police car roared past flashing blue and red, while a helicopter whirred overhead with a roving searchlight. The sirens stopped a half a block away, and she could see the reflections of the emergency vehicles' lights on the side of a block building. She left the window, and had just climbed back into bed, when she heard her boyfriend, twenty-three year old Rafu Saito, and his older brother, twenty-five year old Taro, come storming into the apartment and lock the door. Rafu opened the bedroom door, and glanced in on Kiku. Thinking that she was asleep, he pulled the bedroom door leaving it open a crack.

Kiku, wondering what sort of trouble the men had gotten into this time, slipped out of bed, and tiptoed over to the door. She peeped through the narrow opening, and saw both men standing in the kitchen, both speaking in low tones. Two knitted, black ski masks, a 9mm handgun, and a brown paper-bag sat on the kitchen table.

"Are you crazy?" whispered Taro. "Why did you pistol-whip that lady? She gave us all of the money. She cooperated, and then, bam! You had to smack her."

Kiku put her hand over her mouth, muting her gasp. She knew that Rafu was an incorrigible bad boy, and had served time for petty crimes. His street-tough, gangster life-style is what attracted her to him, but assault and armed robbery frightened her.

"I wanted to send a message to everyone else—that we'll hurt them," snarled Rafu, as he reached up in a cupboard and gripped a fifth of cheap tequila. "The next time, no matter who it is, they will automatically do what we say. We'll be in and out in a flash." Rafu twisted off the bottle's cap, took a swig, set the bottle on the table, and then pulled the cash out of the paper bag.

"Well, we didn't grab very much," said Taro, eyeing the money, while lighting a cigarette. "That'll only buy a couple of weeks of groceries, and I've got Tojo's gang threatening to thrash me for the money I owe him, so," he leaned in closer and spoke even softer, "let's start cashing in Shiga's jewelry."

Rafu, considering his brother's words, picked up the bottle, sucked down two swallows in succession, and then while wincing at the burning taste, he shook his head no. He wiped his mouth with the back of his hand, and spat, "No. If we try to turn it into cash, the cops will be on us, and then we'll both be at San Quentin on death row."

Kiku clearly heard Rafu, and she knew about Shiga's jewelry store robbery; the robbers had wounded Goro Shiga and murdered his wife. However, she had never suspected that Rafu and his brother had committed such a heinous crime. Filled with horror, she backed away from the door. She had been feeling regretful over leaving her grieving father and her home, and now even more so. In her eyes, Rafu was no longer a cool gangster, but a cold killer. She crept over to the closet, and by the lights of the city peeping in the window, she began packing her small suitcase with her meager belongings.

"Never again speak about the jewelry," ordered Rafu, "I'll let you know when it's time. Let's get some sleep. Tomorrow we'll go and buy some food, and then we'll go to Fisherman's Wharf and snatch a purse or a wallet."

Taro stuffed the masks, the gun, and the cash in a beat-up gym bag, and set it down under a small table next to a filthy, worn-out sofa. He snuffed out his cigarette in an ashtray, grabbed up his soiled pillow and tattered blanket, and then lay on the sofa.

Rafu took two more shots of tequila, set the bottle down, and said with a smirk, "I feel like waking Kiku."

"Just keep it quiet," said Taro.

Rafu removed his shirt as he walked into the bedroom. In the dimly lit room, he heard commotion, and flipped on the light. He saw Kiku, slipping on a pair of jeans, and he growled, "What the hell are you doing?"

"I'm leaving," she said, buttoning her jeans. "I'm going home. I miss my father, and I'm tired of this dump and being hungry. Not only that, I'm sick of your worthless brother, your drinking, smoking, and drugs, and you slapping me around all the time."

He scowled at her in the same way he had just scowled at the woman in the adult bookstore just before he had pistol-whipped her.

"You're not going any where," he decreed. "Take your pants off and go back to bed!"

"No Rafu! I'm going home to my father," she stated, as she reached down to put on her shoes.

"No you're not!" he yelled, filling with rage. He then reached out and backhanded her across her face, knocking her back on the bed. He grabbed her legs, and with her kicking violently, he jerked her in close, unbuttoned her pants, and pulled them off.

"What the hell is going on?" Taro demanded, stepping into the room.

In a flash, Rafu wadded up the pants, and hurled them into his brother's face, yelling, "Shut up Taro! Go back to your sofa!"

Taro slinked out and into the kitchen, where he lit a cigarette, and took a slug of tequila.

"Pipe down over there, before I call the cops!" hollered a man with a low gravelly voice, as he pounded on the wall in the next apartment.

In response to his neighbor's threat, Rafu, now even angrier, snatched up Kiku's suitcase, popped it open, dumped out her stuff, and then slung the piece of luggage against his neighbor's adjoining wall.

Kiku jumped up to retrieve her pants, but Rafu slapped her down to the floor, giving her an immediate black eye.

"So, you want to leave me," jeered Rafu, "well, let me help you!" He then reached down, got a fist full of her hair, and yanked her up off the floor. She stood up, screeching in pain, as he dragged her by her hair across the apartment, out the door, and over to the edge of the second floor stairwell.

Taro remained in the kitchen, out of the way of Rafu's rage.

"Let go!" demanded Kiku. "You're hurting me!"

"Okay, you little skank, I'll let go of you!" He then launched her down the stairs.

Kiku tumbled in a heap; head over heals, bumping her head, elbows, and knees, landing with a thud and a groan at the bottom of the steps. Still conscious, with nothing broken, though covered with bumps and bruises, and a bleeding split across the hairline of her forehead, she peered up in a blur at Rafu.

He charged down the steps, pointed down at her, and growled, "I think you heard me and my brother talking in the kitchen, and if you tell anybody about it, I will kill you and your father, and then I'll set his place on fire. You know I will!"

Sobbing now from the pain and fear, she stood up, and with blood oozing down her face, she limped out the door. She staggered down the street in her T-shirt and panties; her bare feet padding down the cold sidewalk. She felt dizzy, and her body ached from the plummet down the stairs. She glanced behind her, and felt relieved that Rafu wasn't following her.

Rafu stormed back upstairs and into his apartment just as the irate neighbor bellowed, "I called the cops!" Both Rafu and Taro, without a thought, dashed out the door, down the stairs, and out the back door of the building.

It began to rain lightly, but in large droplets. Kiku stepped under a freeway onramp, evading the wetness, but not the wind. She shivered, feeling as though she would faint from the jarring that she had sustained. She saw a large cardboard box, and crawled inside.

Goro sat under the dumpster's open lid propped up against Eto's alley wall. He stayed mostly dry, sheltered from the rain, but the wind chilled him through his clothes.

"Sake! And sushi!" he screamed hoarsely, and to his astonishment, the door opened and there stood Hiroshi, holding a Styrofoam takeout box and a Styrofoam cup with a plastic lid.

"Goro," said Hiroshi, "with all of your incessant yelling, you have awakened my kindness. I have brought you hot sake and fresh sushi. You have been awful. Tell me, why must you yell?"

"If I don't yell," responded Goro with a grimace, "I will surely lose the rest of my mind to the grief that haunts me. I had faith that you would not let an old man suffer. Thank you, thank you for your compassion and providing me sake and sushi."

Hiroshi, without another word handed him the containers, stepped back inside, and locked the door. He opened a bottle of expensive sake, poured some in a cup, set it on the table next to the fish tank, and then sat, lost in his thoughts, staring, with glossed over eyes at the swimming *tora-fugu.*

Goro squatted back under the dumpster lid eager to eat the reward for his persistence, but a frigid gust changed his mind, so he hurried through the drizzle back to his cardboard home under the onramp.

Arriving at the box, he stooped to enter it, when he heard a loud gasp, and a girl's voice exclaim, "Please don't hurt me!"

Startled, he almost dropped the food. "Don't worry," he replied, peering into the gloom of the box, "I won't, but what is your name, and why are you in my home?"

"My name is Kiku, and I'm hungry and cold, and my boyfriend beat me, and threw me down a flight of steps. I crawled in here to escape the wind."

"Let me light a candle so I can see you," he said, stepping into the box, and scrunching in next to her. She smelled his filth, but she was too feeble to care.

He took out a candle and matches from a plastic box, and lit the candle. In the flickering light he looked at the girl and saw her black eye and her bloody head. Her small figure and sweet voice reminded him of his own daughter Momoto. He asked, "Do you need to go to the hospital?"

"No, I just want to go home to my father. His name is Hiroshi Eto, and his sushi bar is not far from here."

"I know Hiroshi very well," Goro said with a wide smile. "In his immense charity, he has provided this sake and sushi for me. Eat and drink, and then I will take you to him. Surely, in his great joy at your return, he will then feed me."

Kiku sipped the sake between bites of sushi, consuming them both. Upon finishing she said, "I don't feel well. Please, take me to my father now."

"Mr. Eto! Open the door!" yelled Goro, pounding on Eto's alley door.

Hearing Goro, Hiroshi sat his cup of sake down, and stomped to the back door. "Go away!" he shouted through the closed door. "I have already given you sake and sushi. Leave me alone."

"Please," begged Goro, "I have your daughter, Kiku."

"Kiku," muttered Hiroshi, as he hastily unlocked and ripped open the back door to see Goro standing there in the blustering rain, holding up his daughter; her arm draped around his shoulder. "Kiku, oh Kiku," Hiroshi cried out, "you have come home!" He noticed the bloody cut on her forehead and her bruised, swollen eye, and asked, "What has happened to you?"

"Father," moaned Kiku, as she began sobbing, "I'm sorry. You were right, and I should have listened to you. Rafu hurt me. Please let me come home."

Hiroshi rushed out, embraced his daughter, and then scooped her up under her knees and back, and carried her inside.

Goro stood humbly in the rain.

"Please, come inside," Hiroshi said to Goro, "and close the door."

Goro stepped inside, and shut the door behind him.

"Goro," commanded Hiroshi, "get two blankets in a cupboard just at the top of the stairs." While Hiroshi sat down, cradling his crying daughter in his arms, Goro raced his rickety, elderly body up the stairs.

"Goro Shiga?" Kiku asked between sobs.

"Yes," replied Hiroshi, as Goro returned with the blankets.

Kiku stopped crying, as she contemplated telling her father about Rafu and Taro, and the Shiga robbery.

"Goro, help me wrap a blanket around my little girl, and then please wrap yourself with the other."

As Goro unfolded the blanket and placed it around Kiku, he boasted, "I found her in my box. She was cold, hurt, and hungry, so I fed her the sake and sushi that your generosity had given to me."

Hiroshi's eyes widened, as he queried Goro, "You gave her—and she drank and ate the sake and sushi that I gave you?"

"Yes, Mr. Eto." Goro answered, grinning, puffed up with pride.

Hiroshi gaped up at Goro, and then down at his precious daughter, and then back at Goro. He then bowed his head, hugged his daughter in tight, and wept.

"So, she made it home to her daddy," a gruff voice interrupted, as a cold draft molested the warm room.

Hiroshi looked up to see Rafu and his brother Taro, both drenched from the rain, standing before him. They had crept in through the back door. Rafu pointed a pistol. Taro scowled.

Kiku weakly stood, faced them, and stated defiantly, "I am staying with my father. I never want to see you again Rafu."

"Rafu," said Hiroshi standing next to her, "you and your brother have no business here, so go, and never set foot in my restaurant again."

Goro felt an eerie loathing.

"Oh, we have business here, Mr. Eto, with your daughter and

now you," snarled Rafu, "and we've also have some unfinished business with Goro Shiga, our neighborhood bum." He looked at Goro, barely recognizing the weathered, old man. "How you survived that bullet to the brain is beyond belief. Either my hand jerked or your head moved. You should have died with your wife."

"You killed my Momo!" Goro yelled hysterically, lunging at Rafu.

Rafu stepped back and then pistol-whipped Goro, knocking him to the floor.

Kiku gasped. Hiroshi took a step to aid Goro, but Rafu stopped him, waving the gun in his face.

"Okay, now, before we eliminate our witnesses, and burn this place down, get us some of this sushi that you are so famous for, and pour us some hot sake too.

Hiroshi disregarded Rafu's command, and stood his ground next to his daughter and Goro.

"Do it!" Rafu screamed. "Or I'll start by putting a bullet—and no missing this time—in the center of Goro's head, and then your daughter's." Rafu placed the barrel of the gun against Goro's forehead. Taro fidgeted, keeping silent.

Hiroshi bowed in submission, walked over to the sushi preparation table behind the bar, and brought out a Styrofoam cup of warm sake and a Styrofoam box of sushi already prepared. "You may eat this," he said to the brothers, "the order was changed after I had made it."

Both men sat at the table next to the *tora-fugu* tank. Rafu held the 9mm, pointing it at Hiroshi, Kiku, and Goro; the three of them, sitting at another table. The brothers ate and drank in haste, and finished after a few minutes.

Rafu stood up and said, "Okay Taro, we've got business to take care of." He raised the pistol at Kiku, but suddenly with his other hand, he gripped his stinging mouth. Hit with a wave of nausea, he dropped to his knees and started vomiting. His hands became numb, then paralyzed, and he dropped the gun. His brother also fell to the floor, with his arms curled around his cramping stomach.

Goro sprung from his chair, grabbed the gun, and pointed the weapon down at Rafu. "You killed my Momo and shattered my life," he cried out, breathing heavily, and trembling, "now you and your brother will die."

"Goro," said Hiroshi, reaching out and calmly lowering the handgun, "they have eaten their last meal. They both have ingested *fugu* liver."

"*Fugu?*" Rafu and Taro both muttered in horror.

"*Fugu?*" exclaimed Kiku and Goro.

Hiroshi took the gun from Goro, pointed it at the retching, writhing brothers on the floor, and ordered, "Get up—and get out of here."

Using the chairs and tables for support, they climbed to their feet. Both of them, doubled over in pain, drooling, and wheezing, staggered out the back door and into the wind swept rain.

Hiroshi locked the door behind them.

Rafu and Taro stumbled within a block of their apartment, but could go no further, collapsing on the pavement under an onramp. Spying a cardboard box that could shield them from the wind, they crawled inside it.

Hiroshi hugged his daughter, attended to her injuries, and then assisted her upstairs. He started a hot bath for her, and before he left for downstairs, she said, "Father—please forgive me for the grief and worry I caused you. I'm happy to be home. I feel safe again."

"I do forgive you," said Hiroshi, "and I'm happy that you are back home. We may not have your mother, but we do have each other, and we will work things out. Take a hot bath, relax, and then get some rest, and honey—you are safe."

Downstairs, Hiroshi prepared for Goro a full meal of *miso*

soup, sushi, teriyaki-chicken, *tempura*, and rice. As Goro sat at the sushi bar on Mr. Matsuo's regular stool, and ate a delicious meal, Hiroshi said, "Goro, I must confess that the deadly *fugu* I gave Rafu and Taro was intended for you. But then, I realized that I grieved for Natsuko and Kiku as you grieved for Momo and Momoto. Like you, I ached with loneliness and drank sake. Throughout many weary days and sleepless nights, I have worried: What if I lose everyone and everything like Goro. I saw myself hungry and cold, huddled at Yakamoto's alley door, yelling for sake and sushi. I understood that I too could end up living in a cardboard box under an overpass. My compassion would not allow me to serve the *fugu* liver to you, so I pushed the box of poisonous food aside, and prepared for you fresh sushi and sake. Earlier, when I held my cherished daughter in my lap, I wept from horror when I realized that if I had obeyed my loathing for you—I would have killed my own sweet child. Then I cried from great relief and joy, knowing that I fed you from my kindness, thus saving my little girl, bringing her home and into my arms."

"Your kindness was awakened at the right moment," said Goro, between bites of *tempura*.

"Yes, it was, and I'll make a deal with you Goro. If you stay at the rescue mission, and remain clean and presentable, then you can help here at Eto's. I'll provide your meals, and support you until you can get on your own again."

"I am grateful Mr. Eto. I will not fail you," assured Goro.

Before the sun rose, the Saito brothers had died. The next day, a jogger spied two left feet with different shoes sticking out of the box, and discovered their stiff bodies. The investigators blamed the deaths of the brothers on a drug overdose of methamphetamine found in their blood. Searching their squalid apartment, they found the jewelry, the ski masks, and the 9mm handgun used in Shiga's murder-robbery. The jewelry went to the insurance company. The authorities considered the case closed.

After a few weeks passed, when word got out that Hiroshi's daughter had returned and was helping him, and Eto's no longer had a bum yelling at it's alley door, but a clean, sober, and hard working helper in the kitchen, Mr. Matsuo stopped by for some *tora-fugu-sashi*. Sitting on his usual stool at the sushi bar, the hefty man said to Hiroshi, "Mr. Eto, I am glad that I can now dine in peace. I have missed my *tora-fugu*. Please prepare it for me, and remember—I want to eat *fugu*, but I don't want to die."

BETSY'S GARDEN

Betsy Gardner felt peculiar. She didn't know why. Usually, a youthful vitality frolicked in her eighty-nine-year-old mind and body, and usually, the beauty and serenity of her garden comforted her loneliness and quelled her longing for Walter, her loving husband, long ago deceased. However, on this day, she felt feeble, alone, and she missed—to tears—she missed Walter.

Her lack of vigor began that morning, as the first light of dawn peeked over the stone wall, filtered through the tree branches, and beamed a hearty good morning through her kitchen window. Usually, as she waited for the water to boil for tea, she gazed back at the sunrise, its light diffusing past her eyes, bouncing off her soul, then reflecting back out her eyes as glinting sparks of verve. However, on this day, it glimmered off her tears.

Hearing the whistling kettle, she went to the stove, poured boiling water into her teacup, let the tea bag steep, dunked it a few times, and then swirled in a teaspoon of honey. Usually, she only spooned in one teaspoon, however, on this day, she added one more—the way Walter liked it. Holding her warm cup in both hands, she stepped out the back door and sat in a wooden rocking chair next to a trellis of wide-awake, blue morning glories. Rocking gently in her chair, in the tranquility of daybreak, she sipped her steaming cup of honeyed tea, and beheld the awakening of her heavenly garden.

With an invasion of brilliance, rays of sunshine burst forth upon the landscape, brightening the dew-covered blossoms of every genus and color into a floricultural paradise. Doves cooed. Sparrows chirped. Robins trilled. Two white butterflies fluttered in erratic circles, while buzzing honeybees gathered pollen. A sleek, red squirrel scurried across the manicured lawn and another up the trunk of a towering pine tree. The entire garden bustled in the sunlight.

Usually, while drinking her tea, Betsy planned the chores and errands of the day. However, on this day, she thought about Walter, and the mornings he used to sit in the rocking chair next to her, and enjoy his tea. When it was time, he'd charge off to work, but not before he had kissed her on the cheek. He'd then march out the garden gates, up main street, along the stone wall to his office, where, as a family doctor, he had become well acquainted with the insides and outs, from the nose to the toes of most of the town folks and the farm folks too.

Memories flowed by Betsy with every sip of the sweet, honeyed tea. She visualized the modest, country school, where she and Walter, as small children, had played together in the schoolyard, and the quaint, little church, where they, as teenagers, had married. She recalled the years, while Walter attended medical school, when they lived in a big city far away. The hardships they endured only deepened their devotion to one another. Upon returning to their hometown, their families had helped them purchase a seven-acre parcel on the edge of town, with a large, two-story, Victorian home. The forlorn house sat at the center of the barren land with the entire property surrounded by a six-foot-high stone wall. Walter had worked hard, restoring the house, while Betsy had toiled, creating a garden. She marveled at how, over time, the small town had grown, and their estate had become the heart of the city.

She stopped rocking in her chair, and hung her head in sorrow, reflecting on the nearly two decades she had spent, wanting, trying, and praying for a child of their own, but never to be blessed with one. Then, she thought of all the countless babies that Walter had delivered, and how she had insisted on going with him to each newborn's first check up. Cuddling the infants, she had silently asked God to bestow a blessing upon them. Thinking about the darling babies, her spirits lifted, and she smiled, rocking again in her chair.

With the last sip of her tea, her mind returned to the present. She stepped back into the house, ate a light breakfast, dressed, put on her gardening apron and bonnet, and strode out into her garden.

All day long, as she gardened, the splendid, summer day treated her especially kind, providing warm rays of bright sunshine as she clipped bouquets of flowers for next Sunday's worship service, and sending her a slight, cooling breeze when she had tilled the flower beds. Usually, she hummed a hymn as she worked, however, on this day, she raked, hoed, and clipped in silence, lost in her memories of Walter.

At the end of the afternoon, as the fleeing sun slipped behind the gnarled and knotted limbs of the regal old oak tree, she needed to finish one last task.

Down on her hands and knees, she patted the loose dirt firmly around the skinny trunk of a three-foot tall willow tree that she had just transplanted from under its parent tree to an open spot where it could thrive.

With the young tree standing at attention, she raised up on her knees, placed her small shovel in an apron pocket next to the pocket with her clipping shears, and wiped her hands off on a little towel drooped over her apron string. She then stood up, and peered down at the junior tree. In her elderly, wavering voice, she spoke softly, yet firmly, as if it were her child. "Now, first of all, you tiny tot of a tree, I planted you with love, just like I did with all the plants in my garden, so, you belong here; this is your home. Secondly, I planted you in a perfect spot, where you've got everything you need to grow into a mighty tree—rich soil, bright sunshine, and refreshing water from the rain and that sprinkler over there. The birds will keep the hungry bugs off you, so you can stretch out them branches, and there's plenty of wigglin' earthworms to keep your soil tilled, so you can reach out them roots. Thirdly, there aren't no weeds in my garden, nor them naughty gophers, so none are gonna bully you, and don't fear the unruly wind neither 'cause that burly hedge will shelter you from blowin' over until you can hold your ground. Lastly, I expect you to provide a lot of shade someday for the little critters around here, and for young lovers who come and picnic under your branches. Just delight in the sunrises and sunsets, and every sunbeam, raindrop, or snowflake in between, and just like this old gal, you'll do fine."

When she finished her exhortation to the peewee tree, she removed her sunbonnet, slid it into an apron pocket, placed her hands on her hips, and gazed out at the garden all around her. A quiet stillness subdued the garden in the emerging twilight—no tweets from the roosting birds; no buzzing bees, only the whispering, gurgling water, cascading over rocks in the stone fountain.

She glanced at the large, wrought iron gates at the garden's entrance, then looked away, then back again. She thought that she had seen Walter, coming through the entrance as he had always done. Nevertheless, no one was there. She began to feel faint, as though her knees would collapse. She shuffled a short distance and sat down on a wooden bench. Again, she peered over at the gates, feeling a strange notion that she would see Walter.

Every work day, whether sunny, rainy, windy, or chilly, Walter had come strolling through the gates and into the garden, whistling in the sunshine with his hands in his pockets, pressing his fedora hat down upon his head in the wind, or holding an umbrella in the rain. Over almost four decades of living at the estate, on those bright days, she had sat on the bench waiting for him. As he entered, they'd wave to each other, and then, he'd march directly toward her, with his footsteps clip-clopping on the cobblestones, and his whistle-song in the air.

Arriving at the bench, he'd blurt out with a wide and genuine smile, "Now there's the prettiest flower in the garden!"

She'd jump into his arms, stand on her tiptoes, and kiss her tall and handsome prince upon his cheek. Holding hands, they'd walk over to the bench and sit down, where she'd always have ice cold lemonade mixed with sweet tea, exactly how Walter liked it.

She'd listen as he talked about the interesting lives of his patients, and he'd listen to her share about her activities in the garden, the quilting circle, and the church. They'd converse until their separate adventures of the day became a part of both, and always, before they'd go into the house for supper, they'd pray for those whom her husband was doctoring, and ask God to bless her garden.

On this day, alone in her garden, she ignored her silly notions of Walter strolling through the gates. For a moment, in her mind, she relived that night, twenty-five years ago, when shortly after dinner, he had muttered, "Honey, I feel peculiar. I'm goin' on up-stairs to bed. Will you bring me up a seltzer when you come?"

"Sure dear, I'll be right up with it, after I put Kittyrose out."

Holding the glass of fizzing seltzer, she climbed the stairs, entered the bedroom, and found Walter in bed, eyes closed, sitting motionless, propped up on his pillows. Thinking he had already fallen asleep, she softly called out, "Walter." No answer. She moved to his side, sat the glass on the nightstand, and brushing back his hair from his forehead, she whispered, "Walter." There was no awakening him, and to her horror, he had stopped breathing. She tried desperately to revive him, but to no avail. Suffering from silent heart disease, her beloved husband was gone.

Out in the garden, sitting on the bench, she felt feeble, alone, and she missed Walter so, that she sobbed into her apron. She tried to stand and go into the house, but felt dizzy, and sat back down. She felt peculiar. Her chest felt tight, it seemed difficult to breathe, and she felt pain in her fingers. She decided to lie down for just a minute and rest, placing her hands under her head and curling her knees up on the bench. Though the sun still spied over the stone wall, darkness surrounded her.

"Betsy! Betsy dear!"

She heard her name called out and awoke. She sat up, wondering how long she had slept. Although the sun had dipped below the horizon, a celestial sky of golden clouds illuminated the garden in flaxen light.

"Betsy!"

Hearing her name sung out again, and footsteps on the cobblestones, she peered toward the gates and saw a tall man, wearing a fedora hat, walking toward her. She stood up. No dizziness; no labored breath; no pain. She felt euphoric, and her joy bubbled into girlish giggles.

He continued strolling toward her; his whistle-song in the air; his face obscured in a silhouette. Her heart raced and her skin tingled with excitement. When the man was but a short distance away, he exclaimed, "Now, there's the prettiest flower in the garden!"

"Walter!" she cried out in a youthful, unfaltering voice. She ran to him and wrapped her arms around him, hugging and kissing him.

He embraced her, enveloping her in his arms, and then held her away from him. "Hold on Bet," he chuckled. "Hold on, and let me see you." As he gazed at her angelic face, he whispered, "Truly, sweetie, you are such a lovely flower."

"Oh, Walter," she moaned, seeing that he was but a young man, "you don't want to ogle an old gal like me."

"You're not old Bet," he informed, walking her over to the fountain and its reflecting pool of water, "you're young, just like on our wedding day."

She stared at her youthful reflection, and smiled. Walter smiled too. They turned and faced each other, both still grinning, when he witnessed her face turn somber.

"What's wrong Bet?" he entreated with tenderness.

"Well, I've been feeling peculiar all day—thinking about you and missing you horribly. This morning, as I gazed out the kitchen window at the sunrise—I cried. I sensed your presence, but because we weren't together—I felt lonelier than ever. My longing for you seemed greater than my joy for life. I'm happy now that we're together—but I'm afraid. Walter, are you going away again?"

"No, darling," he said cheerfully, "I've come to take you with me."

"Oh, that's wonderful!" she burst out, then asked solemnly, "But—what about my garden?"

In the faint light of twilight, Walter gazed all around him in awe. "Well, Bet, your garden is a mighty fine garden—the finest. Indeed, it is a piece of Heaven, but it's only a very, small piece. I can't wait to show you the rest of it." He reached out and stretched his arm around her shoulders, hugging her in tight, and said, "Honey, come with me."

She wrapped her arms around his waist, leaned her head on his shoulder, and together, they strolled down the cobblestone walk, stepped off onto the grass, and vanished behind a majestic weeping willow tree.

INSOMNOS

A s MIDNIGHT HATCHED its first millisecond, an unseen presence arrived, shifting unrestrained amidst the darkness of the unlit room.

Stephen slept peacefully in his bed, breathing deeply and rhythmically, with a slight snore that tagged along with each breath. At twenty-five years old, he had a good job, a comfortable place to live, and a loving girlfriend who lived nearby. With few worries, his nights were restful.

All was quiet in his apartment, except the recurrent sound of the refrigerator clicking on, humming, and then clicking off. All the doors and windows were locked and secure.

The being crept to Stephen's bedside and stood silent. Its cat-like eyes widened with intrigue as it stared down at his face. It saw clearly in the dark, for long ago the beast chose to dwell in the darkness, had adapted to it, and eventually embraced it to the point that it abhorred the light.

It moved in closer, perused the smoothness of Stephen's flesh, and marveled at its glowing serenity. Envious, it placed its hand on its own guttered face and scraped its fingernails over the deep and contorted lines engraved by timeless agony.

It turned away from him and looked at a clear glass of water on the nightstand. Although it could reach the water, it could not partake, for they were worlds apart. It licked its dry cracked lips and wondered if just a sip of the earthly element could quench its hellish thirst and revive its parched soul. Even it—a cast down, ugly being from a place void of light, peace, water, and time—had a soul.

It swallowed hard, looking away from the water and back at Stephen. It again concentrated on its purpose—delivering deceit into the man's mind by sowing subconscious sprouts of doubt and timidity. It knew the seeds would grow to eclipse his faith and courage, thus thwarting wisdom with folly and instigating the proliferation of misery.

The shrouded creature leaned in and hovered over Stephen with its shriveled lips pursed close to the man's ear.

Though deep in slumber, Stephen sensed something unseemly and awoke, jerking his head up from his pillow. "Who's there?" he mumbled, then listened, hearing nothing. He glanced at the alarm clock resting on the nightstand. The glaring red numbers 12:05 a.m. bled into the darkness.

The beast grinned. With Stephen awake, its amusement ballooned. The beast watched the clock and waited, breathing heavily with anticipation.

Stephen felt coldness on his face like the chill rolling out of the opened door of a freezer, and snatched his blanket up to his neck.

As the clocked blinked 12:06 a.m., the presence spoke.

Stephen could not see the creature hiding in its darkness, but he heard its coarse inaudible voice in his mind. It uttered the time, as a simple mathematical riddle in the form of a taunting rhyme.

"Twelve plus sixsss. Twelve plus sixsss. Divideth by three is sixsss, sixsss, sixsss."

Like air escaping from a small puncture in an air mattress, its tongue seized upon, and then lingered with a lengthy hiss as it annunciated the x of each number six.

Alarmed, Stephen sat up in bed; eyes open; his heart racing.

The creature ceased whispering, and recited the taunt louder.

"Twelve plus sixsss. Twelve plus sixsss. Divideth by three is sixsss, sixsss, sixsss."

Stephen kicked off the covers, swung his legs around, and dropped his feet to the floor. He shot a glance at the clock's blinding scarlet numbers, still illuminating 12:06 a.m. He endured the message a third time, as the creature shouted at him with seething hatred.

"Twelve plus sixsss. Twelve plus sixsss. Divideth by three is sixsss, sixsss, sixsss."

He heard the words with such clarity; iciness crept over him, melting into dread. He knew that a demon was present. He knew, because he'd studied the scriptures and believed them as truth. He knew, because he expected opposition to his burgeoning spiritual growth. He knew, because only a demon would arrive at midnight, hide in the dark, and whisper taunts extolling 666—the prophesied number of the apocalyptic beast.

He trembled with fear as he snapped on a small reading lamp, glanced around the bedroom, and saw no one. He stood up, shoved his feet into his slippers, took a couple of steps to the dresser, reached for his robe, and slipped it on.

The sneering demon stepped aside, crossed its arms, and watched.

Stephen then hurried out of the room, down the hall, and into the living room, where he flipped on the switch to a table lamp.

The unseeable beast followed a step behind, mimicking every move he made.

Arriving at his lounge chair, Stephen promptly dropped to his knees, leaned over, and rested his elbows on the seat cushion. With his hands clasped together and his head bowed, he prayed, "God, help me, please help me!"

The demon snuggled up close to him, and whispered directly into his ear, "Your God doth not heareth you."

As the whisper wafted into Stephen's mind, he felt turmoil

churning within his soul. Undaunted, he continued, "God, I know you hear me, and love me."

The being spat right back, "Your God doth not loveth you, for amongst the infinite heavensss, you are but a speck of dusssst."

The words rattled Stephen's thoughts. He drew in a deep breath, mustered up his faith, and declared, "God, I know that you are with me and that you will protect me."

"You are alone," it hissed, "in my darknessss."

Stephen ignored its lies, and avowed, "I am not alone, God is with me, and is watching over me!" Before the beast could spew another venomous lie, Stephen implored, "Dear Lord, what is it that would wake me in the middle of the night, taunt me with dreadful rhymes, and whisper lies to me?" As Stephen prayed, the creature hissed loudly in his ear, disturbing his thoughts with a noisy static. Stephen continued undeterred, "God, please show me. Please reveal to me what it is!"

Stephen assumed that God would answer his plea through the human senses over time, as he lived life moment to moment. Instead, God granted an immediate answer to his prayer; an answer from a realm unseen—but now seen in a mighty rush of thoughts.

Though he remained kneeling, he pictured himself in his vision, standing in the dark. A glow encircled him that illuminated twenty feet into the darkness, like the light cast by a lantern on a moonless night.

As he stared out to where the haze of faint light met the edge of murky blackness, he noticed a creature dart past, then vanish beyond the curtain of darkness. Although he only caught a glimpse of it, what he saw walked upright with the stature of a ten-year old boy—though not human. He yelled, "Who's there?" There was no answer. Then, out of the corner of his eye, he saw it dash by again and disappear. He hollered, "What do you want?" Again, there was no answer.

The creature remained soundless and obscured, just beyond the fragments of diffusing light. It stalked the man, encircled him, and eyed him from every angle. Puzzled, it scratched its bald, leathery scalp with its spindly fingers. It wondered why a man of flesh loitered in *its* world. In its lengthy pursuit of inflicting woe, it had never experienced this before. "Ssstrange," it whispered, unheard by the man, "he hath parted my veil of darknesss."

Hidden behind Stephen's back, it crept to the edge of the man's luminescence—the brink of its own darkness. With apprehension, it placed its foot into the ring of radiance, as a person dips his toes into a pool of water. The man's brightness felt harsh, though sufferable, so it decided it could bear it for a short spell, since the gratification of attacking the man would greatly exceed the discomfort.

Stephen spun around and spied the beast just as it withdrew its foot and leapt back into black oblivion.

The creature stood silent in the dark and observed the man. Over the ages, it had marred the mind of many a man, but now arose the opportunity to harm one physically. It smiled at the thought and prowled about for a strategic position to do so.

As the beast treaded between light and dark, Stephen's mind tottered between fear and faith. He peered into the darkness and saw his adversary faintly as it paced cat-like about the haze.

The demon sensed that as the man's fear grew, his faith withered. With a presumptuous smirk, it said under its breath, "Yesss, yesss," sniffing deeply through its stub of a nose, "I sssmelleth hisss fear," then, lightly smacking its lips, "I tasssteth hisss doubt!"

Feeling crude merriment, it started to hum, and added an uncoordinated dance to its pacing. Its deplorable song lacked tempo as if it followed a spasmodic metronome. It danced as though it was sneaking up on an unsuspecting prey; on its toes, arms lifted, elbows bent, and hands drooping, all the while jerking about like a dangling marionette.

Hearing the discordant noise, Stephen shouted again, "Who's there?"

The beast stopped humming and prancing, and stepped backward into deeper obscurity. It narrowed its eyes and scowled at him in silence.

Stephen heard no answer, so shouting louder, he demanded, "Tell me who you are!"

From behind him, and out of the soundless gloom, he heard the creature speak in a hushed, raspy voice, "My Prince hath named me Insomnosss."

Stephen simultaneously took a step back and spun facing the answering voice. The light moved with him, keeping him at its center bathed in brightness.

The beast hunched into an attack position, like a wrestler opposite his opponent, and began slinking in a circle around the man.

"I recognize your voice," Stephen blurted out, as he slowly turned and searched the darkness for the beast. "You are the demon that woke me and whispered to me."

"Noooo, not a demon," muttered Insomnos, as it roved about, shifting turn for turn with Stephen, remaining behind him, "I am an angel, sent by your god to enlighten you."

Stephen pointed a finger toward the voice hidden beyond the vigor of the light, and asserted with clenched teeth, "You are not an angel, nor were you sent from God!"

The demon was not in front of Stephen's pointing finger, but had already slipped behind him. It contemplated for a moment about whether to lie again. Craving violence, it felt impatient with the prattle. Besides, this man knew the truth and stood valiantly upon it, repudiating all of its lies. It tired of its own game of falsehoods and concluded that the truth would add greater fear to its advantage of stealth and confusion.

"Nooo," confessed Insomnos, "I am not an angel, nor frometh your god. I hateth you and want to torment you as I alwaysss have, as I am, and as I alwaysss will."

Startled, Stephen shuffled back and away from the voice, then proclaimed, "I am not afraid of you. God is with me!"

Insomnos snickered at his remark and spat, "I see him not," while it maneuvered in the dark and positioned itself directly behind him. It snarled as it tensed up its body, sucked in a few deep, rattling breaths, and cracked its neck from side to side. It then stooped down like a runner in a starting chock, focused on Stephen's back, and charged out of its hiding and into the light.

Stephen heard the creature's pounding footsteps behind him, but before he could spin around, it lunged at him and landed on his back, knocking him to the floor.

The beast rode Stephen's falling body to the ground. Then, trembling with wrath and drooling with pleasure, it gripped its bony, unhallowed hands around the smooth, fleshy throat of its human prey.

Stephen choked and coughed as he tried to wrest himself free. He rolled to the left and then to the right with no avail. Still in the clutches of the beast, and under its weight, he thrust himself up to one knee, and then stood.

Insomnos rose with Stephen, wrapping its legs around his waist, spewing out horrid blasphemies like raw sewage gushing from a drainpipe.

The impieties of the demon enraged Stephen. He grabbed at it, trying to get a grip on the nimble creature, but there were no clothes to grasp on the sexless beast.

Stephen finally wrapped his hands around its skinny throat. Its hairless skin felt wrinkled, dry, and scabrous like a lizard. He yanked it off his back, and flung it down, banging its head on the floor. The creature cried in agony, scrambling out of the brightness and back into the dark.

Stephen stared into the inky nothingness, and waited in the eerie silence, trying to catch his breath.

The obfuscated beast sat on its haunches, rubbing the knot swelling on its wounded head. It watched the man closely while gathering its strength. It had discovered that the man's physical strength was more challenging than manipulating his mind.

"Go back to your despair," Stephen huffed, "and leave me alone!"

Insomnos laughed, jumped to its feet, and ran directly at him for another assault. As it charged, it yelled, "I thriveth on anguisssh! I will alwaysss be near!"

Stephen saw it rush out of the dark, advance into the glow, and then dive straight toward him.

The grinning creature—with glimmering drool dribbling out of its mouth—soared through the air eager to torment the man.

Stephen caught the airborne beast, shoved it down, and pinned it on the ground.

Face to face, he could feel its cold breath that stunk like vomit. Its yellow eyes were compassionless, like the eyes of a feeding lion. Its skin was the color of greenish-gray algae floating on a stagnant pond. The agony it had plowed into countless thousands had tilled bone-dry furrows upon its vapid face.

It grappled with Stephen, not to escape, but to gain further advantage. As they scuffled, it gnashed its brown rotten teeth and spat blasphemous words against all that is righteous.

In the midst of the tussle, Stephen gasped, "God please—please—free me!"

Within an infinitesimal fraction of a second, there was a flash of bluish-white light. More blasts followed the first, each one accompanied by the sound of a vast orchestra. As the light grew in brilliance and sustained, or pulsated in staccato, the symphony accompanied it in perfect synchronization.

The intensity of the light caused no harm to Stephen, but greatly distressed the beast. Wailing out of tune and its face twisted in pain, it gave up its attack and squirmed free. Trying to cover its eyes and ears with its hands, it crawled awkwardly away from the light, back toward the darkness on its elbows and knees. The light lowered into a low golden shimmer and then surged again into an intense brightness, exacting severe pain upon the creature.

Stephen watched it as it slowly retreated, then as it stopped and rested on its haunches. It squatted, still vaguely visible in the gray vapor at the skirt of the void.

The light advanced, devouring the darkness, unveiling a stone wall twenty feet tall in front of Stephen. The wall continued to his left, into the heart of the light; to his right, into the bowels of darkness. Another twenty-foot wall met the first, forming a corner directly in front of him. There was no ceiling above the lofty walls, only empty night.

The brightness steadily dawned, illuminating the wounded demon trapped and cowering in the corner. Shielding its face with its hands from the ever-intensifying light, it could only steal quick glances in Stephen's direction. As the creature moved within its tight confines, so did its shadow, perfectly projected on the walls behind it.

By now, both Insomnos and Stephen were bathed in bright light. The cornered creature seethed, yelling obscenities and threats of death at Stephen. It clenched its right hand into a fist, and violently shook it in his direction as it repeatedly hissed in its fury, "I hateth you!"

Now that Stephen saw it more clearly, he noticed that it was not looking at him, but beyond him. It cried out in its anguish, "I hateth him," as it pointed at Stephen with its shaking finger. It then pointed over and beyond Stephen's head, directing its wrath past and far beyond him, and whined, "Because I hateth you!"

Stephen watched as Insomnos tried to shield its face and body from the flooding light, but to no avail. It could not run, for the luminosity and the walls held it captive. Weak and injured, it collapsed to the floor and rolled into a ball. Rather than cry for help, or plead for its life, it cursed.

A fire ignited at the toes of the beast, then licked at its ankles. It shrieked, jumped up, and patted its feet trying to extinguish the flames that were quickly ascending its legs and torso. As the blaze consumed its body, a foul green smoke billowed and swirled up into the void. The creature was horrified for its prince had forewarned of a fire so terrible that it obliterated souls. Its callous eyes now pleaded for pity as it looked directly into the searing light above Stephen. It beseeched, "Noooo, not the fire of Absolute Death. I only dideth what my Prince commandedeth!"

Justice overruled mercy as the fire raged hotter, engulfing the demon's head. As the intense heat cooked its mind, it expelled the creature's memories, horrid scenes depicting the abominations that it had afflicted on mankind.

Stephen saw each disturbing image projected onto the swelling green smoke. He watched aghast as graphic incidents of human pornography, violence, and murder flashed into view. He saw the last gasp of the dying and the moaning hopelessness of those consumed with disease. He beheld the shrieking grief of the mothers of dead soldiers and the sullen faces of those caught in the atrocities of war. He witnessed the cries of molested children, the wails of those hungry and sick, and the sobs of those frightened and alone. He saw the ugly, contorted faces of racial hatred and the tortured faces of its victims. As the small inferno roared, a multitude of faces—all portraying the misery from the gross inhumanities that they suffered—vaporized into the dark. As they did—the dark became darker.

Stephen turned away in horror at the sights, and wept with his face cradled in his hands. He realized that these atrocities formed the darkness. Like the woven strands of a blanket; the sadness, greed, lust, hate, and all that extinguishes the radiance of love had intertwined, creating a vast fabric of lightlessness. Since one demon's existence had spawned so much chaos, he wondered how many more workers of woe existed in man's world, engineering sorrow upon people's souls.

The small fire burned hot on the demon's vileness, incinerating its external shell of existence. Then its condemned core steamed away into a soulless finality of non-existence.

Stephen stared in silence at the empty corner. Not a nether world trace of Insomnos remained. With the threat vanquished, he breathed in deep, then whispered, "Thank you God, thank you!"

After a moment of blessed silence, he heard a voice speak from behind. It spoke in a tone of compassion, "Stephen—Stephen—turn around."

Stephen felt hope rather than fear as he turned away from the corner and the darkness beyond, and faced the voice that had called his name. As he did, he looked into the shining beams of an extremely bright light. Squinting, he peered between the fingers of his outstretched hand, looking to see the origin of the emanating light. His eyes teared from the brightness as he saw a huge throne the size of a three-story building. A man sat upon the majestic throne while another being, more spirit than man, orbited it, whooshing about like a gust of wind.

Overwhelmed by a tremendous sense of humility, Stephen dropped to his knees and bowed his head to the floor. He glanced up and saw that giant pillars stood on each side of the throne. Platforms of different levels, like large steps, began halfway up the throne and descended down to floor. Other beings, with flowing white robes, stood upon these landings to the right and to the left of the throne. Behind the throne and descending platforms, he saw more platforms rising like the bleachers in a stadium. Upon these platforms sat an orchestra, and above them stood a great chorus. Not a concert hall on earth could have accommodated all of the singers, musicians, and instruments. They played and sang so melodically, harmoniously, and heavenly, that Stephen wept in awe.

The blinding light and his distance from the throne prevented Stephen from clearly seeing the features of the being upon it, or of those on the platforms.

Beyond the orchestra and choir stood the skyline of a magnificent city, and beyond the city, green hills rolled up against mountains with snow covered peaks that disappeared into the clouds, then reappeared above them. All basked in a golden light.

It seemed to Stephen that he had experienced a long look at the glory before him, but it had been only a glance. Still prostrate, he heard a loving voice call him again by name, "Stephen—My love and grace are with you. Fear not, for the peace that I have—I give to you."

As peacefulness swept over him, Stephen heard a sound like the rapids of a rushing river, and the vision left him. He was still in his living room, on his knees in a prayer position. He looked around the room blinking his eyes into focus as he regained his orientation. He stood to his feet, trembling, not from fear, but from awe.

He prayed to God and worshiped Him, then ended with, "Thank you almighty God for your love, peace, and protection. Amen." He then strolled to his bedroom, drank some water from the glass, and climbed back into bed. After a few moments of fluffing his pillow and getting comfortable, he again slept peacefully. The refrigerator clicked on, hummed for awhile, then clicked off.

LORANT ELLIOT DOPPEL

"BRING ME THE baby!" ordered the dying old man.

With her back to him, the young nurse rolled her eyes. She finished checking his IV tubes, then turned, and looked at the decrepit man lying in his bed. He was already a portrait of death: gaunt, with cadaverous eyes that no longer reflected the faint life that clung to his soul.

Ignoring his rudeness, she replied without anger or compassion, "Yes, Mr. Doppel," then briskly turned to leave the bedroom.

Before she got to the door, he lifted a shaking hand toward her, raised his head up from his pillow, and loudly cleared his throat.

She stopped, closed her eyes, and massaged her headache with the tips of her fingers. After a deep, calming breath, and a silent sigh of exasperation, she turned and faced her overbearing employer. As always, she waited patiently for him to speak and wondered if these might be his final words.

Once he had her attention, he muttered between labored breaths, "I must—see the photograph—and the…" He stopped in mid-sentence, sucked in just a scrap of a full breath, and then coughed, gagged, and choked. His pallid face turned grayish-blue as he drew in three wheezy breaths, then finally sucked in a long, unobstructed inhale. Speaking hoarsely, he demanded, "Get me the photograph—and the baby!" Overwhelmed with fatigue, he dropped his head onto his pillow and closed his eyes.

Again, in a monotone voice, she replied, "Yes, Mr. Doppel," then left to do his bidding. Once out the door, she stomped down the hall complaining under her breath, "Ooh, that ungrateful old man, and after all these months of caring for him."

She knew which photograph he required, and hurried down the stairs of the mansion to the withering man's den. She opened the door and walked into the large room. Bookcases lined its walls from floor to ceiling. She recalled a time, back when he was somewhat healthier, when she had asked him, "Mr. Doppel, have you read all of these books?" He had replied curtly, "Yes, of course, and most of them twice."

In the middle of the den sat a huge cherry wood desk along with a high-backed, leather chair, and on top of the desk sat the five by seven portrait that he so desperately desired. She noticed, next to the portrait lay a manila, letter-sized envelope addressed to Lorant Elliot Doppel. She pondered the envelope, but decided to ignore it. She then snatched up the photo, left the den, and rushed up the stairs to the nursery to retrieve the baby.

Though death hovered eagerly over Mr. Doppel, he did not fear it, not its instrumentality, nor its probable agony. Nor did he fear the cessation of breath, nor the final throb of his heart, nor the last twitch of a finger. Furthermore, he dreaded not the aging and withering decay of his physical body, nor the claustrophobic darkness of a sealed coffin. He had no sympathy for the few, if any at all, who would grieve over his death, nor had he concern for the welfare of his family—for he had none. He rejoiced not at the thought of heavenly rewards, nor did he tremble at the thought of an eternal damnation.

Simply put, he feared obliteration of his life's stamp—the earthly imprint of his mortal existence. He knew that time soon erases any remembrance of those who have accomplished nothing beyond the ordinary. For some, eternal fame may stem from a marvelous good, or from a horrendous evil. He had lived with—and at times intentionally without—the restraints of morality, but not noticeably so.

To him, his quest for earthly continuance was not born from psychosis, nor was it rooted in phobia. It was not because he needed more time to recompense his regrets, because he had little remorse. He merely pursued his vehement desire to sustain his self—a personal perpetuation beyond his own end.

The young nurse entered the nursery, telling a middle-aged nurse who was more of a corporate scientist than a caregiver, "Mr. Doppel wants to see the baby. I think he's close to death."

The older nurse, reading in a rocking chair, looked up from her magazine, and said, "Everyday, for the last two weeks we've thought that he was close to death. But I'm glad you're here, I need a smoke break." She stood up, and dug in her purse for her cigarettes and lighter.

The young nurse looked in the crib, seeing the little three-month-old boy sucking on his pacifier and staring up at a colorful mobile hanging from the ceiling. The little guy spit out his binky and smiled up at her while kicking his tiny legs with excitement. She said, "I hope all of the prearranged adoption and inheritance works out for this cute little guy. I've really come to love him."

"It's hard to believe," the older nurse replied, "but he is adorable. But I can't wait until this is over, so we can all get back to our research projects."

"I hope when it's all over," the young nurse stated with concern, "I'll have another job to start. I have bills to pay."

The older nurse left the room, then popped her head back in, and with an unlit cigarette dangling out of her mouth muttered, "Oh, and by the way, I just changed his diaper and fed him."

"Good, thanks," said the young nurse, slipping the photo into her smock pocket, scooping up the baby, and cradling him in her arms. Rocking him gently, she spoke softly to him. The tot smiled, eyes twinkling, murmuring happy coos and squeaks.

The infant had been conceived and birthed with great care and concern, unlike the birth of Mr. Doppel, eighty-five years before.

On the day that Mr. Doppel had entered the world, he came near to nonexistence—no life stamp at all. Only the woman who bore him knew of him, and she had callously discarded him in a downtown trashcan. A scrounging transient had heard his muffled cries escaping from the rotten garbage. The vagrant had nothing but the clothes on his back, and just enough compassion left in his destitute life to save a newborn infant.

The foundling was placed in an orphanage and named Lorant Elliot Doppel after the bum who found him. Over all the cheerless days of his childhood, Lorant was never adopted, so the name stuck. Inadvertently, the tramp had left his own life's stamp.

Mr. Doppel bounced from one abusive foster family to another, until he ran away. At eighteen years of age, after living on the streets for a time, he secured a job working for a pharmaceutical drug company. He cleaned the laboratories and the cages of the rats, guinea pigs, and monkeys used for testing. The company allowed him to live in the supply room, as long as he pursued an education. He attended night courses earning a high school diploma. He went to college and studied hard to gain a degree in biochemistry. He eventually worked with the other scientists in the lab, earning enough money to move into a small apartment. He was obsessed with his work, abstaining from any friends or social life. After working his shift and on his own time, he developed a few products for anti-aging. He left the drug company and invested his meager savings into his own creations. With relentless drive and hard work, he built a vast company of products—energy pills, wrinkle-vanishing cremes, and hair growth inducers—all for feeling and looking young. He marketed them aggressively, playing into the fears that people have about old age and death. After fifty years he retired, letting those younger and more educated manage his company. He still delved into his own projects, integrating great minds and new technology in the pursuit of his life's stamp.

Mr. Doppel did not know his lineage. For sixty-five of his eighty-five years, he had hoped and painstakingly searched for a clue to his unknown clan, but to no avail. He never loved a woman, married, or started a family. He lived his entire life blaming the 'woman who bore me' for his bitterness toward all women. He desired to father children, but could not. The drugs and alcohol consumed by his mother had left him impotent.

All that confirmed his mortal footprint was his company's accomplishments in biochemistry. Personally, he received no accolades, though it had been his investment. His hired young scientists wrote in the journals and received the credit.

All of his achievements were rapidly fading from contemporary notability—as well as the ledgers of human remembrance—into the dusty archives of "who cares." Maybe his obsession would have waned if he had introduced an invention that graced a person's life, such as the works of Thomas Edison or Henry Ford. If he had authored a book, painted a chapel, or composed a masterpiece, then his life's stamp would be secure. However, his name did not circulate in high society, nor was his life lauded in the annals of science, medicine, religion, politics, literature, or philanthropy. He knew that soon after his death, he would be forgotten. Time would quickly evaporate the misty droplets of his existence, and nonchalantly discard his life stamp like an unwanted baby in a downtown trashcan.

The young nurse returned to Mr. Doppel's bedroom. He did not move, and he looked to be dead. She called to him, "Mr. Doppel—Mr. Doppel." He snapped open his eyes and gasped for air, as if someone had held his head under water. "Mr. Doppel," she said, "I have the photograph and the baby."

"Give me the baby!" he growled.

She laid the little boy in his arms, then placed her hand over her mouth, distressed to see the sweet, healthy baby in the arms of the feeble, old man.

Mr. Doppel gazed down at the baby with a long, scrutinizing look, then bluntly ordered, "Hand me the photograph!"

"Yes, Mr. Doppel," she said, handing him the photo.

He cradled the baby in the elbow of his right arm while he stretched out his left hand and seized the timeworn photograph. He stared at the picture, then the baby, then the picture, back and forth numerous times. The photograph, taken at the orphanage eighty-five years before, was of Mr. Doppel as a three-month-old infant.

As the nurse peered down at the aged man cradling the infant, she saw the deep creases around Mr. Doppel's eyes gather, and his eyes faintly twinkle. A thin smile formed out of the wrinkled corners of his mouth. The rosy-cheeked baby sucked contently on his tiny index finger as drool glistened on his chin. The infant stared wide-eyed up into the man's elderly face without making a sound. Mr. Doppel stared silently back, hoping that the boy would grow to be a healthy, productive man. An amazing man who might leave an incredible life stamp.

After a few moments of silence, the ailing man mumbled in a hoarse whisper, "The baby—is me—the baby is me."

Mr. Doppel grinned, inhaled a deep rattling breath, closed his eyes, and then exhaled for the last time. At eighty-five years old, Lorant Elliot Doppel died. In his arms—his life's stamp—the infant Lorant Elliot Doppel—his clone.

DRIVE-UP BUBBY

THE LAST TIME Bubby trudged onto a scale, he weighed five hundred and thirteen pounds, and he had gained weight since then. At five-foot-six, he appeared as wide as he was tall. He used to work at home entering data on his computer, but that job went away. A year later he was still unemployed and receiving financial assistance. All day, every day, he watched TV, ate, and felt worthless.

One afternoon, Dr. Singh, Bubby's doctor from social services, made a scheduled house call to administer a complete medical check-up. He knocked on Bubby's door and heard a garbled holler, "Come on in!"

As the young doctor entered, he saw Bubby sitting on the couch, watching TV, and stuffing a huge meatball sandwich smothered in marinara sauce into his mouth. As Bubby bit down on the sandwich, the red sauce oozed out, dripping onto the colorful collage of food stains on his size-4XL white T-shirt. Littered all around him were empty pizza boxes, fast food bags, Chinese food cartons, and one-liter diet rootbeer bottles.

"How'ya doin' Doc?" Bubby muttered between chews.

Dr. Singh set his medical bag down, stroked his well-trimmed beard, and scrutinized Bubby through a physician's eyes. He spoke with a sharp accent from India, articulating each word in a singsong, airy voice, beginning each sentence in a high tone and then dropping low. "Ooh Bubby, I am fine. But, I am shocked! You have gained so much weight. It is obvious that you did not follow my recommendations from my last few visits."

Bubby set the sandwich down, turned off the TV with the remote, swallowed the mouthful of food, and in his country drawl apologized, "I'm sorry Doc. Ya'know I've tried, but I've got five fast food restaurants at the end of my block servin' up burgers, pizza, tacos, chow mein, and sandwiches, not to mention everything that goes with'em." Bubby closed his eyes and sniffed the air like there was a bouquet of roses under his nose. "All them smells float down here twenty-four-seven, creep in through my windows, and tempt me with every breath I take. Now combine that with my humongous appetite, and you're lookin' at a big, big, guy. Me!"

"By the looks of you and this room, it seems that you have been on a fast-food frenzy. That is a very bad thing. Bubby, you must control what you eat, and how much you eat," admonished Dr. Singh.

"I'm tryin' Doc. I've stopped eatin' them fried apple pies that always burn my tongue and those little French toast sticks that'ya dip in syrup."

Dr. Singh shook his head and advised, "That is not enough Bubby. You are slowly but surely killing yourself with all of this fried food. You must stop. Now, please, stand up and take off your shirt."

Bubby squirmed to the edge of the couch, then grunted as he strained to push himself up using all the strength he had in his legs and arms. The incredible exertion made him breathe heavily and caused beads of sweat to form on his forehead. Once upright, he wrestled off his T-shirt. Trying to catch his breath, he wheezed, "Okay Doc, do your thing!"

The doctor reached into his medical bag, withdrew his stethoscope, and then walked around the girth of Bubby, checking the big man's breathing and heartbeat. He then plucked the instrument out of his ears and cautioned, "Bubby, you must reduce your intake of calories, carbohydrates, and fat, and begin lightly exercising. By the way, how is it that you can hardly get off the couch, but you are able to drive to the fast food restaurants every day?"

"I don't," confessed Bubby. "I pay Marco, my pizza delivery guy, to do it for me. All I have to do is call his cell phone, tell'im what I want, and he brings it to me. It could be any kind of food, as long as it's not too far from his delivery zone. If he's not workin', then Richie, my back-up delivery kid, takes care of me. I still buy a lot of pizzas, plus, they're earnin' a little extra cash. It's all good."

"I see," said Dr. Singh with a frown, "it is all very convenient for you to continue this bad habit." Next, he checked Bubby's blood pressure, which was much too high. After that he put on a pair of latex gloves and drew a blood sample. He then ordered, "Now drop your shorts and lift your belly for me." Bubby wrapped his arms around his gut like it was a keg of beer and held it up while the doctor continued, "Ok Bubby, turn your head to the side and cough, and again please. Thank you. Now turn around, bend over, and put your hands on the arm of the sofa."

"Oh come on Doc, do I have to?" whined Bubby.

Without sympathy, Dr. Singh shot back, "Absolutely, and believe me Bubby, it is no party for me either."

Bubby reluctantly bent over.

For about ten seconds, Dr. Singh spelunkered around with two of his gloved fingers as Bubby groaned with discomfort. As the doctor backed away, he removed his gloves and tossed them in Bubby's trash container. He asked casually, "Do you have burning and itching?"

"Yessir," said Bubby sheepishly, still feeling somewhat violated.

"I will prescribe some ointment and have it delivered. Okay, that completes the examination." The doctor then picked up the urine sample that Bubby had ready for him and placed the sealed container in his bag. As he was leaving, he turned, waved a long finger at Bubby, and scolded, "You are a good man Bubby, a very good man, with a very dangerous habit. You must stop this over-indulgence right now! I will be back next week. Have a good day."

"You too, Doc," said Bubby as he plopped back down on the couch, clicked on the TV, and snatched up his meatball sandwich.

A week later, Dr. Singh returned with the results of Bubby's tests. Again, he found Bubby sitting on the couch and watching TV. Speaking in a solemn tone, the doctor warned, "Bubby, you have a serious medical problem. I have confirmed it with your tests. Your Body Mass Index that correlates your weight with your height is way over 80. A score of fewer than 25 is indicative of a healthy person. I hate to sound harsh, but you have to hear me: Your heart can only support one man, not the weight of three. Unfortunately, you suffer from a…"

There was a lively knock at the door and Bubby interrupted the doctor. "I hear'ya Doc, but Marco's at the door. Please 'scuse me a minute." Without getting up, he shouted, "Marco, come on in buddy!"

As Marco, an eighteen-year-old young man entered through the door, he rattled off in a Spanish accent, "Hey Bubby! Wuz up?"

They greeted by slapping hands as Bubby replied casually, "Oh, just Doc givin' me the lowdown on my health."

"Oh yeah, well, you'd better be okay," quipped Marco, "you're my best customer! And just to let you know, I put extra cheese on the pizza, just like you wanted it."

"Right-on Marco. You're so cool man! Hey Marco, this is Dr. Singh."

"How do you do?" said Dr. Singh without smiling.

"Everythang is everythang," replied Marco, which really didn't make any sense, but he had heard a rapper say it, so, he thought it had to be cool. He then slid the box of pizza out of its hot pouch—releasing its zesty aromas—and set it on a TV tray in front of Bubby.

When the scent of the Italian pie smacked Bubby in the nose, he grinned broadly, and his neon-blue eyes twinkled with excitement. He moaned, "Mmmm, that smells soooo gooooood!" He then grabbed his black, shoulder-length hair, pulled it away from his face and bound it in a ponytail. He was ready to eat.

Dr. Singh waited impatiently, scowling at them both, tapping his pen on his clipboard of test results.

Bubby paid for the pizza, tipping Marco generously. As the delivery boy walked out the door, Bubby said, "See'ya tomorrow dude, and remember, no matter what I order, make it with extra cheese!"

"You got it man," chimed Marco. "Thanks for the nice tip. I'll see you mañana Bro!"

As Marco shut the door, Bubby opened the box, and with a big grin, asked, "Want some pizza Doc? You'll love it!"

Dr. Singh replied curtly, "No, absolutely not!" Anxious about being the bearer of bad news, he removed his glasses and began cleaning them with a soft cloth that he kept in his pocket. "Like I was saying Bubby, you suffer from congestive heart disease, and since you are so big, with such a weak heart, any exertion will most likely kill you. It is ironic, but your sitting on the couch and hiring a delivery boy has probably saved your life. Your condition will worsen though, with each pizza, with each passing day. I recommend confinement to your bed. I do not think you have the time or the health to endure any bariatric surgery. Nor do you demonstrate the will power for a strict diet." Dr. Singh slipped his smudge free glasses on and looked Bubby in the eyes. "Bubby, I cannot be more serious. One day soon, your heart is just going to give out. You must get your affairs in order. I am sorry."

Bubby felt distressed as the doctor spoke, but shoved a hot piece of the thick-crust, all-meat pizza in his mouth, and mumbled, "I hear'ya Doc. I learned in counselin' that because I hurt inside, I'm deliberately killin' myself by overeatin'. Instead of drownin' myself with booze, or swallowin' drugs to feel better, I eat. Look at that pizza. Believe me. It tastes great, and I'll eat every bit of it. It'll be gone, but not my sadness. To be honest with'ya Doc, I'm tired of fightin' this battle. I just don't care what happens anymore."

"Bubby, I care what happens to you, not only as your doctor, but also as your friend," assured Dr. Singh, as he opened the door to leave. "You are a good man, and I am sorry that you are suffering, but please try to eat healthy foods, reduce your portions, and maybe you will have a chance. If not, you will spend your final days immobile in your bed. Bubby, do something that will bring you happiness—except eating. Okay? I will see you soon."

"Okay Doc, I understand. See'ya." After the doctor left, Bubby felt the impact of the doctor's words. He hung his head and wept. He was weary of the flab fight, the weight war, and the ongoing oppression of obesity. He did not want to just lie in his bed and wait to die, letting the delivery boy find him dead with cold chow mein noodles dangling out of his mouth. Depressed, he turned on the TV. Seeking comfort, he grabbed up another big, steamy, slice of pizza with stretchy, melted cheese hanging off it. He took a big bite, but chewed it without delight.

Bubby always assumed that he was doomed to die just like his mother Bridgett. Overweight, she had died five years before from a heart attack. Since his father, Bobby, a long haul trucker, died in an icy freeway accident twenty years ago, both Bubby and Bridgett had developed eating disorders.

Bubby, an only child, was twelve at the time of his father's death. He idolized his dad; they were pals. In fact Bubby's given name was Robert, just like his father's, but people called his dad Bobby and him Bubby.

Whenever Bobby returned from a haul, he'd park his eighteen-wheeler on the street at the trailer park's entrance. As the air brakes of the big rig squealed to a stop, he'd blow the horn and young Bubby would race down the driveway to greet him. His dad would jump down from the cab, and wrestle-hug Bubby, and then they'd walk back to the singlewide, with their arms around each other's shoulders. Bobby would greet Bridgett with a long kiss, and a tight hug. Then, smiling mischievously, gazing into her big blue eyes, he'd slide his hands down her waist, and squeeze her butt cheeks with both hands.

After every trip, on the night of his return, Bobby would take Bridgett and Bubby out to their favorite all-you-can-eat restaurant—the Hooray! Buffet. They'd connect again as a family while they eagerly chowed on savory fried chicken, roast beef, mashed potatoes with gravy, hot fresh rolls with butter, and for dessert: cookies, cakes, pies, pudding, and ice cream with candy sprinkles on top. No matter how much Bobby would eat, he remained thin; not so with Bridgett and Bubby.

Bubby remembered the last time they had dined together before his dad's death. Bobby had entertained them, as always, with the adventures—and mishaps—of hauling freight across the country. "Man oh man, Bubby," he had said, "I wish'ya could've seen it, right out the windshield, the Grand Canyon." He then described it in every detail. "From there, I hauled a load north. Oh my word, Bubby, ya'would've loved it, right in front of my eyes, Mount Rushmore. Man, what a sight!" He talked about battlefields, historical monuments, and state parks. He described snow-covered mountains, crystal-clear lakes, and red sand deserts. He saw wild animals and snarled traffic. He rambled on about good weather, bad weather, and worse weather. He talked a lot about the people he met, and how good they were.

Bridgett had chattered about keeping house, and about the people in the trailer park. As her husband took a bite of food, she had interjected, "Bobby, I know you're tired from the road, but tomorrow will'ya take a quick look at the dryer? It ain't dryin'. It takes over an hour for just a small load."

He had replied simply, "Okay baby."

Then she leaned in across the table and reported in a hushed tone, "Hon, you 'member Billy and Marlene in the blue trailer a couple rows over and down at the far end, well, their daughter Darlene's goin' to move back in with'em. I guess she's 'spectin' soon."

Bobby had replied, "Is that so?" He didn't get involved with the gossip of the park, so he changed the subject asking, "Sugar, how's our son treatin' his mama?"

"He's doin' fine, 'cept he keeps gettin' behind on his homewor..."

Bubby had interrupted and started rattling on about his video game, and how he'd conquered the next level. His dad had smiled, listening patiently. Then said, "That sounds like a lot of fun son—but, how's your homework comin'?"

When all three were done with trips to the buffet table, and while Bobby had sipped his coffee, he concluded his stories, "Bubby, there's a lot of good hearted people across our big, beautiful country, and remember: You can never—now pay attention son—Bubby—you can never have enough friends. I only hope that someday, someway, you'll get to experience it all like I have."

The next day Bobby had fixed the dryer. The day after that, he had left on the road again. A few days later, Bridgett had received a phone call from the Colorado State Patrol. In her shock, the only words she had really heard were, "Mountain pass—snow and ice—horrible crash—sorry, so sorry, but Robert didn't make it."

Grief consumed them both. After Bobby's death, the only joy they ever felt was eating at the Hooray! Buffet.

Bubby knew that he couldn't lose weight. He was too overweight to exercise and he craved food too much to diet. He believed losing weight was impossible, so he gave up on the fantasy of being thin. He accepted the fact that he did not have long to live.

Confined to his bed, the boredom tortured Bubby. The only things that remotely excited him were the next mouthful of French fries dipped in mustard and swirled in ketchup, the extra-crispy fried chicken with a side dish of sticky-thick mac and cheese, or a good movie on TV. The mesmerizing fumes of fast food constantly wafted into his house, inciting his raging hunger.

Bubby had not had a girlfriend since his high school days when he was a trim 260 pounds. He had no extended family that he was close to, and most of the friends he had were busy with their careers and their own families. He feared that he would die alone.

After a month of bed-ridden isolation, he decided that if he only had a short time to live, then he would do—as Dr. Singh suggested—something that would bring him happiness. He determined not to squander the last few days, weeks, or months of his life lying on a mattress. Like his dad had hoped, Bubby would travel America and see the sights his dad had seen, and all along the way—make some friends.

He made a plan and started working it immediately. He sold the house that he had inherited from his mother, who had bought it with his dad's life insurance money. He received a sizeable equity, insuring that he would have more than enough money to pursue his quest. Next, he sold most of the home's furnishings, then the junker of a car that had sat in his driveway for the last two years. He replaced it with a brand new, bright blue, convertible Volkswagen Beetle. He had it customized to fit all of his needs.

One sunny day the retrofitters delivered the car, and a few hours after it arrived, a crane with a hoist and an operator showed up, then a roofer, then the nosy neighbors gathered out front. Bubby had gained a ton of weight since Dr. Singh's visit and could barely walk because of his heart condition. Even if he could walk, he couldn't fit though the door. The workers would have to cut a hole in the roof and lift him by crane to his car. Bubby waited on his bed, eager to embark upon his adventure.

Above Bubby's bed, the roofer cut a Bubby-size hole. The crane operator lowered a hoist through the hole, strapped Bubby in, lifted him up, and swung him around in midair over the housetop. Bubby laughed like a youngster on a Ferris wheel. Then, with the beetle's convertible top down, they lowered him delicately behind the steering wheel into the front seat of the car. The operator and his crane left, while the roofer repaired the roof.

Bubby fastened his extended seat belt, slipped on his knockoff Ray Ban sunglasses, waved to the curious bystanders, beeped the horn twice, and sped off.

At the end of his first week on the road sightseeing, and as the setting sun eased behind the 'W' on the Wal-Mart sign, Bubby pulled into the store's parking lot. The mega store had a gracious policy permitting overnighters. He drove to the perimeter of the lot and saw an old pick-up truck with a camper shell, a man sitting in a folding lawn chair, and an average sized dog chained to the truck's bumper. The man waved at him. The dog barked. From front to back, the chalky white truck had rusty dents and long, raking scratches. The bulky camper piggybacked the truck extending over the cab, making it appear top-heavy, as if it would flip over when turning a corner. The man wore a soiled, straw cowboy hat, a long sleeved, red-white-and-blue plaid shirt buttoned up to his neck, faded blue jeans, a large glinting belt buckle, and dusty boots. His silver hair hung out of his hat to his shoulders. The dog was gray and fuzzy, like a large ball of dryer lint—with teeth.

Bubby parked within shouting distance from them, and lowered the top. The man stood up, patted the tail-wagging dog on the head, and then strolled toward Bubby. The dog followed, but the chain stopped it short. The old man walked bowlegged and tilted to his left side at the waist. With a wad of chew in his bottom lip he hollered, "Hello there! Ya'stayin' for the night?"

Bubby stretched up and spoke over the top of his windshield, "Yessir, I am!"

"Well then, welcome neighbor." The cowboy hobbled up, reached into the car and shook Bubby's hand, "Hi, I'm KaBob. That's what people call me." Wrinkles and deep creases like an old map of rough roads and dead ends lined the man's weathered face. He had a wide jack-o-lantern smile with a few teeth missing, and his gleaming eyes snitched that he was younger than he looked.

"Hi KaBob, I'm Bubby. That's what people call me."

"Well, nice to meet'ya Bubby. Oh, and that mangy dog over there—his name's Bite-u. He tends to growl and snap at folks. I call'im that so they'll leave'im alone, and don't get bit." KaBob turned his head and fitzed out brown juicy spit onto the ground. Leaning against the car door, he peered into the vehicle and exclaimed, "My god son, ya'got some stuff goin' on in here, don't'ya?"

Bubby, proud of his car, sucked in a deep breath sticking out his chest and replied, "Well, since I live in this car, it's got all I need."

"Tell me it ain't so. How can a big guy like you—live in this bug of a car?"

"Check it out!" Bubby said with enthusiasm as he began pointing around the vehicle. "I had my retrofitters remove the seats and install this wide, heavy-duty one. The back swivels up and down so I can lay back and sleep. All the fabric is breathable to prevent rashes. See, they moved the steerin' wheel, instrument panel, and both pedals to the center of the car."

The old cowboy shoved his hat back, whistled, and burst out, "Well, ain't that somethin'. Now, don't tell me that's a TV in the dash."

"That's right. It's a 10" flat screen. Not only that, I got this killer stereo, a phone with a headset for drivin', and this talkin' map to help me find my way."

"Dang, don't that beat all. Since you're livin' in this car—what'a'ya do for food?"

"I go to drive-up windows. No pots and pans that way."

KaBob scratched his head just under his hat. "So I reckon the only time'ya git out of your car is for a toilet."

"Nope, I can't get out. With my heart condition, it'll most likely kill me. But look, this car's got everything." Bubby leaned over lifting his rear off the seat. "See, the seat's equipped with a toilet. This slidin' cover opens underneath me. My pants have a Velcro flap, and I ain't wearin' no skivvies. After I use it, I push this blue button, and a small high-pressure spray washes me where the sun-don't-shine. Then I push this green button, the lid closes, and it flushes into the dump tank."

"Partner—that's wild," said KaBob, shaking his head in disbelief.

"How 'bout this?" Bubby reached over and turned on the water in a small plastic sink mounted on the driver's door. "It's got hot water. I use it to wash up, brush my teeth and shave. In case you're wonderin', it all works on pressurized air. When its time, I drive into a trailer station where the attendants empty the dump tank and fill up the air and water tanks."

"I don't see no shower nor no bathtub," KaBob said smartly, thinking he had found a loophole in all this auto automation.

"You're right. But bathin's easy. I got my sink, soap, and a giant sponge. I put the top up, crank on some tunes, and get to scrubbin'."

"Son, it sounds like'ya got it all figured out," said KaBob, spitting a wad of chew juice onto the asphalt.

"Not only that—when I need money—I drive up to an ATM. When the car's dirty, I drive through a car wash. When the car needs gas, or oil, or the tires need air, I just drive into a gas station, honk, and ask for some help. I treat people nice and tip'em well. I always get help."

"That's amazin'. I'm truly impressed son. Hey, how 'bout'ya back up that Buck Rogers car of yours next to my lawn chair, and I'll round us up some grub."

"Now that sounds like a plan my man!" Bubby said, then backed up the car, and parked it next to the chair and camper.

Bite-u barked, then jumped up, leaning his paws against the car. He panted, smiling at Bubby. Bubby reached out to pet him on the head. The mutt snapped at him, yapping loudly. Bubby jerked back his hand and scolded, "Bite-u, how'ya gonna make friends bein' so ornery?"

KaBob cooked. Bite-u stood against the car staring at Bubby. Bubby ignored him, chose a travel destination for the next day, and then programmed its location into his GPS unit. It wasn't long before KaBob came out of the camper with a couple of plates of fried liver and onions, fried potatoes, and string beans with bits of bacon.

"Wow, KaBob. It smells good! I ain't had no liver'n onions since my mama used to cook'em," said Bubby.

KaBob went back in. He then came out with a large plastic cup of sweet tea in each hand and a plastic bottle of ketchup pinned under his arm. He set down the cups of tea and asked Bubby, "Ya'like ketchup on your liver'n onions?"

"Oh yeah. Thanks," Bubby gripped it, flipped it, and squirted.

They ate and talked, while Bite-u curled up nearby waiting for scraps.

"How'd'ya get a name like KaBob?" Bubby asked.

KaBob finished chewing, swallowed, took a deep breath like it was going to be a long story, got real serious, and explained, "Well, Bubby, my real name ain't KaBob, it's just Bob. I've been workin' rodeos for darn near forty years. I started out as a cocky, young bullrider. Did real good; won some prize money; made a name for myself. Never feared any them bulls—until I sat upon the brick-red back of Destruction. He was considered a lucky draw, earnin' a cowboy higher points—if the cowboy survived. I'll tell'ya, I felt like I was sittin' on a load of dynamite." KaBob stopped talking for a couple of seconds, and just stared off at the sunset while the memory became clearer. "Anyway, while I was cinchin' my suicide grip on my bullrope, that crazy bull darn near bucked me out of the pen. First time I ever thought about turnin' a bull out, but…" Kabob snugged down his hat, sucked in a deep breath, and gritted his teeth, "once it's your go'round, it ain't the cowboy way to get off. So, I gave the head nod. That rank beast exploded out of the chute like a freight train bound for hell—takin' me with'im. He spun so fast, everthang blurred. He'd spring into the air like a ballerina, then come crashin' down like a cement truck jarrin' my bones. He'd buck, whippin' my face into his skull. He'd kick, slammin' my head into his rump. I knew it to be day, but I swear I was seein' stars. I'll admit it. It wasn't skill or courage that kept me on that bull; it was powerful fear. I rode'im out—eight seconds—makin' me that rodeo's champion. But, I didn't think about it much bouncin' in that am'lance speedin' to the hospital."

"An ambulance? What happened to'ya?" Bubby asked, stabbing his fork stacking up a mouthful of string beans on it.

"Ya'see, Destruction charged out of the chute, chippin' a horn on the gate, makin' that horn a razor sharp spear. When I tried to dismount, he kicked up his hind legs, tossin' me over the dashboard right onto that horn. It skewered clean through me." KaBob stood up, lifting his shirt and said, "Right here." He pointed at a nasty scar where the horn had pierced through his abdomen. He turned around saying, "And this is where it poked out. I nearly lost a kidney and part of a lung. My drinkin' partner, Wace Needles, one hell of a bullfighter, jumped off the fence, gave chase, grabbed hold of my belt, and yanked me down from certain death. While draggin' me to safety, he took the same gol-durn horn to a butt cheek. He's tough as tires, so he patched up okay. Wasn't long after that, over some ice cold beers, ol' Wace got all smart-alecky and nicknamed me KaBob."

"Man, oh man, that's amazin'! Did'ya ever ride a bull again?"

"Nope—gave it up for ropin'. Eventually, I gave that up too, and got a job workin' the chutes with the Pro Rodeo circuit. Bite-u and me—we go where it goes. When its time to move on—I just fold up my lawn chair, unchain Bite-u, and hit the road. We're on the road now 'cause we're headin' up to a rodeo in Idaho."

"Well, I'm on the road too, seein' the sights and makin' new friends like you. My dad always told me, 'Bubby—you can never have enough friends.' Anyway, that's a heck of a story KaBob. Thanks for tellin' it to me—and thanks for fixin' that tasty dinner." Bubby yawned and stretched. "I guess I'll pull up over there, put up the top, and get some sleep. Nice to meet'ya, KaBob. Goodnight."

As KaBob stacked the plates and cups, he said, "Nice to meet'ya too Bubby, be safe on the road, and in everthang'ya do—be a hero like ol' Wace Needles. Goodnight."

Bubby moved the car. Bite-u barked as KaBob raked him off some dinner scraps to shut him up.

The next morning Bubby awoke with the sun peeping out from behind the green Starbucks sign across the street. KaBob, Bite-u, the lawn chair, and the truck were already gone and on the road. Bubby buzzed over to the Starbucks drive-up window and ordered a Venti mocha cappuccino. From there, he drove to the nearest Krispy Kreme for a box of jelly-filled donuts, then hit the freeway.

Bubby drove all over the country, east and west, north and south, never leaving his car. If he had a flat tire, he called AAA on his cell phone. If he needed anything at all, he'd simply call the appropriate store, explain his situation, and they brought it out to him. He drove to wherever and whatever interested him. Whether the weather was sunny or stormy, the top down or up, Bubby moved and grooved to the soulful sounds of Motown. He saw historical sites and earthly wonders, state parks, monuments, and the changing colors of the seasons. He met interesting people in interesting places. All the while he gained more weight.

He treated everyone with love and respect and tipped those who helped him. People started calling him "Drive-up Bubby," and as newspapers and TV news reported on his adventures, he became quite a celebrity. America was quick to adopt him. After losing John Candy and Chris Farley, Bubby filled the large void that they'd left behind. He conducted interviews from his car, and as people saw his kindness, humor, and charisma, his popularity grew.

People parked their cars up next to his; they rolled down their windows, and talked with him for hours. When they passed him on the road, they'd honk their horns and wave. Bubby would honk twice, smile, salute, and wave back.

When he pulled up to a drive-up window, the workers would yell, "Hey everybody, its Drive-up Bubby!" The young people would leave their stations and gather at the windows and gawk at him. Some would even ask for an autograph. More often than not, the manager would say, "You don't have to pay for a thing, Bubby. It's all on the house."

The corporate executives of all the restaurant chains wanted Bubby to endorse their food. He refused to do it; he was too busy making friends and touring America.

Out of all of the thousands of people Bubby met, there was one person who was special—and pretty. He met Brenda at a campground in the Rocky Mountains. The day was friendly with a slight breeze that tweedled through the pines. Bubby had parked the car on a scenic bluff and lowered the top. He was taking in the view of a waterfall down in the river valley when he noticed a woman on a trail, hiking toward him. Bubby swallowed hard and stared at her. As she drew closer out of the shade of the pines and into the sunlight, he saw that she had violet-blue eyes and shiny, golden hair with one curl flipping up at the ends just above her shoulders. Although she looked a couple of inches shorter than him, and three hundred pounds lighter, she was still a big girl with most of her plump in her rump. Bubby sat up straight, stuck out his chest, and sucked in some—but not much of his belly.

She strolled up to him and said, "Hi, I'm Brenda. I'm from Minniesooodah." She spoke with a Norwegian sounding accent that played out in a phonetic rhythm—do de der de do de der de. "I'm stayin' with my folks in da motor home in da next campsite."

Bubby, speaking all deep and sexy, sounding like singer Barry White, said, "Hi, nice to meet'ya Brenda, I'm…"

"Yah, sure, I know who ya are," Brenda playfully interrupted, "geeez, ya don't have ta tell me. Yer Drive-up Bubby. I know all about ya from watchin' TV. Yer cute ya know."

Bubby blushed, and said in his normal voice, "Ohhh, that's just TV stuff. There's a lot more to me than bein' a biggie-size, fast food eatin' c'lebrity in a car."

"I've nothin' ta do but take in da scenery," she said. "Cripes sake, my mom's doin' her greetin' card stampin' an' my dad's installin' some new gadget on da motor home. I'd love ta get ta know ya. Do ya want ta sit an' talk?"

"Sure! It'll be tight, but if'ya don't mind—come on in."

"Yah sure, you betcha."

Bubby popped open both of the car's doors and slid over to his left as far as he could with a large part of his derrière dangling out the car. Brenda scooted in to sit next to him with most of her tushy resting on the seat, but some overflowed out the right door. Both were in the car—mostly. Both seemed to be comfortable, and both seemed to enjoy the tight squeeze. After getting to know each other for awhile, Bubby slipped his arm around her shoulders, locking him and her together in a sort of snuggle.

They talked for hours, gazing at the vast panoramic view before them. The sun set in the west amidst a backdrop of fiery orange clouds, and the first star appeared in the vacant purple sky of the east. The full moon rose, then stole across the heavens, grandstanding in front of infinite, brilliant stars.

He told her about his adventures, the sights, and the people. She shared about her hometown and about going back to college studying nutritional psychology. At twenty-six, she was committed to her goals of helping herself first, and then opening a center for those who needed support establishing their self-worth and a balanced diet. He talked about his parents and their deaths. She told him about the death of her older brother, a soldier in Desert Storm. She cried for Bubby's loss; he cried for hers. They both reached for the dispenser under the dash, filled with brown recycled paper napkins, and wiped each other's tears.

As it was getting late, Brenda's folks peeked out the window of their nearby motor home and saw that she was okay. In fact, they were happy for her. She had met Drive-up Bubby. From what they saw of him on TV, he seemed to be a nice man.

As shooting stars streaked now and again across the midnight sky, Bubby and Brenda shared about hurting and eating and the cyclical perpetuation of depression, food, feeling good, and gaining weight, more depression, more food—on and on.

Brenda became quiet, cried softly, then burst out sobbing,

"Cripes Bubby, I try so hard ta lose weight. My parents, my friends, my doctor—everyone—is always sayin' I need ta 'slim down.' I want to, I need to, I strive to, but no matter how hard I try—I just can't. I feel so ugly."

Bubby reached for another napkin, then tenderly turned her moonlit face toward him, and dabbed at the shimmering tears that trickled down her cheeks. She sniffed and stared back at his face glowing with lunar radiance. He spoke softly, almost in a whisper, "Brenda, to me, your beauty is breathtakin'. Your kindness, your enthusiasm for life, and your desire to help others adds sparkle to your eyes and dazzle to your smile. Your lovely face is soft, like a rose petal. Everything about you—your walk, your voice, your giggle—is adorable."

The entire time Bubby was speaking, Brenda gazed up into his compassionate eyes and let his sincerity liberate her from the cumbersome chains of her self-loathing. For the first time, in a very long time, she felt pretty and sexy. She smiled shyly and cooed, "Thank ya Bubby. I think yer such a handsome man, an' ya have such a big heart."

He smiled and said, "Thank you, Brenda." He then sighed heavily.

She asked, "What's wrong Bubby?"

Bubby held both of her hands in both of his hands and said, "I hate to tell'ya this, Brenda, but the very reason I'm on this great adventure, is that…" he hesitated as he searched for the right words, "well—I have a serious heart condition. Most likely—I'm goin' to die soon."

"Oh nooo," she gasped, then hugged him, burying her head into his chest. He pulled her in tight. They held each other in silence. A coyote howled somewhere out in the canyon. An owl hooted nearby.

After a while they talked, smiled, and joked again. As the night cooled down, Bubby reached into a compartment behind them and pulled out a quilted blanket. They snuggled under it and chatted quietly the rest of the night, giggling at times in hushed tones. As dawn appeared, sadness came with it. The sun had coursed half way around the globe to peek out the other side, proclaiming it time that they go their separate ways. Their budding romance would never bloom.

"Well, my knight in shinin' VW," whispered Brenda, "I guess I should go in an' help my folks ready the RV. We're headin' back to Minniesooodah today. Before ya leave, would ya like some breakfast? Some blueberry muffins or a bowl of Wheaties?"

Bubby didn't feel hungry. He felt sad. It was time to leave his newfound friend. "Thank you Brenda," he replied, "but no thank you. I really must hit the highway. Thanks for the wonderful evenin'." He then hesitated, wondering whether or not to ask her what he wanted to ask her, and then he just asked, "Could I—maybe, uh, kiss'ya goodbye?"

Brenda leaned in closer and purred, "Yah, sure, you betcha Bubby, I'd love a kiss."

Bubby cupped her angelic face in his hands and gazed into her inviting eyes. He said softly, "You're the purtiest woman I ever did see." He slowly leaned in, closed his eyes, and kissed her on her moist, soft lips, and held it, held it, held it, held it—with a little kissy smack at the end.

"Mmmm," she moaned, as if under a spell, "geeez, Bubby that was a humdinger. Yer such a wonderful man an' a great kisser!"

"Thanks Brenda," blushed Bubby, "you're pretty hot yourself!"

"I'm happy ya think so, Bubby."

"Bye bye, sweetie. I'll call'ya from time to time, if it's okay."

"Yah, sure, okeydokey. I'll be waitin' ta hear from ya."

Bubby backed his car away from the bluff, stopped, slipped on his sunglasses, and gazed at Brenda. She looked sad, but mustered up a smile, waved, and threw him a kiss. He waved back, caught the kiss with both hands, honked the horn twice, and drove off. He saw her in the rearview mirror until he made a turn though the pines. She was gone, and Bubby felt sad until he thought about calling her later, and then he felt happy again.

Bubby traveled on and saw many of the wonders that his dad had talked about. He had more fun than he could remember, and, at times, he almost felt as if his dad were with him. Bubby felt loved and was grateful for all the new friends he had made. Seeing America and meeting its people instilled in him a great pride. As time passed, Bubby grew bigger, and his heart became weaker. He thought about Brenda a lot, and called her often. They became best friends.

After a day of sightseeing, Bubby pulled into a K.O.A. campground for the night. He could think of nothing else but Brenda. He didn't even think much about food.

Bubby put on his headset and spoke, "Brenda," into his voice-actuated cell phone.

Brenda looked at her caller ID and answered. "Oh Bubby, I'm so glad ya called. I've been thinkin' about ya all day. I miss ya so much."

"I miss'ya too sweetheart. I've been thinkin' seriously, if I ought not come on up there."

"Oh yah, sure Bubby," she squealed with delight, "I'd love for ya to. Ya know yer welcome. My folks said, you could stay with us until ya find yer own place."

"Until we find *our* own place sugar."

"Really, Bubby, really?"

"Oh yeah, really Brenda. We'll get a place close by your school. We'll help each other and I'll put my mind, body, and soul into regainin' my health. Then, when you're ready, we'll open that clinic'ya talked about."

"Oh Bubby, dat sounds so wonderful!"

They talked and talked, then finally whispered goodnights. Both were so excited they had trouble falling asleep.

The next morning, with the first coos of the morning doves, he left the campground, and headed north to Minnesota.

On the way, at a highway rest stop, while he was eating only one western double bacon, double cheeseburger layered with extra onion rings and drenched in honey barbecue sauce, without an order of French fries, he heard the loud screeching of rubber tires braking on the asphalt road. He stopped in mid-chew, looked out at the two-lane highway and saw an old blue pick-up truck swerve, trying to avoid a head-on collision with a passing sports car. When the pick-up veered, it lost control and shot off the road onto the grassy area of the rest stop. The passing car stayed in the lane, zoomed by the other vehicle barely missing the careening truck, and then accelerated on without stopping. The pick-up slid sideways, just missing the block walls of the restrooms on one side and a large shade tree and picnic table on the other. It then flipped over. The force popped open the doors, and snapped the truck's worn seatbelts, ejecting both of the passengers. One body soared away from the truck, while the other tumbled with it.

Bubby watched through his windshield in disbelief. It seemed as if it were all happening in slow motion. The truck rolled again, losing a wheel that whirled across the grass, bouncing off a large plastic trashcan. Then its hood ripped off, landing on top of a picnic table. The pick-up then jolted to a stop upside-down, pinning one of the occupants underneath. Steam escaped from punctured radiator hoses. Gas trickled out from a rupture in its tank, forming a pool on the ground under the tailgate. A small fire sprung up in the engine enveloping the truck's front end with swirling black smoke.

A burly trucker at the rest stop was already running to help before the vehicle came to a stop. Bubby tossed his burger on the dash, called 9-1-1, then watched incredulously as the other passenger scrambled up from the ground. He was a boy of about twelve. He had miraculously survived and was running toward the smashed vehicle screaming hysterically, "Where's my dad? Where's my dad?"

The boy's unconscious father did not move, trapped from the waist down under the cab of the truck between the spreading fire and the swelling pool of gas.

The trucker grabbed hold of the boy, and asked, "You okay?"

The horrified boy—only suffering a few scratches on his forehead and arms—stared at his dead-like dad, and silently nodded.

"Okay, son," the trucker told him calmly, "we've got to get him out from under there, before the fire ignites that pool of gas and the tank explodes!" Right then, a mammoth recreational vehicle drove into the rest stop and an elderly, mostly bald man in blue coveralls jumped out of it and ran over to help. His gray haired wife followed a step behind him.

The boy's dad regained consciousness. Wild-eyed, he careened his head around. Realizing the danger, he cried out, "Get my boy away! Don't let him get hurt! Get him away!"

The wife of the RV man hurried over, and tugged the boy away from the vehicle. The youngster jerked free of her, charged back and shoved at the truck along with the other two men. He glanced down at his dad and started screaming, "Dad! Dad! Don't die!" Through the fear and tears in his eyes, the lad looked up at the men and pleaded, "Please don't let my dad die!"

The men dropped their shoulders into it, yet their combined strength was not enough to lift the truck up and off the distressed man.

Bubby watched in horror as the scene unfolded before his eyes. He wondered where the paramedics were. He knew he could help, and deep down he knew it would make a difference.

With courageous resolve, he shoved open his car door, squirmed and wrestled his heft over, and then placed one foot at a time out of the car. His legs felt weak, but he had to try. A man's life was at stake.

The pool of gas crept toward the fire at the front of the truck soaking into the trapped man's jeans. The wife of the RV man screamed, "The gas is going to catch fire. Hurry Ben, save him!" The two men and the boy struggled with all of their might, but to no avail.

Bubby stood up; he was out of the car; the first time in a long time. He held on to its door. His legs quivered, then shook, as his weight bore down on them. He dropped to one knee, then the other collapsed, and he let go falling face down onto his stomach. He looked up to see the flickering fire, the billowing smoke, and the dauntless rescuers.

Bubby heard the man coughing and the boy screaming hysterically, "Dad—please don't die! Please don't die!"

The boy's shrieking plea pierced Bubby's mind. It all made sense. He ate because he missed his own dad. All the good times that they had shared were at the Hooray! Buffet. Security, comfort, and love revolved around heaping helpings of food. It was as though every time he ate after his own dad's death, his mind was shrieking: *Dad, please don't die. Mom and me are waitin' for 'ya at the Hooray! Buffet. Please don't die!*

It was now clear. Eating could never bring back his dad. But, he was who he was, and how big he was, and where he was, so, he could save this kid's dad. With gallant determination, he pushed himself up and off of his huge gut and then, clinging to the car door, he pulled himself up on one leg and then the other. Fighting dizziness, with sweat pouring down his temples, and with labored breaths—he stood up.

He peered through the dense smoke and focused on the pick-up truck. He shuffled his feet sluggishly at first, then gradually built the momentum to a walk, and then increased it to a jog. Perspiration soaked him as he willed his body to move faster and faster. "Everyone," he bellowed like the horn of a freight train, "get outta the way! Get outta the way!"

The rescuers stopped, looked out through the thick smoke that engulfed the scene, and saw this gargantuan man running toward them. The wife of the RV man recognized Bubby from TV and shouted, "It's Drive-up Bubby!" They hastened to move aside.

Bubby bounded up to the burning truck, and, like a swinging wrecking ball, slammed his entire weight into it. The sheer impact lifted it off the ground.

The injured man looked up, saw huge Bubby and gasped, "Push man. By god, push with all your weight!"

The truck teetered on two wheels. The others feared Bubby's weight was not enough to hold it up, and that it would come crashing down killing the man and Bubby. They watched and waited until it would be safe to slide the injured man out of danger.

Bubby grimaced as he leaned his weight against the hot metal of the truck. His grunts increased into a warrior's battle cry. Sweat soaked his shirt. He strained, dug his feet into the ground, applied his mass, and pushed the pick-up onto its side. It teetered once each way then stood still.

The trucker and the RV man each grabbed an arm of the crushed man and dragged him a safe distance away. Bubby staggered backwards, just as the flowing gas reached the fire and ignited. Everyone took shelter behind the restroom's block walls. As the flames reached the gas tank, it caused a deafening explosion, shooting hot shrapnel through the air.

Immediately after the fiery blast, an ambulance and a fire truck sped onto the scene. The paramedics administered medical attention to the man and his son, while the firemen fought the fire. The trucker and the RV man helped Bubby back to his car. He climbed inside to rest.

The local news crew showed up. They were overjoyed to find out that the man and his son survived the crash, but even more excited to find out that the hero was Drive-up Bubby. They interviewed and videotaped everybody, spending most of their time with Bubby. They left with their hot story, and, within an hour, the interview titled, *Drive-up Bubby—Highway Hero* was on every news channel across the entire country. Brenda beamed with pride as she watched from Minnesota. KaBob saw it from Nevada. Dr. Singh, Marco, and Richie viewed it from California.

Bubby needed to recuperate from his daring rescue. He watched as the paramedics raced off to the hospital and the trucker revved-up his semi to hit the road. The RV man and his wife drove off to their next scenic spot. The firemen finished putting out the fire and loaded up to leave. A tow truck hauled away the still smoking mass of twisted metal. Bubby saw himself on the six o'clock news as the sun was setting in a cloudless sky, and all was again peaceful at the rest stop.

Bubby sighed with a groan. He did not feel right. His legs hurt, his arms and shoulders hurt, and his back hurt. What bothered him worse was that his chest felt tight. It seemed difficult to breathe. Bam! He gripped his chest with both hands. He slumped over the steering wheel. He heard the sounds of a truck turning into the rest stop, and glanced up over the steering wheel. In the twilight of sunset, he saw an eighteen-wheeler come rolling to a stop next to his car, its air brakes squealing, and a short blast of its horn. Bam! Bubby felt another sharp pain, winced and looked up into the cab of the semi-truck. The driver reminded Bubby of his father. Bubby reached for his cell phone to call emergency but felt an explosion of pain in his chest. He could not breathe. His entire body felt cold and numb.

His vision blurred. He slumped over the steering wheel and whispered, "Brenda, I'm so sorry."

Bubby died from a massive heart attack. For Bubby, the flab fight, the weight war, and the ongoing oppression of obesity were over. A tow truck picked up the car with Bubby inside, covered it with a black tarp, and transported them both to a funeral home. The mortuary dressed him up, washed, and waxed the car and trucked both of them back to his hometown of Fresno, California.

Bubby had indeed put all of his affairs in order and had prearranged all of the necessary services for his burial. A multitude of his newfound friends and onlookers showed up at the cemetery for the graveside memorial. The mayor of Fresno, Alan Alright, spoke, lauding him as a local hero. G.L. Jenkins, the pastor of Fresno's largest church, conducted the eulogy. A gospel choir sang some hymns as well as a few Motown ballads. A network news team covered it all, planning to broadcast it that night as a special interest story with heart warming interviews from many of the people who had met Bubby. The rest of the country mourned.

Brenda had caught a flight from Minnesota and sat in the front row with Dr. Singh, Marco, and Richie. Bubby had left her the remainder of his estate—enough money to start her clinic. She sobbed into a pink handkerchief, while Dr. Singh sat stoically cleaning his glasses. Marco wiped tears from his eyes with the back of his fingers, and Richie just hung his head and stared at the ground. KaBob—in town for the Clovis Rodeo—stood nearby. The creases on his face looked deeper. Bite-u was chained to a tree near the gathering, but he didn't bark.

At the conclusion of the service, and as the crowd looked on, a large crane lifted the VW car-coffin with the body of Bubby inside and lowered them down into a huge rectangular hole.

The crater encompassed four burial plots next to the gravesites of his father and mother. The highly polished VW gleamed in the sunlight. The body of Bubby sat in the front seat, as though he was driving up to his next drive-up window.

As the cemetery workers bulldozed the dirt over the massive grave, Brenda, Dr. Singh, Marco, and Richie walked away from the cemetery together.

Dr. Singh turned to Brenda and the delivery boys, and warmly said, "I will miss Bubby. He was a good man. I must say, I am very, very proud of him. Instead of lying in bed waiting for a heart attack—he saw America, made lots of friends, fell in love, saved a man's life, and died a hero."

"He was such a cool dude," expressed Marco.

"Totally," agreed Richie.

"Geeez, ya know," said Brenda, dabbing her tears with her hanky, "I loved Bubby dearly, an' he'll forever be in my heart."

In silence, they all sighed heavily.

Dr. Singh looked at each one of them, grinned, and then blurted out, "I feel like pizza! Who wants pizza?"

EQUIPOISE

J USTIN AND JULIE studied the deli's wall menu. The young
lovers stood intertwined with her arms around his waist, and
his arms about her shoulders.

"The Plymouth Rock sounds yummy," suggested Julie.

"Hmm, let's see, roasted turkey, cranberry sauce, Havarti
cheese, and red leaf lettuce on Dutch crunch bread. Yeah, that
does sound tasty." Justin faced the man slicing prosciutto behind
the counter and ordered, "One Plymouth Rock please."

Grabbing a loaf of bread, the deli man asked, rolling the r of
each word, "For here or to go?"

"To go, please," replied Justin. He unraveled his embrace
with Julie and said to her, "Okay, while he makes the sandwich,
how about you grab a bag of chips, and I'll get a bottle of
wine."

With a turkey sandwich, a bag of Sun Chips, and a chilled
bottle of *Gewürztraminer* all in a bag, they left the deli and
walked across the street to Justin's parked car. He popped open
the trunk, placed the food and wine in a picnic basket, and then
picked up the basket. Julie reached in the trunk and pulled out
a folded blanket. She shut the trunk, and then slipped her free
hand around Justin's arm. Side by side, they stepped up on a
broad cobblestone sidewalk, and headed for the entrance into
the city park.

Along where they strolled, honeysuckle climbed the stone
wall that surrounded the park. After a few steps, Julie stopped,
leaned over, and smelled the scent of the yellow flowers flushed

with reddish-purple. Justin smiled as he watched her. She breathed in another long sniff of the fragrant blooms, turned to him, and sighed, "Ohhh, I just love a picnic on a sunny spring day!"

"Me too," said Justin, leaning in and kissing her on her forehead.

They walked a bit further coming upon the noble iron gates of the entrance. Blossoming purple flowers of wisteria beautified the walls around the hinges of each opened gate. Just within the entrance, in the middle of the sidewalk, stood a granite memorial:

Betsy's Garden
In memory of
Walter and Betsy Gardner
Behold the vibrant colors,
Breathe the fragrant scents,
Hear the bird songs,
Sense the peace of God.

Betsy's Garden was once the grand estate of Walter and Betsy Gardner. He had been one of the town's founding fathers and most everybody's family doctor. He knew not only the intricacies of local politics, but he was well acquainted with the insides and outs, from the nose to the toes of most of the town folks. Walter and Betsy had attended the same small, country school, and had married each other while still very young. They purchased a seven-acre parcel on the edge of town with a large, two-story Victorian home. Throughout the years, they were at the center of most social and civic affairs. Over time, the city grew and their estate became the heart of the city. Not long after celebrating their fortieth wedding anniversary, Walter passed away. Betsy continued her gardening for another twenty-five years, creating a floricultural paradise. Upon her death, with no heirs, she bequeathed her beautiful estate to the city. The city made her home into a museum of local history and her magnificent garden into a park for all to enjoy.

As Justin and Julie sauntered past the memorial, they came upon a panoramic view of the garden. They stopped and delighted in it. Their senses were overwhelmed. Flowers of every genus and color imaginable decorated the landscape. A scent of Jasmine wafted in the air. A frivolous breeze rustled the slightest of tree limbs, creating a soothing shushing sound. Not far from them hovered a ruby-throated hummingbird amongst bright yellow daffodils. Varicolored pink and white peach blossoms floated about like floral snowflakes. Birds chirped and trilled as red squirrels scurried across the lawn and up and down trees.

"Wow! It's breathtaking," exclaimed Justin.

"I feel like I just stepped into heaven," said Julie. "It makes me wonder if we're still alive and here on earth."

"Oh, we're still here," said Justin, as he tickled her, causing her to giggle.

They continued walking, following the cobblestone path as it turned a corner around a bed of Crimson Glory roses, and a small gurgling fountain, providing a bathtub and a drinking trough for all the critters.

"Oh good," announced Julie, "*our* spot isn't taken like last time." Then kidding, "The nerve of some people, picnicking in *our* spot without first asking us."

Justin peered over at the shady place under the drooping limbs of a weeping willow tree and joined in, "I agree. They need to contact us, apply for a permit, and then we'll approve it, based on whether or not we intend to use it." They both chuckled. Then Justin remarked, "Well, in any case, it's all *ours* today."

As they stepped off the sidewalk and strolled across the

plush lawn toward *their* spot, a bumblebee dived at them. Julie screamed. They ducked, bobbed, and weaved, as it buzzed around and around. It finally zoomed off and they laughed about how they must have looked in their panic. Reaching their enchanting hideaway, Julie spread out the blanket on the grass, and then Justin set the basket down. Julie sat on the blanket and opened the picnic basket, pulling out the wine and food, her magazine and his sketchpad, some plates, napkins, wineglasses, and a corkscrew. As she placed a half of a sandwich and some chips on the plates, he uncorked the wine, and poured it into the wineglasses. After handing her a glass of the golden nectar, he raised his glass and said, "A toast—to springtime, Betsy's Garden, and our love." They clinked glasses, and sipped, then ate lunch, chatting about friends, family, and work.

After Justin finished his sandwich and the rest of hers, Julie put away the picnic things, except the wine and glasses. As their wonderment of the park settled into tranquility, she lay on her stomach and read a magazine. He leaned against the willow's trunk and sketched his view—between the tree's dangling branches—of the Gardner mansion. Every so often, they would gaze silently at each other and smile.

Justin and Julie were both born at the local hospital. They had attended the same schools, and through the years, knew of each other, but since he was two years older, they had not been close. Both earned their degrees at out of town universities, returning to their hometown to find jobs. She taught at the elementary school and he worked as an architect.

They had met at the wedding of a mutual friend, where they ate cake, danced, talked, and fell in love. After dating for six months, they discussed marriage, and both agreed that they would shop for rings, and that someday soon, he would make a romantic proposal.

As they relaxed under the willow, the tweets and twitters of various garden birds sang out, along with children's laughter on the other side of the park. Justin was sketching the ornate woodwork framing the home's gable roof, when Julie said, "Justy, this article talks about something interesting."

Justin looked up from his sketchpad as she continued.

"It discusses a concept for heavenly happiness in a relationship. It's called," she read its spelled out phonetic pronunciation slowly, "Ek-wuh-poiz," then repeated it, "Equipoise. It means a state of equilibrium or equal balance."

"Read on, my love," said Justin.

"To sustain this delicate balance, both partners must concentrate on, and nurture the other's physical and emotional needs. As both partner's needs are met, a oneness of contentment is consummated, ergo happiness. If every disagreement began with, 'I want *you* happy—No, I want *you* happy,' then the best solution for both would be discovered."

"Fascinating," interjected Justin

"Ignoring selfish desires," she kept reading, "along with the quest to please the other will create *equipoise*. To live happily ever after, *both*—with virtue—must seek the *other's* happiness."

"Okay, so in other words, if I live for your happiness, and you live for mine, then both of us will be happy. Right?"

"Right."

"Well then, Julie—I shall live for your happiness," declared Justin.

"And Justin—I shall live for yours," pledged Julie.

Justin raised his glass and said, "I would like to amend our earlier toast. To springtime, Betsy's Garden, our love, and equipoise. We shall both live in the pursuit of the other's happiness. Thereby, we shall live—happily ever after." They clinked glasses, sipped a taste, then leaned in, and sealed their promises with a long kiss.

Not much later, a chilly breeze kicked up, swirling dry, dead leaves onto their blanket. A moment afterward, the clouds hid the sun, stealing away the sunlit vibrancy of the park. Julie closed her magazine. Justin set down his sketchpad.

An elderly couple, out walking their dog, hastened down the sidewalk. As they neared Justin and Julie, the lady shouted, "Hey, you young folks need to heed the storm that's comin'! It's a bad one!"

Justin and Julie glanced at each other, and simultaneously asked, "What storm?" Both jumped up and left the canopy of the willow tree, peering behind them, beyond the treetops, to the northeast horizon. From under the tree, their view to the southwest had appeared calm and sunny. They were unaware that a violent storm approached from behind them.

Lightning streaked across the black threatening sky. Justin counted aloud, "One-one-thousand, two-one-thousand, three-one-thousand, four-one-thou..." Boom! The thunder crashed. He knew that five seconds from flash to bang meant that the lightning was a mile away.

"The lightning is very close! We need to get out of here!" he asserted.

Raindrops began splatting on the tree leaves. The wind whipped. Birds darted overhead to shelter in the trees. All of God's creatures vanished, taking cover.

Again, lightning stabbed at the sky, with thunder roaring a second later.

Trembling, Julie placed the glasses and wine bottle into the picnic basket, then tossed in the sketchpad and the magazine. Justin gathered up the blanket. Arm in arm they hurried across the lawn onto the sidewalk, back toward the entrance. The clouds burst. Rain fell. They passed the memorial, nearing the iron gates.

"The car's not far! We'll be safe in it!" shouted Justin.

A few steps later, they heard crackling noises. Their

eyebrows, the hair on the top of their head, and on their arms stood on end. Justin and Julie glanced fearfully at each other. They dropped the blanket and the picnic basket, and hugged each other tightly.

The senior couple with the dog sat in their car parked in front of the entrance. Horrified, they peered out the windshield at the young couple hurrying toward the gates. There was a blinding flash, a horrendous boom, and an explosion of sparks. The elderly couple ducked below the car's dashboard. Their dog barked. The gates glowed red hot. The wet wisteria steamed.

Witnesses across town saw the jagged three-fingered bolt jab down and touch the earth, followed by a resounding thunderclap.

Justin and Julie fell in a heap onto the wet sidewalk. An ambulance came.

In the hospital's emergency room, they were conscious, but disoriented. They couldn't speak in sentences, only short answers. Their extremities tingled with pain. They had a ringing in their ears combined with dizziness. Justin sustained lightning burns in the shape of his wristwatch, the coins in his pocket, and his belt buckle. Julie suffered burns from her necklace, an ankle bracelet, and her watch.

The doctor said they were "lucky." The lightning had struck the metal gates, not them directly.

Justin and Julie stayed in the hospital for a couple of days. The doctors evaluated their mental awareness and physical mobility. Their burns were dressed and redressed.

After their release, both experienced too much sleep, then difficulty falling asleep, and then insomnia. They felt fatigue, then total exhaustion. In the months that passed, they were irritable, arguing over trivial things. At times, one would ask the other, "What's the matter?"

"Nothing," was always the reply.

"Come on, you're acting different, what's wrong?"

With a scowl, the other would snap back, "I don't want to talk about it," putting an end to the inquiry. Both assumed the other still suffered the effects of the lightning.

They never shopped for an engagement ring, and stopped visiting Betsy's Garden. She spent more time at her apartment; he at his. Both alone. Unhappiness settled in. Their relationship crumbled.

One morning, toward the end of summer, they met at a coffee shop, near the deli, across the street from the park. They picked up lattes and walked over to Betsy's Garden. The day was sunny, without a cloud in the sky—or on the distant horizon. They strolled up, somewhat timidly to the iron gates. A section of the gate, where the lightning had struck, was discolored a chalky white. The wisteria grew heartily. They entered the park, walking past the memorial. The garden was vibrant with flowers, and teeming with fluttering butterflies and singing birds. Squirrels bounded on lawns and up in trees. Turning the corner, around the red roses, they peered over at *their* picnic spot. A family, with two children picnicked under the willow tree. Justin and Julie sighed, then sat on a park bench.

In silence, except for the plaintive calls of morning doves, they each sipped their coffee, until Justin erupted, "Jules, what's happened to us? The last time we were here, we talked of living happily ever after."

"Yes," she answered softly, "I remember." She took a sip of coffee, while staring at a few pigeons clustered on the ground, then whispered, barely audible, "The last time we were here—when the lightning struck—I saw things." She paused and gazed into his eyes. "I saw the future. It was so clear—so real. I think about it all the time." Her eyes became moist and she sniffed her nose. "I saw you," she muttered, as she reached into her purse, withdrew a tissue, and dabbed around her eyes careful not to smudge her mascara.

Justin reached over, held her hands, and gently asked, "What did you see?"

Their eyes met again. "You were at the hospital, in a waiting room. A sign above the elevator marked the ninth floor. It was as though I floated in the room above you—watching you—but you couldn't see, nor hear me. You were alone—pacing. You were distraught. You were as handsome as you are now, but you appeared older. Your hair had receded a bit and shorter than you wear it now. You were still in shape, but you had gained a little weight."

Justin looked down at his stomach, rubbed his hand across it, and sucked it in.

"I watched as you walked over to a window and peered out into the night at the city. It was late. Droplets of rain drizzled down the glass. There were a few lights on at the Walter Gardner building and only a few headlights on the causeway. The landing lights of the airport glowed south of the city. From the northeast; a storm. You were lost in your thoughts. A three-fingered bolt of lightning snaked across the sky followed by a loud clap of thunder. It startled you; you stepped back from the window. With a ding, the elevator door opened. Your dad and mom stepped into the room. Your dad had gotten balder; your mother had stopped dying her hair, so it was gray. Your mom asked, 'How is she?'"

Justin listened intently, leaning back against the park bench without letting go of Julie's hands.

"You turned to your parents and stated that there were severe complications; an emergency c-section. You said that the doctors were trying to save the baby without losing her. I could see the tremendous fear in your eyes; fear that you would lose the love of your life. You waited, pacing from the elevator over to the window and then back. Tears filled your eyes. You bit your lip to keep from crying. Your dad and mom sat in chairs. Your dad stared silently at the floor. Your mother quietly prayed. The doctor entered the room. You rushed over to him asking how they were. The doctor smiled and said that you had a healthy baby girl. He said it was a tough go, but that both mother and baby were doing fine. You sighed with relief, and then wept into the palms of your hands, releasing all of your fears and worry. A nurse escorted you from the waiting room to the recovery room. I followed. When you stepped into the room your face beamed with happiness. You gazed at your sweet baby girl and then smiled at…" Julie stopped and began to cry.

"I think I know, what you hesitate to say," said Justin softly.

"You do?" said Julie, sniffing her runny nose.

"When the lightning struck—I saw things too."

"You did?" Julie asked incredulously.

"Yes, and I think it is what we saw, rather than the lightning's aftereffects that is so disturbing to us. I saw the future too, and it seemed very, very real. I can't get it out of my mind. I saw you—at the airport, at a terminal, waiting for an arriving flight. Like with you at the hospital, I floated above you—you couldn't see or hear me. It was storming. You were staring out a large window looking out at the puddles on the runway reflecting the terminal's lights. The wind surged, hurling rain upon the window, obscuring your view. You looked distressed. Your hair was stylish, but shorter. You were still incredibly beautiful, but you dressed more conservatively. You were pregnant and looked close to your due date."

"I was pregnant?" Julie asked, her spirits lifting a bit.

"Yes, and you rested a hand on top of your baby and with your other hand you dabbed at your tears with a tissue, just like you always do when you cry. You just stared out the window lost in your worries, until a bright flash of lightning streaked across the sky, followed by crashing thunder. It had three fingers, like what you said I saw up in the hospital, and like what really crashed into the garden gates here. Well, it scared you pretty bad. You backed away from the window. An airport official walked in amongst all those waiting for the flight and shouted to gather around. He said that lightning had struck the plane and that it was experiencing trouble. Emergency crews were standing by. You started crying. A young woman asked if the plane was going to crash. The official replied that they were doing everything possible to bring it home safely."

As Justin talked, Julie stared at him, captivated by his words.

"You peered again out the window as the red lights of ambulances and fire trucks blurred by. Seconds later there was the roar of the plane landing, and then zooming past the window. After a short while, seeming more like an eternity, the official again entered the waiting area and announced that the flight had landed and that all on board were safe. All those waiting, as well as you, applauded with joy and relief. A bus pulled up to the terminal gate. A group of stunned and weary travelers began coming through the door. You stood on you tiptoes trying to see over the people greeting their loved ones. You couldn't see him. You were trembling. Finally, in the midst of the crowd, you saw him, and broke through them to embrace him. He dropped his carry-on baggage on the floor and enveloped you in his arms. You beamed with happiness and cried for joy. You kissed and kissed and..." Justin paused, and sighed, "Julie, honey—it wasn't me."

"Really?" she whispered. "How strange. In the hospital—it wasn't me either."

They both sat silent, emotionally processing what they had just heard.

"Justin," spoke Julie softly, yet with resolve, "I can't be happy knowing that another happiness awaits you. Every day that I'm with you, I think of the vision, and I feel that I'm keeping you from your future."

"I understand Julie," stated Justin calmly, holding back his twisted emotions. "I can't be happy knowing that your happiness awaits you. Because the vision was so clear to me—I also feel that I'm in the way of your fate. I don't understand it, but I know it was that three fingered bolt of lightning that revealed it to us. Strange—hard to believe—but, I believe it to be true."

"Me too," she whispered, then trembled, and then cried. He helped her up and hugged her tightly. She squeezed him back. The young lovers stood intertwined; her arms around his waist, and his arms about her shoulders.

"I love you," Justin said kissing her forehead.

"I love you too," Julie said resting her head on his chest.

"Because I love you, I want *you* to be happy."

"No, because I love you, I want *you* to be happy."

Both of their distraught faces expressed a meager grin.

"I suppose we just experienced a bit of equipoise," said Justin. "Right over there under that willow tree, we promised each other to live for the other's happiness. When the lightning struck, something dreadful, yet wonderful happened."

"I can't explain it, but I truly believe that we saw beyond ourselves, and into the other's future happiness," stated Julie.

"Me too," concurred Justin. "It's bizarre how our oath to live for each other's happiness was tested so quickly, and far beyond our anticipations. Although no longer lovers, we shall remain as friends, remembering the visions and abiding in faith, knowing that a greater happiness awaits us both."

"I feel sad," sighed Julie, "that we're no longer a couple. I would never have imagined, without the lightning strike, that we could both be happier apart than we were together. But, I also feel a tinge of excitement, because I believe and hope in our visions that blissful lives await us."

Leaving the park, they walked hand in hand past the flowers, the memorial, and out of the iron gates. Standing on the cobblestone sidewalk, they kissed, followed by a long hug. The fragrance of honeysuckle filled the air. Their hearts hurt, and both were on the verge of breaking down, when Justin took a step back. He pretended he had a wineglass in his hand, holding it in the air. Julie played along, as Justin proclaimed, "A toast—to Betsy's Garden, our futures, and equipoise. We shall both live in pursuit of the other's happiness." They clinked their make-believe glasses and pretended to sip, then slowly withdrew from each other, turned, and walked in opposite directions to their cars. As they drove away, both smiled, thinking about the other living happily ever after.

THE LETTER

O H, Chris," called out his father, stepping into the entertainment room, "will you stop playing your video game, and come into the reading room please. Your mom and I need to talk with you."

"Just a minute," hollered Chris over his shoulder. He sat cross-legged on the floor in front of a fifty-two inch flat screen TV. His thumbs and fingers fired rapidly on the controller's buttons and toggles as his body flinched with the action. Behind him sat a comfortable U-shaped sofa, and to one side a Ping-Pong table and to the other side a pool table. An electronic dartboard hung on the wall amongst framed movie posters. His parents had just given him the video game at his thirteenth birthday party, and two hours later, he had nearly mastered the game's assault level five.

"Christopher," said his father, now standing behind the sofa, "I'll give you one minute to be in the reading room, or that game gets returned to the store."

As his father marched out of the room, Chris quickly annihilated the last Explo-bot of the Evil Alien Invaders on level five, paused the game, left the entertainment room, and raced down the hallway of the opulent mansion into the reading room. Books in bookcases covered its walls from floor to ceiling. On one side of the den sat a huge cherry-wood desk along with a high-backed leather chair, and on the other side, his parents sat next to each other on a couch. He plopped down in one of two chairs across from them.

"What'd I do?" he asked, expecting a lecture about something he had done or didn't do during his birthday party.

"Son," began his father with a serious tone and holding a manila letter sized envelope between his hands, "you didn't do anything wrong, it's just that we need to talk, and we need to give you one last thing on your birthday. It's very important."

Chris's mom sat quietly, nodding in agreement, but wringing her hands.

"What is it?" asked Chris, speaking in a tone on the edge of disrespect.

"Well son, I need to give you this envelope containing a letter, but before you open its seal, your mom and I need to tell you something. First and foremost, we love you very, very much…"

"I know you guys love me," interrupted Chris, "but what's the matter? Are you guys getting a divorce?"

"No son, absolutely not. I love your mom and she loves me, but what I'm trying to say is that—well—it's your thirteenth birthday, and we are under legal obligation to tell you that you're not—well—it's difficult to say—but, Chris—you're not our biological son. Your mom and I adopted you."

"I'm adopted," he blurted out, with his face scrunched up in disbelief. "But—but you have all of my baby pictures with me in your arms."

"Yes, yes we do," said his mother. "We were present at your birth, but we've only raised you since you were three months old."

"But, come on, I look like dad—brown hair and blue eyes."

"Yes, you do, and quite handsome I might add," said his dad with an uneasy chuckle, "but son, our looks are purely coincidental."

"But—but why? What happened to my real parents?"

"The answer to that question," replied his father as he passed the envelope over to Chris, "is in this letter. Please, read the letter first, and then we'll answer all of your questions."

"And remember," interjected his mom, "we love you very much."

As Chris reached out for the envelope, a short, elderly man, wearing a three-piece suit and carrying a briefcase, whisked into the room and sat in a chair next to him.

"Please excuse me for my tardiness," said the man bluntly, "but my court case detained me."

"Chris, this is Mr. Isaias," said his father. "He is our family attorney, and is here to witness and then notarize your possession of the envelope and your reading of the letter."

"Happy birthday, Chris," said Mr. Isaias stoically, as though he was presenting a legal deposition.

Chris, still in adoption shock, stared at the man and then down at the envelope. His mother handed him a letter opener, and he slid it under the gummed lip and sliced open the wax seal. His anxious parents watched him, worried that once he read the letter, he would reject them as his mom and dad. Mr. Isaias set his briefcase in his lap, opened it, and retrieved a notary stamp and an ink pen.

Chris withdrew the document, along with a five by seven, black and white portrait of a baby, and then silently began reading the handwritten letter.

Dear Lorant.

"My name's not Lorant," said Chris.

"Chris, yes—yes it is," said his mother. "Lorant was your name before we adopted you and called you Chris. Legally, your name is Lorant."

Chris's stomach hurt. He felt as though he would barf birthday cake, ice cream, and tropical punch. Just a few minutes before, he had been in a fantasy world detonating Explo-bots, and now his real world was exploding. He resumed reading.

Dear Lorant,

Happy thirteenth birthday. I hope you are healthy upon this day. My name is

Lorant Elliot Doppel, as your legal name is Lorant Elliot Doppel. Your parents adopted you when you were three months old, under the conditions that they present you with this letter upon your thirteenth birthday, and that they never legally change your name. I personally chose your parents out of many candidates, and they are more than simply foster parents or guardians, they are your mom and dad, and they love you as their own. They are good people, as I am sure you are a good boy. No matter what your feelings are after you read this letter, I want you to continue to love and respect them.

You were conceived when I was a very old man, so old, that I could not care for you properly. At this time, as I am writing you this letter, I am very near death. You, in contrast, are healthy and perfect and still at the beginning of your life.

Although I didn't raise you, I know you like I know myself. You have a small knot on your right ear, and you are left-handed.

Chris touched the knot on his right ear with his left hand, and then glanced at his father pacing the room, his mother dabbing a tissue to her silent tears, and Mr. Isaias bearing witness. He then focused back on the letter.

I know that you wear a size nine shoe, and that you are now five-foot-five inches tall. I know that over the next few years, you will grow to an adult height of five-foot-ten. I know that you have blue eyes and brown hair, and that you have a ruddy face with freckles across your nose. You can roll your tongue and you can whistle real good. Soon you will have acne, but when you're nineteen, it will vanish. At twenty-five you will begin gaining weight, something you will have to control with exercise and diet. In your early thirties, you will need reading glasses. In your mid-forties, you will have a sensitive stomach and chronic heartburn. In your late fifties, you will start taking medication for diabetes, something that you have a predisposition toward but can avoid with proper diet. You will live into your eighties and maybe longer. You are allergic to cat hair, shellfish, peanuts, and ragweed. You have rhythm, but you can't carry a tune. You are okay at art, good at English, better at math, but you excel at science.

Chris stopped reading, astounded at the accuracy of what he had read. He gazed at the photograph of the baby and marveled at how the baby resembled his own baby pictures. He then asked, "Dad, how come this man knows so much about me, and how come this baby looks like me as a baby?"

"Keep reading," replied his dad.

I know that when you catch a cold, you suffer sinus infections. I know that when you become upset, your stomach hurts. I know that you shy away from sports because your knees hurt when you run. And, how do I know so much about you? Because genetically, you are a duplicate of me. We have the same bones and blood. The same ruddy skin. The same hair and eyes. The same height and foot size. The same smile, and the same laugh. Lorant, my lad, I am you and you are me. The only way we differ is in our emotional matrix, but even that is driven by our same propensities.

My life began as a foundling, dumped in an alley trashcan, forsaken by the woman who bore me. I grew up at an orphanage without parents, without love, without tenderness, and my life ended in bitterness. However, it was this bitterness that propelled my creation of you—a new me—healthy and perfect—my second me.

My presence upon this earth will not be forgotten. I will not be discarded in death as I was in birth. It will not be dust to dust. From trashcan to coffin. I will most certainly advance from sick to healthy, from old to young, from wrinkled to smooth, from weak to strong, leaping past the dead-end of mortality and alighting on a path to eternity. Since you are my representative beyond my death, I made certain that you would mature in a nurturing environment, so that you would live out the days of our glorious future with a joyful spirit.

Chris glanced up from his reading again and saw his parents now sitting together on the sofa, waiting for his reaction to the letter.

"How are you doing honey?" asked his mother.

Chris, lost in his thoughts ignored her, and continued reading.

Lorant, I am the first. The original. The pattern. You are the second, but not merely a copy of the first—an absolute duplicate—more precisely the same than a set of identical twins, because you and I are constructed with the same genetic code extracted from the cells of my blood.

How do I know what you look like? I have looked in a mirror. How do I know how you will mature? I have lived out my lifetime. You are me and I am you, because Lorant, my dear boy, you are my life stamp—my clone.

Chris stopped reading and looked up in hushed astonishment. His eyes met his father's eyes, then his mother's, and then the mindful eyes of Mr. Isaias.

"I'm a clone?" Chris asked, as though in a trance.

His parents and Mr. Isaias silently and in unison nodded their heads.

"I'm adopted—my name is Lorant—and—and—I'm a clone?"

Without saying a word, they nodded.

As his mind reeled, his eyes began again reading the letter.

But please, though you were conceived and birthed in my laboratory, do not fear the genesis of your existence, because indeed, though you are a clone, you are still human. Therefore, you must live and laugh, marry, and beget many happy children.

But Lorant, my dear me, you also have a legal responsibility. For you and your family to inherit a sizeable portion of my vast fortune, there is something you must do. You must do as I have done. Near the end of your life, you shall secure loving parents for the next Lorant, an infant Lorant dependent upon you for a happy life. According to my last will and testament, upon your seventieth birthday another Lorant will enter our world. If you die before you are seventy, or you refuse to carry out my wishes, then others, that are paid very well, will step in and fulfill your responsibilities. Know this, I have set forth legal and monetary checks and bounds to assure that my will is executed. You must pass this letter to the parents of the next Lorant and they are to present it to him on his thirteenth birthday. Because, surely as I existed and you now live, there will be another Lorant, and another, and another—for I have cryogenically frozen a thousand Lorants, and have made provisions for more. Each me is eager to live a lifetime, waiting his turn, and anticipating his birth. My life stamp—the life stamp of Lorant Elliot Doppel—will live on beyond my death, for I have engineered and established my everlasting life.

Sincerely,
Lorant Elliot Doppel
The First

A Patriotic Sneeze

Reporter Harley Castle piloted the twin-prop, all-gray Vulcanair P68 aircraft, while peering out the cockpit down at the Afghanistan landscape—dry, hot, and uninviting, except to scorpions, snakes, and a hiding horde of Allah-obeying terrorists training for *jihad*. The early morning sun cast long shadows across the jagged, mountainous terrain slipping by beneath him. Arriving at his coordinates, midway between the capital Kabul and the Tajikistan border, he descended beneath the wispy clouds, and spotted the designated landing strip—a flat, barren patch between the rocky mounds and deep gulches of two sun scorched ridges. He maneuvered the plane toward the clearing, flew over it, and dipped his wings as a signal to his infidel-hating greeters. He then circled for an approach, and noticed a khaki-color, off-road vehicle in the shade of a large mound of rocks. He dropped over a wrinkled hill and set the plane down quickly on the short runway, sped past the vehicle, and stopped in front of a massive boulder, with just enough room to turn the plane around. As he taxied back to the land rover, he pulled out of a shirt pocket a small aerosol canister similar to a metered-dose asthma inhaler. He placed its mouthpiece up to his lips and then hesitated, knowing that once he breathed in its contents—there was no turning back.

As a foreign correspondent for over thirty-five years, covering up-close, wars and disasters around the globe, he had survived explosions, gunfire, riots, hurricanes, and earthquakes, all while gripping a microphone and staring into a camera. He never worried about sacrificing his life for the story, hell, it was his job; it was expected—get as close to the story as possible and survive by grit or by gusto for the next one—but in this situation, Harley Castle was the story, and he was destined to die.

Before using the canister, he inhaled a slow, deep breath—inflating with resolve: for America; for his brother; for his career—and then slowly exhaled. He placed the inhaler past his lips and inside his mouth, followed immediately by a quick breath along with a burst from the pressurized canister. He grimaced as its bitter contents burned the back of his throat. He then stuffed the inhaler into a seat pocket, and halted the airplane near the vehicle where a man stood holding an automatic weapon.

Harley switched off the engines, crawled out of his seat, released the latched door, and swung it open. First, he felt a blast of arid, hot air broil his face and then the barrel of a rifle thrust into his gut. He peered out at the man, who epitomized the photos of the world's most-wanted terrorists: bristly, black full beard and mustache, bushy, black eyebrows shading dark, scornful eyes, and olive-colored facial skin clinched in a scowl of hate. Upon his head, a dusty, gray *pawkul*: a lamb's wool beret, with a long cylindrical side rolled up around his forehead; worn by the Afghan soldiers who had fought the Soviets. On his body, tan-colored *payraan tumbaans*: loose fitting pajama-like shirt and pants, and over them a reddish-brown *chapan*: a robe-like coat. On his feet: black army boots.

"Get down pig!" ordered the man with a coarse Arabic accent.

Harley, clean shaven and ruggedly handsome for fifty nine years old, was dressed in light brown bush shorts with numerous pockets, a white cotton, button-up shirt with two chest pockets, a New York Yankees baseball cap, white socks, and hiking boots. He climbed slowly out of the plane, ducked under the overhead wing, and stood to his six-foot height, facing his armed escort.

"Hey Abdul," growled Harley, shoving the gun away from his chest, "I'm Harley Castle, here to do an interview with your leader, and then broadcast it to billions around the world. How about a little respect?"

"I know who you are. You have reported the news since I was a child. Even if you are world renown, you are an infidel, and my enemy. Though you are a filthy dog, you are here only to serve Allah."

Harley reached into a shirt pocket, withdrew a lighter and a flip-top box of Marlboros, pulled a cigarette out, and placed it between his lips. With it dangling from his mouth, he retorted, "Well—now I'm confused. Am I a pig," he lit the cigarette, inhaled a long drag, and then spat, "or a dog?"

"Shut up, pig!" yelled the *jihadis*t, reaching out and slapping the cigarette out of the journalist's mouth, causing his Yankees hat to fall in the dirt.

Harley wiped his mouth with the back of his hand, bent over, and picked up his hat. He slapped it on his leg, swept back his full head of gray hair, and plopped the cap back on his head. "You know," growled Harley, glaring at his Arab captor, "maybe if you guys, as kids, would have had some fun playing baseball, instead of training day and night for *jihad*, you wouldn't be so damn bitter and hateful toward the rest of the world."

"We don't live for fun, but to slaughter our enemies, and my name is not Abdul, it is Aziz Izz al-Daed. Now, we will load the camera and equipment into the truck."

Harley leaned into the plane—where the seats had been removed to accommodate the two aluminum instrument cases holding the camera, tripod, and satellite broadcast equipment—and slid the containers to the edge of the door. With one man on each end of each case, they loaded them into the back of the vehicle. Al-Daed shoved Harley around to the passenger door, tightly blindfolded him, and pushed him into the vehicle. He started the truck and then drove down a rugged passageway into the mountains.

Harley pitched and bounced with every rock and rut on the difficult, gully-raked passage. He felt nauseous, not only from the heat, dust, and jostling vehicle, but from the beginning effects from the inhaler. In his blindfolded darkness, he thought about the day, two-weeks before, when this one-way trip had begun.

"Tell me straight doc, just like I report breaking news," said Harley. "I see it. I say it, and it's the news. No time in between to make a B.S. sandwich."

The tanned, in-shape, middle-aged doctor sat quietly at his desk, engrossed, scrutinizing Harley's test results.

"Oh, come on doc," Harley said in a huff, as he scooted his chair sideways, so he could see the doctor instead of the back of his computer monitor. "Talk to me."

In the silence of the room, the doctor continued clicking the computer mouse, bouncing from one screen to the next of blood work, biopsy reports, and MRI scans.

Harley stood up and paced the room looking at the vacation photos hanging on the wall of the doctor, and then he burst out, "Just tell me doc!"

"Okay, Mr. Castle, okay!" blurted the doctor. "You've got lung cancer and cirrhosis of the liver."

Harley leaned his head against the wall—next to a snapshot of the doctor surfing in Fiji—and sighed, mumbling a few choice cuss words under his breath.

"That explains the pain in your chest," the doctor continued professionally. "It also explains that persistent discomfort in your upper right quadrant, plus the muscle and joint aches, and the fatigue. I'm sorry, but both conditions are advanced, so, one, or the other, or both, are going to end your life within the next six months. You look great at fifty-nine. Obviously you exercise and eat right, but all those years of smoking and drinking, well—again Mr. Castle, I'm sorry, but, you need to get your affairs in order."

"I hear you doc, and thank you for not patty-caking around with me."

"I'll write you a prescription for the pain, and schedule you for more tests to determine radiation and chemo treatments, but please Harley, stop smoking and drinking, and maybe you'll have an extra month or two."

"I'll keep that in mind," said Harley, as he walked toward the door. He then stopped and turned saying, "Oh, and doc, please, remind your staff, that I don't want the media to know about my private health matters. If I see my mug in *The Enquirer*, the network's attorneys are going to inquire about who that smiling, bikini-clad girl is in the background of your Fiji pictures—and I doubt that she's your wife."

Harley marched out of the oncologist's office, and then once outside, he shuffled in despair over to his car. He climbed in and cranked the ignition, letting the car idle, as he sat thinking about his mortality, staring out the windshield at nothing. He had expected bad news from the doctor, but not, "get your affairs in order, you're going to die." After a minute, he backed out of the parking space, and pulled up to the street. As he waited for an opening in traffic, he reached habitually into his shirt pocket, and pulled out a pack of smokes. He took out a cigarette, placed it between his lips, flipped open his lighter, and then paused, pondering the doctor's prognosis and whether to smoke or not. After a couple of seconds, he muttered, "Ahhh, screw it," lit it, and then merged into traffic.

As he drove out of the city and up the winding road through wooded hills to his home on Lake Pleasant in upstate New York, he thought about getting his affairs in order. What affairs? He hadn't seen any of his three ex-wives for at least five years. And his twenty-five-year-old son? He hadn't seen him since the boy turned sixteen. He had lived for the story, reporting the news from wherever in the hell it was unfurling, to wherever in the hell people were watching TV. Yeah, he had missed birthdays, anniversaries, and sit-down family dinners. Regretful, but nevertheless, even when he was at home, he was restless to leave again. The wives and son took it personally, even though he had truly loved them. But his job couldn't be curtailed anymore than the planet's chaos. Since the last divorce ten years ago, he hadn't had a serious relationship. Oh, he had plenty of exotic ladies all over the world; but they were more of a sport thing, like playing golf, except with only a driver and a pitcher of margaritas. They wouldn't give a damn either. His folks had passed on, and he hadn't stayed in touch with the rest of his extended family back in his hometown of Buffalo. The only person he had remained close to over the years had been his younger brother, Jake, a fireman, who died in the Twin Towers on 9/11. It had taken four months to find his body, and another month to identify it. They used to attend Yankee games together—beers, hotdogs, hollering; they had had a lot of fun—but Harley hadn't been to a game since Jake's death. He missed his brother and the New York Yankees. As for his house, and all the other stuff, he had already set it up; he'd just leave it to his son as an apology for being a rotten dad. As for his ashes? Dump them into the lake.

Arriving at his modern, two-story cabin on the lakeshore, he strode directly to his wet bar and poured himself a Dewar's scotch on the rocks, no water, and then stepped out to his redwood deck with a scenic view of the lake. The setting sun cast a calm across the water, a big contrast to the frenzy of hotels, traffic, and airports that came with his job. He lit a cigarette, inhaled, coughed, and immediately felt a sharp pain in his lungs. He drank a big swallow of scotch and felt an ache in his side. He looked down at the drink in one hand and the cigarette in the other and quipped, "I knew you two little fun-bastards were going to get me, and since it's too late now—you can take me all the way."

So he sipped and smoked, standing at the deck rail, wincing at the pain in his lungs and side, gazing out at the reflective image of the pines, the surrounding hills, and the setting sun upon the water's surface. He thought about contacting his ex-wives, and made a decision. To hell with them. He thought about calling his son, but cringed, thinking about how his ex-wife had turned the boy against him.

An angler in a small fishing boat motored across the lake and up to a private dock on the lakeshore a few cabins down from Harley's home. The man waved. Harley waved back, regretting that he never made an effort to get to know his neighbors, or even taken the time to fish. Tranquility, he loved it, but hated it. It was great for a week, and then he'd get antsy for an assignment. He snuffed the cigarette out in an ashtray on the deck rail, then unclipped the cell phone off his belt, and called his boss Russell Davenport at the network.

"Hey Russ, Harley."

"Hello Harley, I was just going to call you. Something weird is going down, but first, what'd the doctor say about you feeling like crap lately."

"Well, it's bad, real bad," mumbled Harley. "Apparently, I smoked and drank myself into an early exit, and well—hell—I've only a few months or so. How pathetic, I'm going to die from lung cancer and cirrhosis of the liver, both, self-inflicted injuries. There'll be no heroic glory. I'll just wither, drop out of sight, and die."

"Oh no, I'm sorry, so sorry," said Russ. "Whatever you need Harl, you just say the word and I'll be there." He became quiet for a moment, then continued, "Harl, regarding heroic glory, you might just have an opportunity, but it is totally up to you and how you feel. A man belonging to the al-Qaeda terrorist group contacted me here at the network. His name is, hold on—let me read my notes, Ahmed Mohammed Ali Abdullah Bin al-Badarab. The bastard wants to share with the world a *fatwa*, you know, a fanatical Islamic religious decree, and he wants you to be Johnny-on-the-spot for an interview."

"Me?"

"Yeah you. He's speaking for Osama—whether he's still alive or not, who knows. Apparently, you are the only infidel who they believe will report the truth."

"And where would this interview take place?"

"In Afghanistan, in the mountains. But get this, not more than a couple of minutes after the call, I received a call from the CIA, who had scanned the international call and listened in on it. They want to meet with you and me in the early morning up at your place."

"My place?"

"Yeah, your place. It's secluded. Again Harl, I'm sorry that you're in bad shape. Hell, I'm probably next in line right behind you. For over thirty years, we've been friends, and I don't want you gone, but I know you want the truth straight up. If you're up to it, this could be your last great story. You'll most likely receive the Nobel and a Pulitzer."

"Yeah, probably—posthumously."

The next morning Harley sat in a chair out on his deck, smoking a cigarette, and drinking a cup of coffee—no cream, or sugar. He coughed between each drag, and cringed from the side ache the coffee caused, but he smoked the cigarette and drank the coffee anyway. He watched as a white four-door sedan pulled into his driveway, and saw Russ and another man climb out of the car. The thin, middle-aged man was tall, but somewhat hunched over; most likely from the weight of all the secrets he carried, and pale, from sitting under fluorescent lights in front of a monitor. Russ looked the same as always, a balding, sixty-year old, silver-haired man with a paunchy stomach—his excuse, "I love my pizza and beer."

The man introduced himself as agent Dryden Nale, from the

CIA Counterterrorism Center in Virginia. Harley poured them each a cup of coffee, while his retired neighbor fired up his outboard, waved, and then set a course for his favorite fishing hole across the lake.

"Okay, Harley, let's talk," said agent Nale, as he lit a cigarette. "My task force intercepted an international call to your boss Mr. Davenport here. We listened in on it, and then immediately contacted him. And just for the record, it's only certain calls from particular international regions—not domestic—that we intercept."

"Of course," muttered Harley incredulously.

Agent Nale inhaled a long drag, and then exhaled, while flicking his cigarette's ashes mostly into the ashtray. He furrowed his brow, as his entire demeanor became serious. "For the past few months we have listened in on communications from the shrouded terrorist cells around the world to their insurgents who have infiltrated our country. According to our data from email scans and cellular taps, they are about to launch an attack on four U.S. cities—Washington, Chicago, Los Angeles, and Miami. All simultaneously. We know that it'll be bacterial, or viral, or both—in our drinking water, in our food, or in the air we breathe. It's an extremely serious threat, and our country is still highly vulnerable; we may or may not stop them. Now, because of the international accords, the terrorists believe that we are cowards and won't fight fire with fire. Normal policy wouldn't allow it, but what I'm about to tell you came down from the top."

"The President?" inquired Russ.

"The President, the Trilateral Commission, Donald Trump. Who knows? I have my orders. All through the night my team brainstormed a plan, and has already initiated it. The plan relies on you Harley. We've already hacked into your doctor's database and have your complete medical records. We know you are terminal, which we are not happy about, but maybe it will make your decision easier. We also know that your younger brother Jake died in the Twin Towers. Again, we're sorry for your loss, but maybe stirring up some revenge will help you decide."

"So much for privacy," retorted Harley. "So what's this brilliant government plan? Isn't that an oxymoron—brilliant government?"

Agent Nale ignored him and continued, "Okay, the man who requested you to interview him is al-Qaeda's second-in-command—Ahmed Mohammed Ali Abdullah Bin al-Badarab. He most likely wants to show that terrorists have a human side, so that we Americans will let down our guard, but at the same time, he'll try to proliferate terror. Our counter-plan is a preemptive biological attack on them—before they attack us."

"Whoa, hold on," demanded Harley. "That sounds crazy."

"It certainly does," agreed Russ.

"I know it sounds crazy, but we must safeguard our families from another 9/11. A horror that will be four times worse. This is not one of those weapons of mass destruction political scare tactics. This is real. Our strike will more than eliminate that threat. So, maybe you'd be interested, or even honored, to save your country and your fellow citizens from the terror of another 9/11—times four. And let's not forget your brother."

"Harl, you've always lived for the story," chimed Russ. "Now you can die for it. You know, I don't want to see you go buddy, but I know you'd rather go out with the breaking news than slowly suffocate and melt away in a hospice bed."

"How exactly would I go out?" asked Harley.

"The details are classified," replied agent Nale, "but I can tell you this much, in three weeks, we fly you to Kabul, the capital of Afghanistan. You fly a small plane—we know you have a pilot's license—to their designated meeting point. You inhale a cocktail. They take you to their camp, and…"

"Wait a minute," interrupted Harley, "a cocktail?"

"It's a bacterial-viral contagion of Pneumonic Plague, Small Pox, and Clostridium Botulinum. You cough, they breathe it in, and they die. You sweat, shake their hand, and they die. If the bacteria don't take them down, then the virus will. They may even have a vaccine or antibiotics for one, but not for all three. Regardless—they die. The concoction is perfect, because it's stable until it encounters living host cells. Then it rapidly multiplies. It has a controlled incubation period, and it has a high infectivity and lethality. In other words, it will increase in severity, it spreads fast with human contact, and it leaves no survivors."

"Including me," mumbled Harley.

"Uh, well, yes, Harley, eventually," he said, crushing his cigarette out in the ashtray, "But you have an interview to conduct, so your cocktail will be time released, though theirs will infect them instantly. You will give your life for your country, for your viewers, and for your brother. Although, I'm sorry to say, that, um, no one will know it. The world will simply see it as your last great story, and think that the terrorists executed you. Once you transmit the germs, our Special Forces will convene, surround the area, follow the trail of dead bodies, and clean up the evidence, containing the deadly microbes within a specified circumference. Harley, you will be an American martyr, no, an international savior."

Harley sat silent, so did agent Nale, and so did Russ. All three lit cigarettes. A trout splashed in the lake.

"Well," said Harley interrupting the serenity, "I'll do it, so, I guess that makes me a terrorist's terrorist."

"We have arrived," blurted al-Daed amidst the sound of squealing brakes. The vehicle lurched to a stop, and Harley, still blindfolded, sensed that it had become cooler and darker. His Islamic chauffeur had spewed hatred like crude oil from an uncapped well, ranting the entire two hour trip about capitalism,

Christianity, decapitating Americans and Jews, and waging *jihad* against all infidels. Harley, feeling feverish, nauseous, and fatigued, had remained silent, refusing to engage the Muslim extremist.

Al-Daed shut off the engine, got out, slammed the door, walked around the vehicle, and ordered Harley out. Harley carefully stepped down, and the Arab removed the blindfold. He rubbed his blinking eyes as they adjusted to the dim light, and he saw that he stood in a magnificent cavern, the size of a domed football stadium. Bare light bulbs hung every twenty feet along its clay and rock walls. More than thirty armed and sneering men encircled him. Automatic weapons, cases of ammunition, rockets, and rocket launchers sat stacked in hewed out areas. Troop carriers and jeeps, along with drums of fuel and oil sat at the far end of the cave near another opening. Aromas of food seasoned with curry wafted in the musty air amongst the odors of gasoline fumes.

"This is where we train for *jihad*," boasted al-Daed, holding his arms out with palms up as though praising Allah. "Even if the American military has tracked us, they cannot bomb us from the sky. Allah will protect us with this holy mountain. And once you broadcast our message to the world, we will depart from this place, and find shelter within another noble mountain. Our enemies will not find us." He then ordered four soldiers to grab up the instrument cases. "Come, we need to set-up," he said to Harley, "al-Badarab has been waiting for you."

Al-Daed led Harley into a smaller chamber of the cave, followed by the four terrorists carrying the cases. The empty, rock-hewn room had a multicolored Afghani blanket hanging on the wall for a backdrop. The men set down the cases. Harley, feeling weak, thirsty, and suffering a pounding headache, started setting up the tripod, camera, and the lights. He worried he might die before the interview. Al-Daed plugged the equipment into the power generators, and set up the portable broadcast equipment outside the cave.

A short man strutted into the chamber. He was dressed in the same attire as al-Daed, but this man wore an elegant, varicolored *chapan*, and a white *lungee*: a turban wrapped about his head with its end draped over his shoulder resting upon his chest. Loathing and outrage filled his eyes that lurked under a prominent mantle of dark, wooly eyebrows. A foot-long black beard with streaks of gray hung down next to the end of his turban. He had the same rigid scowl of hatred as all the other soldiers, but with deeper creases on his forehead and around his eyes from scowling with greater frequency, and for longer periods, and with more zeal than his subordinates.

"Mr. Castle," spoke the man, lacking a smile or a salutatory intonation, or even an extended hand, "I am Ahmed Mohammed Ali Abdullah Bin al-Badarab."

Harley instinctively reached out to shake al-Badarab's hand.

"I cannot shake hands with you," said al-Badarab, speaking with a viscous Middle-East accent, "for you are an unbeliever and therefore my enemy. Although you are an infidel, I have asked you here because you are highly respected in your field. I have watched you on television, and I have seen you fearlessly report the news, amidst blowing hurricanes, rising floods, and raging wars. You have captivated the world with your courage and won their trust with your zealous commitment to the truth. And so, you are not so different from us. We risk our lives for our faith—serving Allah. You risk your life for the news—serving your viewers."

"You're right, in my business, it is the almighty viewers," agreed Harley, but he noticed, as he talked, his mouth felt painful with little bumps on his tongue, and there was a pink rash developing on his upper arms. He turned his Yankees cap backwards on his head while he persisted at adjusting the video camera's focus and settings, and then plugged in the microphone. Al-Daed had returned from setting up the small satellite dish and stood with a band of soldiers off camera. He held his rifle and glared at Harley.

"I remember when you were reporting the aftermath of an earthquake," continued al-Badarab, "and the building you were reporting from collapsed without warning. You and your cameraman dove under a table as the falling rubble trapped you in darkness. From your entrapment, and by the light of your cell phones, you continued reporting—your feelings and fears, your thirst and hunger, and your hope of freedom. Piece by piece, by hand and by hammer, the debris came off, until two days later you crawled out from your imprisonment. You and your cameraman drank and ate, and rejoiced at your liberty. Someday soon, we will rejoice, as you did, when we celebrate the universal sovereignty of Islam."

"Yeah, it was a pretty horrible ordeal, but it made a good damn story, and brought me international recognition."

"And then," said al-Badarab, "while reporting the carnage of a car bombing in Baghdad, a second bomb exploded. Hot shrapnel ripped through your right shoulder, slamming you to the ground. You scrambled back to your feet, clutched the microphone with your left hand, and then winced through the rest of the story. We are fortunate that we did not kill you at the time."

"That was you guys? It took me six months to heal. So, uh, thanks for more international attention, and the extended vacation."

"Anyway, we must begin," said al-Badarab, "and I trust that you will not try and be a hero here, because we cannot let you go home until we see my message broadcast worldwide. I have read the prepared questions your network has sent me, do not detour from them, and remember, al-Daed will not hesitate to shoot you in the head for all to see."

Harley locked the camera on record, set the equipment to broadcast, and then walked around to stand in front of it. He turned his ball cap back around with the Yankee trademark to the front. "Let's do it," he said, raising the microphone to his mouth and staring into the camera, "This is Harley Castle. I see it. I say it, and it's the news. I'm reporting to you from inside a vast cavern, somewhere in the remote mountains of Afghanistan. I flew here in a small airplane, by myself, and was then escorted for two hours, blindfolded, to this secret location, and now, I'm here interviewing al-Qaeda's second in command," he checked his notes, "Ahmed Mohammed Ali Abdullah Bin al-Badarab. He has a *fatwa*, a religious proclamation, for the world. My first question to you al-Badarab: Is Osama bin Laden alive or dead?"

Al-Badarab stroked his long scraggly beard with his hand, and then peered directly into the camera. His face transformed from a terrorizing glare into a glowing innocence. "Our great leader Osama is alive and serves Allah tirelessly. He spends more and more time in worship and supplication with God, receiving spiritual instructions on how we shall abide in our Islamic faith. He will soon pass the honor of Muslim leadership, and commander of God's army to me, his humble servant."

"To the world, Osama seems a coward, hiding under a mountain."

"America is the coward, using her military machines from the safety of the sky and striking from great distances. Her soldiers could not withstand our wrath face to face."

"Maybe, if you crawled out from under this rock, then you would get to meet, face to face, America's Green Berets, and then we could see who could stand whose wrath."

Al-Daed, off camera, poked him in the side with the end of his weapon.

Harley moved on to the next question. "You have crashed 747s and toppled buildings, killing thousands of innocent civilians, crippling a grieving nation, but the American people and their faith survived, and they, as a nation, are only stronger. Your terror did not make them bow their knee. It only made war."

"War is what we desire," he snapped, his face losing its radiance, as he capitulated to his brutal inner nature. "War is our means to an end: Islamic dominion."

"Most religions are based on compassion for their fellow humans, but you operate in a theatre of extreme violence. Why do you slaughter innocent civilians?"

"Islam does not differentiate between civilian infidels and military infidels. Whether man, woman, or child, or whether a businessman or a soldier, an infidel is an infidel, deserving death. The people who died in our glorious attacks were not innocent; they were unbelievers, therefore guilty and sentenced to death. We have no love for those who do not know Allah, we only know hate and disgust for them. They are an infestation of Allah's paradise. Obedience to Allah commands us to spill infidel blood before they corrupt us, his true believers. For us, it is permissible to butcher them and cut off their heads."

"So, if you conducted a crusade like the Reverend Billy Graham, and invited people to receive forgiveness and a relationship with your god—in your crusade, when they humbly stepped forward, you would annihilate them?"

"Yes, because they are unbelievers. We would slaughter them like sheep."

"How does a man become a suicide bomber?"

"We are taught as children that it is better to die, than living on this earth with the unbelievers amongst us, making a mockery of our religion and our prophet."

Harley thought of his innocent brother's death, and felt his anger welling, but contained his temper, knowing the aftermath of the interview. Feeling sicker by the minute and wanting it all to be over, he continued his questions without arguing.

"Why can't we discuss our religious differences and agree to disagree?"

"Islam does not coincide or make a truce with unbelief, but rather confronts it. There is no discussion, no debates—only a dialogue of bullets, the ideals of assassination, bombing, and destruction, and the diplomacy of the cannon and the machine gun."

"What about Iraq?"

"Your president is an insane, warmonger!" al-Badarab spat, as his face quaked into ripples of hatred, and when he pronounced the letter P, a wad of spit launched from his lip like a scud missile, hitting the lens of the camera, and then remaining there for the rest of the interview. "The war in Iraq is not about weapons of mass destruction," he bellowed. "It is not about democracy. It is not about the Jews. It is about oil and greed. It is about pride and revenge. Many of your young soldiers must die unless you impeach him."

"Leaders around the world are only responding to your threats and actions of violence. You provoked their aggression. So, what is your religious message—your *fatwa*?"

"Our edict to all unbelievers: Submit to Allah, or he will rain down great suffering upon four U.S. cities—Washington, Chicago, Los Angeles, and Miami."

"Your message sounds more like an attempt to instill terror rather than to declare a *fatwa*," interjected Harley.

Al-Badarab ignored him, saying, "We, his fearless servants will—with the power and blessings of Allah—explode your buildings, bomb your schoolbuses and commuter trains, blow your planes out of the sky, and poison your air, food, and water, killing fathers and mothers, sons and daughters, brothers and sisters, and husbands and wives."

Harley, feeling almost delirious from his rising fever, asked, "How about ex-wives?"

"Yes, they will die."

"What about pets—our cats and dogs?"

"We will destroy all pets."

"Including parakeets?"

"Yes, we will annihilate every pet. We know how Americans love their pets."

"Well, how about the farm animals?"

"We will kill all of them—cows, chickens, horses, goats, and especially the pigs." He stopped speaking and glared in silence at Harley, then snapped, "Do you mock me, Mr. Castle?"

Al-Daed muttered in Arabic as he pointed his rifle at Harley's head.

"No," replied Harley, "It's just that I want the viewers to fully understand the magnitude of your hatred. I want to ask you: Can you be stopped?"

"You would have to cut off our heads before we cut off yours. We are growing in numbers. Allah wants us to gather our Muslim armies, united as one, and meet the infidels of the world, on a great battlefield, face to face. It will be a magnificent feat of valor, and another blessed Tuesday, as Judeo-Christian blood floods the earth. Allah will give us a mighty victory, and we will destroy the great American dream and the myth of democracy, and then you will be faced with your filthy, naked reality."

"Wow—that's quite a visual: Blood flooding the earth. So, al-Badarab, what would sum this up?"

"Kill all infidels." He stated, as a judge casting sentence upon the condemned. "We will butcher them, slaughter them, and wipe them off the face of the earth." He then, like the hypnotist Svengali, stared at the camera with his hate filled, penetrating eyes, and threatened all of the people, watching all around the world, "If you do not abandon the path of falsehood and walk on the path of Allah, your doomed destiny will be annihilation, as we prevail with Islamic sovereignty."

Harley turned his attention away from al-Badarab, and gazed directly into the camera. "This has been Harley Castle, from Afghanistan, meeting with," he glanced again at his notes, "Ahmed Mohammed Ali Abdullah Bin al-Badarab. I see it. I say it, and it's the news."

The broadcast had gone out to the network live, and then around the globe, and people of every nationality tuned in. As proof of the broadcast, the small black and white TV in the chamber had lit up with the faces of Harley and al-Badarab. Viewers saw Harley as brave, risking his life, alone, engaging the unpredictable terrorists. They praised him as tough to suffer the torment of a blindfold, and then traveling over such rugged terrain. In contrast, they thought that al-Badarab appeared as a psychotic fanatic, an Osama wannabe, and a coward, hiding far away under a mountain of stone.

Harley walked past al-Daed and shut off the camera. He started to take it off the tripod, when al-Daed reached out with his gun and tapped the back of Harley's head. "Just leave it," he ordered, "it is now the property of Allah—for future broadcasts."

Harley turned and faced al-Daed and al-Badarab. His nose itched and he sniffed. He sniffed again. His eyes squinted and his face scrunched up. He drew in a quick breath, with another quick breath on top of it, held it, crinkled his nose, and then sneezed; a powerful sneeze; a blessed sneeze; a sneeze that would exact revenge for 9/11 and his brother's death; a sneeze for the Nobel and Pulitzer; a misty, germ-saturated sneeze that disbursed a cavernous blast of bacterial-viral contagion into the scowling faces of al-Badarab and al-Daed; a patriotic sneeze that would save thousands of American lives.

"Take him back to his plane," commanded al-Badarab, as he unknowingly inhaled a pulmonary phthisis of Pneumonic Plague, Small Pox, and Clostridium Botulinum.

"Make him video us, cutting off his head," bid al-Daed, as he breathed in the microscopic germs into his sinus cavities.

"No, we must let him live," said al-Badarab. "We may need

him again." He then walked out of the chamber a diseased man, a weapon of mass destruction, and as a biological bomb of suffering, horror, and annihilation. The bacterial-viral contagion exploded within the biotic constitution of one man, then two, then ten, then hundreds, then thousands, multiplying exponentially with every cough, with every sneeze, with every touch. Though ignorant to it, al-Badarab would become the match that ignited an inferno of human suffering among the terrorists, thus, forfeiting a temporary safety for infidels around the world.

Al-Daed shoved Harley out of the chamber and over to the off-road vehicle. Harley checked his watch—it was late afternoon. Al-Daed blindfolded him again, commanded him into the vehicle, and they drove out of the cavern. Back on the harsh road, Harley felt the heat, the ruts, and the ever-increasing effects of the time released contagion: high fever, chills, nausea, a rash upon his arms and stomach, and a swollen bumpy tongue. He also felt the painful coughs of his lung cancer, and the sideaches of his cirrhosis, but remained silent, huddled up against the door.

Al-Daed ranted the first hour, but became quiet, as the brutal symptoms of the relentless disease crushed him.

Arriving back at the plane, al-Daed stopped the rover, ordered Harley out, removed the reporter's blindfold, and then said, "I have noticed that you are extremely ill—beyond your smoking hack. You look feverish and you are soaked with sweat. There are red blotches and bumps on your arms. I believe that you have infected me with some sort of disease."

Harley could barely stand, overwhelmed with weakness, but with a grin, he muttered, "I see it. I say it, and it's the news. And you Aziz Izz al-Daed—is all dead."

He pointed the gun to Harley's head and snarled, "You will fly me out to get the antidote or you will die right here. Once at our destination, if they don't give me the antidote, fuel for the plane, and let you fly me back, you will die right there. I am destined to die as a martyr for Allah in Los Angeles, killing a multitude of unbelievers, not by the sickness of one infidel."

"With my remaining strength, I will fly you, but I must tell you, that I am not afraid of you or any of your hate-filled, psycho Islamic brothers. You don't terrorize me—and you sure as hell don't terrorize the American people. We as a nation don't always get along, but by God and by constitution, we stand united against your cowardly threats."

"I can't believe," muttered al-Daed, experiencing a wave of nausea, "that your government broke international accords, releasing a biological weapon upon us. You have sent all my brothers to death. You pig! You dog! It is not fair, for we are the terrorists, not the infidels."

"Well, we reached a conclusion: We needed to cut off your heads before you cut off ours."

"Get into the plane, pig!" Al-Daed yelled.

Harley fired up the engines, knowing that there was only enough fuel to take off and gain some altitude. Al-Daed sat in the co-pilot seat moaning in agony from his illness, pointing his gun at Harley. Harley taxied the plane back to the huge boulder, turned it around, and then raced down the flat barren patch, slowly lifted off, and barely missed the crest of the wrinkled hill.

The plane climbed quickly into the drab light of dusk. Just as al-Daed shouted, "Allah, save me from this sickness, for I am destined to kill the infidels!" one propeller stopped, followed immediately by the other. Out of fuel, the plane glided in total silence amidst the pale clouds, and then abruptly dropped below them, plummeting toward the jagged landscape. With wild eyes of certain death, both men stared out the cockpit at the fast enlarging, ominous mountains. Harley flew the dead plane steady, but there was no spot to land. An instant before the aircraft slammed into the stone face of a mountain, and while al-Daed screamed hysterically in Arabic, "Allah" every other word or so, Harley cinched his baseball cap down on his head, and spoke the last words of his life, "God bless America—and the New York Yankees."

THE SKY CHARIOT

GREG STEERED HIS car onto the asphalt driveway leading to the ranch house of his mom and dad. It was 5:35 a.m. and still dark, except for a creamy orange glow ascending on the horizon. Driving by the eucalyptus trees lining the entrance, he glanced out at the silhouettes of three horses standing in the pasture. They stopped grazing, lifted their heads, and stared at him with curiosity. He drove past the barn, and around the circular drive in front of the house.

All the lights were on in the house. The cars of his older sister Susan, and his two younger brothers, Ryan and Ricky sat in the driveway. As he parked and shut off his car, he glanced east to see the first light of the sun bursting over the highest peaks of the Sierra Mountains. Though the sunrise was magnificent, he grieved.

With a heavy sigh, he climbed out of his car and shut its door. As he took a step toward the house, a loud bellowing sound and a man shouting startled him. He turned, looking skyward, and saw a gigantic hot air balloon descending out of the sky. It was yellow, almost golden, with bright panels of red, green, and blue. It whisked over, scraping its wicker gondola through the treetops of the towering pine trees on the east edge of the property. The frantic pilot peered down at the rising ground and then at the looming house. He hollered commands at his co-pilot, then calmly reassured the petrified passengers. The co-pilot fired the balloon's propane fuel jets, blasting a roaring flame up into its nylon envelope.

Greg watched in horror, as the balloon and its terrified occupants soared toward his parent's home.

That same morning, a little after 5:00 a.m., the telephone rang. Greg sat up in bed, and grabbed the cordless phone resting on the nightstand. With his eyes still closed, he muttered, "Hello," already knowing, and dreading the reason for the call.

"Hello, Greg."

"Yeah, Dad."

"Your mother—she's—she's gone."

Greg breathed in deeply, rubbed his eyes, and then exhaled, saying, "Okay, Dad. I'll be right over."

Greg's wife, awake and lying next to him, placed a comforting hand on his shoulder.

He hung up the phone, swung his legs out from under the covers, and placed his feet on the floor. Sitting on the edge of the bed, he whispered, "Hun—mom's gone."

"Are you okay?" she asked, her voice faltering.

"Yeah, I'm okay. Are you okay?"

"Yeah, I'll be okay," she answered, reaching over to her nightstand for a tissue.

"I'm goin' on over there. I'll call you later."

In the next rooms slept three little boys—six, four, and two—undisturbed by the ringing phone; unaware that their grandma had just died.

Greg got dressed, brushed his teeth, and put on a baseball cap. His wife heated up a cup of instant coffee in the microwave, poured it in a travel mug, and handed it to him as he shuffled out the door into the predawn darkness. A cool autumn breeze brushed across his face, causing him to shudder. He climbed into his car, started it, and then leaned his head on the steering wheel as he let the motor warm up. After a couple of minutes, he sat up, took a sip of his hot coffee, and then drove off.

A few miles away, under the parking lot lights of the Sierra Vista Mall, more than thirty hot air balloons began launching for Clovisfest.

As Greg drove, he thought of his mother, Joy, and the first time he had noticed the symptoms of her illness. It was June, Fresno, California, and hot—plus ten degrees. His mom was attending his softball game. The setting sun was homerun high over the left field fence. She sat with the families of the ballplayers, on the wooden bleachers behind the chain-link backstop. He stood in the batter's box, smiled, and tipped his cap to his wife, and then, feeling like a ten-year-old little leaguer, he grinned sheepishly at his mom.

After the game, as they walked to their cars, he noticed that his mother had trouble saying words and completing sentences. Over the next couple of weeks, the rest of her family and friends also noticed her altered speech pattern; a stark contrast to her normally chatty manner. Speaking with a Floridian accent, sweet like honey drizzled on cornbread, and with an excited childlike wonderment, she usually talked and talked about all the beauty around her, but now something was very wrong.

In the hospital's radiology waiting room, her husband, George paced about nervously, along with their three sons, Greg, Ryan, and Ricky. Their daughter, Susan, cried softly, leaning her face against the shoulder of her husband. The spouses of the sons sat in chairs and conversed quietly.

The oncologist called the family into a consultation room. As everyone squeezed into the small room, he slipped Joy's x-ray into the light box. The doctor pointed at the gray image of her brain, and then at a darker mass.

"It is a large, highly vascular tumor," explained the physician, "which means it is rapidly growing. We suspect it is a type of brain cancer called…" he called it by a name that one tries to forget and wishes never to hear of again.

Weeks passed and then a biopsy was taken. Joy's family and friends hoped that the doctors could remove the tumor and that she would be healthy, happy, and talkative again.

After the surgery, the brain surgeon—a deeply compassionate man—met with her family. It was in an empty room, recently painted, down the hall from surgery's general waiting room. The new, uninstalled light fixtures sat in a corner so only natural light shined in through the bare windows. The doctor, still dressed in his blue surgical scrubs, stepped in and shut the door.

All the family members waited stoically for the doctor to speak; each fearful of what he would say. They knew that he had grave news. The fallen lines and creases on his sullen face revealed it. He started out speaking as a doctor of medicine, using words like diagnosis and prognosis, until he focused on the tears welling in their eyes. He knew that they loved Joy and needed her in all the ways that a family does.

He stopped speaking, hung his head, and muttered, "I'm sorry, but we can't…" He looked into their anguished faces, and saw their shock—that death would dare take a member of their family. With tears welling in his own eyes, he cleared his throat, and spoke, barely audibly, "I'm sorry." Then, with his voice breaking, "I'm sorry, I'm so sorry. If we remove the tumor, the quality of her life will suffer greatly. She'll lose most of her motor skills and her memory. She'll be confined to a bed, unable to speak, not knowing who she is or who you are." The doctor sighed deeply, then continued. "If we leave the tumor, it will eventually take her life, but until that time, you'll have Joy to love, and you'll have her love in return. Please understand. We did all that we could."

The family gathered around the doctor and embraced him. They knew he had tried his utmost and they released him of the burden.

As he opened the door to leave, he paused and said, "Please forgive me for my tears, but your sorrow was too much for me. Joy, indeed, is a wonderful person, and I, too, do not understand—why her?"

"What should we do?" asked Susan, dabbing a tissue to her eyes.

He knew the tragic answer; he had given it a multitude of times to other grieving families. "Take her home, make her comfortable, love her and hold on to her, as long as you'll have her."

"How long?" asked George, his face displaying his anguish.

"Three to six months—if that. Again, I'm so sorry." The doctor stepped into the hall to leave, then turned, saying, "When you have more questions and concerns, please, call me."

Her family took Joy home. Over the next few days, she wept, sat lost in her thoughts, and wept. Everyone wondered why her life, of all people, would end at fifty seven years of age. Especially since she was so busy loving her husband, children, and grandchildren, and her elderly widowed mother, and visiting those dying in the cancer ward at the hospital, and teaching stitchery to the abused women at the rescue center, and helping with the errands of all the silver-haired octogenarian ladies from the church.

During a visit with her mom, Susan sat next to her. Joy sat in her blue reading lounger by the window with a scenic view of the Sierra foothills.

"Mom, what are some things you'd like to do?" Susan asked, holding her mother's hand.

Joy peered silently at Susan. She heard the question and understood it, but the tumor affected her speech. She cupped her hands around her face and started crying, speaking in halted sentences, "I want—to see my—grandchildren—grow up."

Susan had three girls, all under the age of twelve. Greg had the three little boys.

"I know Mom. They love you, and they know how much you love them," Susan said as she started crying. Joy reached out, as her daughter leaned in, and they hugged for a long while, rocking each other gently. Susan sat up, dabbed her eyes and her nose with a tissue, then again asked, "Mom, what can we do for you? Where would you like to go? What would you like to do?"

Joy stopped weeping, and while wiping the tears from her eyes, she concentrated on her speech. "I want—to go to—the beach—and to the mount—tains," she paused drawing in a deep breath, "And—ride in a ba—balloon."

Susan smiled, happy that her mother had spoken her wishes, then confirmed that she had heard her right, "So you want to go to the beach and to the mountains?"

Joy nodded her head.

"And do you really want to ride in a hot air balloon?"

Joy nodded again, concentrated, then spoke clearly, "Yes."

Susan shared Joy's requests with the rest of the family.

The family visited Pismo Beach. The sun brightened their gloom. The breaking waves quieted their thoughts. Joy smiled.

The family toured Kings Canyon National Park. The gigantic redwoods reinforced their courage. A panoramic view of the snowy peaks fortified their faith. Joy smiled.

Greg contacted a hot air balloon company and reserved a ride for his mom. The thought of floating above all of God's creation excited Joy, and her spirits lifted.

The cancer continued ravaging her brain. It stole away the mobility in her right arm and leg, confining her to a wheelchair. Suffering the effects of radiation, she lost her hair.

The day arrived for Joy to ride in a balloon. She wore a beautiful purple scarf. Greg called to confirm, and explained his mom's condition, hoping they would assist him. The balloon's owner denied Joy a ride, explaining that the balloon could not accommodate wheel chairs, nor would he risk the liability of having a passenger with such a grave illness onboard. Joy cried.

Over the next months, Joy's condition worsened. Greg and his two younger brothers played their guitars and sang hymns for her. The songs comforted her. On many days, Greg pushed her in her wheelchair to the end of the driveway where she could view the sunsets. On one trip, as Joy treasured the setting sun, Greg picked her a yellow daisy. Before he could stop her, she bit off the flower and ate it. Greg stood behind her wheelchair and silently wept.

Another day, Joy sat in her wheelchair on the front porch. Greg walked up next to her. Not recognizing him, she recoiled in terror.

"Mom, it's me, Greg. Don't be afraid," he said softly. He reached out slowly and gently touched her hand. She knew the man was kind and would not hurt her. He pushed her to the end of the driveway. Greg stood behind her wheelchair and silently wept.

Over the months, Joy's mind and body surrendered to her illness. She completely lost her capacity to speak. She lay in her rented hospital bed, and in her silence, gazed out the window upon the serenity of the foothills and the hope of the sunrise. She faced her plight with great courage and faith.

There were many trips to the emergency room, most of them in the middle of the night. Family members raced to the hospital to spend what they thought would be a final moment with Joy. Each time, she survived to go home. Surrounded by her loving family, she lived months beyond all expectations.

Her mother, Audie, flew out from Tampa, Florida. She kept telling her grandchildren, "It ain't right that my daughter will die before me. A parent ain't supposed to bury their child; it's supposed to be the other way 'round. I can't bear it. It just ain't right."

On the eve of Joy's death, she struggled to live; her labored breathing echoing a coarse rattle from within her lungs.

The family braced for the inevitable, as each loved one spent time alone with her.

Greg sat next to her, on the edge of her bed. She seemed unconscious with her eyes closed. He held her withered hands and whispered to her, "Mom, it's Greg. I love you. You have been a good mother and have taught me to seek out and appreciate the beauty in everything and everyone. Thank you."

She twitched her hand. Greg was surprised.

"Mom, I think you need to hear what I am about to say." He got choked up, cleared his throat, and said, "Mom, I want you to understand—that it's okay to leave us. We'll miss you terribly—but we'll all be okay. You need to remember that God watches over all of us. All of your prayers, over all of these years are set in motion. They'll live on, and we'll always be blessed. By spending time with you, we've all, as a family, become closer than we've ever been. I want you to know that you don't have to fight any more for the sake of your family. We have each other. You can let go. Okay? You can let go. We'll all be alright." He leaned over, kissed her on her forehead, squeezed her hand, and whispered, "I love you, Mom." He stood up and lingered, staring down at her. He did not want to leave. He knew it would be the last time he would see her alive.

As he left the room, Susan hugged him, then with a box of tissues in her hand, she entered the room to say goodbye. Passing down the hall, he squeezed the shoulders of his dad and two brothers.

Overwhelmed by physical and emotional exhaustion, Greg went home. Once there, he sat down on a footstool, called his wife and three boys together and wrapped his arms around them all, pulling them in close and tight. His wife cried softly, holding his head against her chest. The little boys squirmed.

On that early morning of his mother's death, Greg stood in the driveway gawking up at the balloon careening toward the house. To his relief, it slowed its descent and nearly leveled off. Just before it did, the sky chariot swung low, bouncing its gondola lightly off the roof's wooden shingles above Joy's bedroom. With another mighty blast from its burner, the balloon rose away from the house.

Greg's father, two brothers, and sister rushed out onto the back porch to see about the commotion they had heard. They stood in awe.

Vivid, multicolored hot air balloons floated everywhere across the blue sky. Some near, others far. Some soared high, touching heaven's orange-tinted clouds; others sailed low, skimming just above earth's golden foothills. On the horizon, the sun beamed over the summits of the picturesque mountains bestowing a new day upon the San Joaquin Valley.

As the balloon gained buoyancy, floating away from the house and beyond the treetops into the sky, the puzzled pilot and passengers peered down at the smiling man standing in the driveway waving and hollering up at them.

Certain that the spirit of his mother was riding in the wicker basket, Greg waved, yelling, "I'll see you on the other side, Mom! Someday—I'll see you on the other side!"

STOP

ALL THE CELLULAR phones, all around the world, all at once received a call. Millions rang with ringtones—some soft, some bright, and some loud and annoying. They beckoned. Millions played a song—some jazzy, some classical, and some cutesy, most of them annoying as well. They beckoned. Others vibrated gently, as others shook with erotic intensity. They beckoned.

In homes and classrooms, restaurants and bars, retail stores and corporate towers, in the cities, in the suburbs, and on farms, they beckoned, and in cars, trucks, taxis, buses, subways, and on airplanes, they beckoned. Across global latitudes and longitudes, ringing, vibrating, and singing in unison, they beckoned answer me—answer me—answer me.

People thought it strange, startling, disturbing that all the cell phones, all around them, all at once received a call. For some people it was daytime; for others nighttime. For some breakfast; for others dinner. Some worked, some watched TV, some slept, others made love, and then suddenly the phones rang, vibrated, and sang, spurring an international, echoing clatter of commotion, as people snatched their phones from a belt clip, a pocket, a backpack, a purse, or out of a briefcase. The fast-paced, stress-filled world rang to a halt, as everyone stopped and answered their phones, with the exception of lovers—they continued making love.

Millions of people simultaneously answered the call, some timidly, others boldly. They answered in their native language:

"Hello; Buongiorno; Olla; Ni hao; Salamu; Hallo; Gashi." They listened, and heard a voice, and they wondered if it was a high-pitch man, a low-tone woman, or a life-like machine. Some people missed the call, but the message recorded into their voicemail, and then, when it was convenient, they too heard the message. The voice spoke clearly, and articulated the same word three times with a three-second interval between each word.

"Stop — — — Stop — — — Stop."

The population of earth pondered the peculiar message. Who sent it? And why? From where? And how did all the cellular phones, all around the world, all at once receive a call? Was it a hoax? An advertisement? A warning? A message from terrorists? From the government? Or—plastered on the front page of the tabloids—contact from aliens? Many "Hearers" of the message of "Stop" met in small circles and crowded meetings. There were voluminous discussions, heated debates, loud arguments, and scrappy fistfights as they sought the answer to the question—what did "Stop" mean?

Bosses seemed to know. It was a message to their employees. "Stop" meant: stop wasting time, stop taking so many bathroom breaks, stop showing up late for work, stop going home early, stop talking about the boss behind his back, and stop acting disgruntled. They trained their employees in just what "Stop" meant in the workplace. It meant more profits.

Parents seemed to know. It was a message to their children. "Stop" meant: stop eating so much junk food, stop watching so much TV, stop staying up so late, stop fighting with your siblings, stop messing up the house, stop talking back to your parents, stop talking on the phone so much, and stop instant messaging so much. They lectured to their children as to just what "Stop" meant in the home. It meant more family time.

Wives seemed to know. It was a message to their husbands. "Stop" meant: stop groping me all the time, stop drinking too many beers, stop watching every game of football, and stop hanging around with your weird friends. They nagged their husbands in just what "Stop" meant in a marriage. It meant more intimacy.

Husbands seemed to know. It was a message to their wives. "Stop" meant: stop nagging me, stop denying me sex, and stop trying to change me. They griped to their wives in just what "Stop" meant in a marriage. It meant more sex.

Artists—painters, writers, actors, dancers, and sculptors—seemed to know. "Stop" meant: stop censorship, stop the war, stop the Republicans, stop the paparazzi, and stop the tabloids. They narrated to their audience just what "Stop" meant in art. It meant free expression.

Environmentalists seemed to know. It was a message to the industrialist. "Stop" meant: stop toxic dumping, stop using aerosols, stop emitting smog, stop over-forestation, stop black market poaching, and for the sake of us all, stop contaminating the soil, the sky, and the oceans. They demonstrated to the apathetic just what "Stop" meant on Mother Earth. It meant ecological equilibrium.

Generals seemed to know. It was a message to their soldiers. "Stop" meant: stop the advancement of the enemy, stop them from far away, stop them without sacrificing your life, stop them in their own country, and stop them with all you can be and with all you got. They commanded their army in just what "Stop" meant in a hostile world. It meant freedom and democracy for all.

Intellectuals seemed to know. Not really. They couldn't agree. They met in an assemblage of pedagogues, philosophers, psychologists, and physicists. Their pomposity swelled with their bombastic interpretations, as they elucidated stop from every point of view. They explained to the so-called ignorant of society just what "Stop" meant in a puzzling world. It meant what one thought it meant.

Politicians seemed to know. It was a message to their

constituents. "Stop" meant: stop voting for their opponents, stop paying such close attention to government, and stop grumbling about paying taxes. They politicked to the people just what "Stop" meant in a bi-partisan government. It meant re-election.

Preachers seemed to know. It was a message to the believers. "Stop" meant: stop smoking, stop drinking, stop overeating; stop swearing, stop stealing, stop killing, and stop having extramarital affairs at work, church, and around the neighborhood. They preached to their congregations just what "Stop" meant in eternity. It meant—with a waving finger and fist upon the podium—Heaven or Hell.

Missionaries seemed to know. It was a message to those poor, unfortunate citizens of the planet that did not have a cell phone or even know what one was. It meant: stop the savage's uncivilized ways. Pursuing their divine calling, they organized, appealed for donations, and sent many messengers into the remote villages of the world. They started TV shows, and solicited more donations to enable them to send more messengers to the far away places. Missionaries shared with the primitive peoples just what "Stop" meant in an unenlightened world. It meant more "Hearers" of the message of "Stop."

But what was the true meaning of "Stop?"

"Stop" really, truly, only meant the same as it always had meant. Since the first chiseled message of "Stop" into the stone tablets of the Ten Commandments, it meant what it meant. Stop hurting yourself, stop hurting others, and stop hurting the planet. It was as though over the centuries the toy top of stop had stopped spinning as people pursued and fulfilled their selfish desires regardless of the suffering they themselves sustained, or the harm they caused others, or the irreparable damage to the planet. But the mysterious message of "Stop" sent the top whirring again as people opened their hearts and minds and embraced "Stop," and with great zeal, they practiced "Stop," and the people began to restore their broken world. Workers worked harder. Children obeyed their parents. Husbands and wives experienced greater intimacy and made love more. Artists expressed and exhibited decency. Preachers brought people to God. Generals negotiated peace. Politicians made promises and kept them without regard to re-election and special interests. Intellectuals broke it down into bite-sized morsels that fed the ignorant, and the missionaries worked tirelessly spreading the message far and wide. All in all, all around the world, after all the cell phones rang, the world transformed, as people simply stopped a lot of what was wrong and harmful to them, to others, and to the planet. Smoking, cussing, greed, gluttony, drug and alcohol abuse, crime, racial and sexual prejudice, pollution, and wars diminished dramatically as the citizens of the world didn't merely stop what was selfishly wrong, but started what was sacrificially right: sharing, helping, communicating, and loving for the good of the whole. The message of "Stop" burst forth as an enduring, universal fellowship of joy and peace, constituting a golden age for humanity as mankind celebrated the reclamation of paradise.

But—who sent the message of "Stop"? And why? And from where? And how did all the cell phones, all around the world, all at once beckon?

One man knew. John Herold knew. He worked as a satellite systems analyst at the S.O.C.C. (Satellite Operations Control Center) in Suitland, Maryland where they manage the satellite constellation, track satellites, control their orbits, and scrutinize spacecraft telemetry and command data. His responsibility: The satellite launched as Jarwin Engineered Satellite United States # 7, one of forty-eight LEO (Low Earth Orbiting) satellites consisting of a spot beam antenna, a trapezoidal body, two solar arrays, and a magnetometer, operating at an orbital inclination of 52 degrees at an altitude of 876 miles above the earth.

John, 31, never married, and an avid reader, read through a

science fiction novel every two or three days. He was a simple man living in a sci-fi fantasy world, without aspirations to improve himself or change the world. While reading the riveting last chapter of his current book—instead of analyzing # 7's endless download of data on his computer monitor—a metallic fragment of orbiting space debris the size of a dime struck # 7. It nudged the craft slightly out of orbit, and also, caused a breach—unbeknownst to John—in the encoding systems that ensure voice and signaling security for individual transmissions. He finished his book, set it down, and then noticed # 7's skewed orbit. Since he failed to react immediately to the problem, and so he wouldn't lose his cushy job, he erased the alert data—and his lapse of responsibility—from the hard drive, and then began the voice sequence for realigning # 7's orbital plane.

With three second intervals between each spoken "Stop" command, he programmed the X coordinate, then audibly commanded it to "Stop." He set the Y and said, "Stop," and then lastly, he set the Z and said, "Stop," thus, restoring and then locking in the satellite's correct orbital path—though the craft was still malfunctioning. Thinking all was well, he began reading a new sci-fi novel.

Instantly, his vocal commands were uplinked to the satellite's damaged encoders and then faultily beamed back down to the terrestrial gateways, coursing the pathways of telecommunication networks, and then internationally transmitted, causing all the cellular phones, all around the world, all at once to receive a call. They beckoned. Millions answered their phones and heard John's nasally voice commands as he spoke them to satellite # 7, "Stop —— — Stop — — — Stop."

HOWL

RESPONDING TO REPORTS of a seven vehicle accident, a hazardous waste spill, and unrestrained wild animals, veteran California Highway Patrol officer, Mike Rhodes maneuvered his motorcycle down the white dotted line, slicing between two lanes of standstill, bumper to bumper vehicles. Startled motorists cringed, sinking into their seats, as he roared past with his lights flashing lights and siren blaring. Speeding north on the 110 Los Angeles freeway, past the elongating, afternoon shadows of the downtown skyscrapers, he wondered: *What sort of wild animals?*

The end of the summer heat wave had scorched the asphalt clogs and tangles of Los Angeles with searing temperatures much hotter than normal, and with weeks of breezeless, sweltering days, the stagnant smog had become noxious, making motorists weary and irritable.

Nine minutes before Officer Rhodes received the emergency call, radio and TV reporter, Ty in the Sky, Tyler Worley described traffic conditions from a helicopter whirring above the freeway. As the pilot, Roger Helms flew the copter, the wry remarks of Ty in the Sky only fueled the wildfires of frustration blazing hotter amongst commuters. "Man, oh man," he spouted, "the 110 is jam packed and in this broiling heat it must be hot, hellacious hot down there!" He focused the craft's camera on a wide aerial shot of the long chain of creeping vehicles, and then as he panned the camera over to the downtown skyscrapers, he continued tormenting. "From up here the sun reflecting off all those skyscraper windows makes it look like we're all being fried by not one, but by a thousand scorching suns. And the freeway," he added, pointing the camera back on the vehicles, "it looks like a long cement Hibachi grill, and the cars—link sausages, smokin' in dingy exhaust fumes. And oh my!" he burst out, zooming the camera in for a close-up on a RV, "what a lot of fun for the folks in the immobile motor home down there vacationing in Trafficland!"

"Flippin' Californians!" gruffed Ben Dover. "And their flippin' crowded freeways, and their flippin' smog!" He used the word 'flippin' because his wife, Eileen scorned him when he cussed.

They rode in their new, forty-foot, Fleetwood American Dream motor home all the way from Iowa to tour Southern California. Ben, outfitted in a bright-blue jumpsuit, and a navy-blue Camping World baseball cap, sat behind the large steering wheel. Eileen, dressed in comfortable slacks, and a button-up blouse, rode in the passenger seat. They both had curly gray hair, his springing out from under his hat and hers sharply styled. Both donned large and boxy BlueBlocker sunglasses, and wore new, white tennis shoes. Both were pushing seventy years old and both were recently retired—Ben as a hard-nosed production supervisor, and Eileen as a soft-spoken elementary school teacher. They had looked forward to a slower, leisurely life, but not the snail pace of L.A. traffic.

Instead of sightseeing, they sat virtually parked, idling away the time on the congested 110 freeway. Adding to the noise and irritation, a news helicopter hovered in the sky above them. Navigating through the intense traffic, Ben had become tired and grumpy. His shoulders ached from gripping the steering wheel, and his foot hurt from hitting the brake pedal a thousand times in the stop and go traffic. Furthermore, they would most likely miss a taping of their favorite game show at Universal Studios.

"No good, flippin' slow-heimers," griped Ben again.

"Now Ben dear," interjected Eileen, "don't get your blood pressure up."

"I take pills for that!" he snapped.

"Well, then don't flare up your IBS," she urged. "You know getting mad will irritate your bowels and then how are you going to sit there in your captain's chair, in that jumpsuit, stuck in traffic, and deal with Dinah Rita?" She called diarrhea, Dinah Rita, after one of her little first graders had mistakenly called it that.

"Oh, just leave me alone," he growled, removing his sunglasses and rubbing his itchy, strained eyes.

"Okay, Ben," she spurted, unfastening her seatbelt and standing up to leave, "I'll just go and lie down on the sofa until you're finished griping us through all of this traffic!"

"Good idea," he stated, as he put back on his sunglasses, checked his rearview mirrors and glanced out his passenger window at a semi-truck two lanes over, hauling bright orange barrels, "because, I'm goin' from gripin' to all out cussin'!"

Two lanes over, Cody Wild sat in the cab of his white Freightliner truck. He wore a soiled, straw cowboy hat, straight-leg jeans, scuffed-up boots, and a tight, muscle shirt with frayed, scissors-cut sleeves that showed off his rattlesnake tattoos. The skin-ink serpents slithered from their rattles on his shoulders all the way down each arm to their fanged heads needled onto the backs of his fists. His rig pulled an open, flatbed trailer hauling fifty-five gallon steel drums of hazardous waste, destined for offloading at the waste management site in the remote Kettleman hills. Each fluorescent orange barrel displayed large black decals of the word *Biohazard* and the odd cloverleaf-like biohazard symbol. The barrels were secured onboard with numerous straps and winches, except for two barrels, unbeknownst to Cody, that were held barely snug by a loose strap with a defective winch.

Driving on the 110, Cody peered out the windshield into the fetid haze at the hundreds of red brake lights flashing on and off in front of him. He thought about Regina, his girlfriend, and he became enraged. He snatched his hat off his head, and violently slapped it two times on the dashboard, shoved it tight back upon his head, reached over, jabbed the cigarette lighter in, and then cranked up a Lynyrd Skynyrd song. After half a minute the lighter popped out, he lit a cigarette, and puffed on it hard. He was anxious to get up and over the I-5 Grapevine to his home in Bakersfield, before his ol' lady went down to Trout's bar, chugged her third Bud Lite, and sped off with her ex-ol' man on the back of his Harley. A glinting in his driverside rearview mirror prompted his glance down at a shiny Liquid Silver Jaguar.

Bupinder Singh, riding in his new '07 Jaguar XJR, less than an hour off the lot, with a paper license plate taped inside the back window, drove on the 110. He dressed in a tailored, three-piece suit, and sported a short, well-groomed beard and slicked back, black hair. A few minutes before, he had been happy, singing along with his CD player—but then the phone call. As an up and coming realtor to the large population of Punjabis in Southern California, he had sold an expensive property. Upon close of escrow, he stood to make a lot of money. So banking on the commission, he bought a costly, new car and expensive clothes. The dream shattering phone call had been from the escrow officer. Escrow would not close—the buyers dropped out —there would be no commission. He would have to return the car with a substantial financial penalty. He shot a look to his left at a motor home with an angry elderly man, who looked to be spewing out cuss words. To his right, he glanced up into the cab of a truck and saw its driver slamming his cowboy hat on his dashboard. He peered in his rearview mirror and saw a man driving, yet leaning over his backseat talking to a pair of bare legs in the air.

"Hurrrrrry Carlos," screamed Yolanda Ruiz, lying with her legs in the air, in the back seat of their yellow 1989 Toyota Corolla inching up the middle lane of the 110 freeway. She gripped the unbuckled seatbelt in one hand, and with the other hand, she clutched the front seat headrest. "Carlos," she begged, wincing in the middle of a contraction, "pleeeease get me to the hospital. The baby is coming!"

"Yolanda, I'm trying, but we're stuck in traffic," whined Carlos, her husband, trying to sound calm to keep her calm. "We barely get going, and then we stop again. Basically, there's no place to go." He glanced in the rearview mirror at his wife moaning in agony in the backseat. Her long, black hair, now damp and stringy, stuck to her pain contorted face, glowing red from the heat. Sweat poured down her neck and pooled in her cleavage, soaking her pink T-shirt. Her blue skirt was hiked up around her waist, with her large white maternity underwear on the floor. Carlos thought to call 9-1-1, but his cell phone was out of minutes. With their air conditioner broken and all their windows down, the smog and heat occupied their car along with them. Sweat trickled down his temples to his sopping white T-shirt and into his damp boxers exhibited above his low-hanging baggy, denim pants. The noise of the idling diesels on either side of him gave him a headache, plus, his throat felt scratchy and his eyes itched from the smog.

"Ahhhhh," Yolanda screamed, gripped by a contraction. "Please, pleeeease, Carlos, get me to the hospital."

"I'm trying," he snapped in frustration, feeling his stomach knot up, "but the freeway is jammed. Traffic isn't going anywhere!" He turned in his seat, reached an arm over, and grabbed her hand. "Breathe baby, breathe like we learned in class!"

"Owwwwohhh!" she yelled, followed by short, controlled breaths. "I don't want to have the baby out here on the freeway. Oh Jesus! My water broke!"

"Stay calm and breathe," encouraged Carlos, trying to sound calm. "We'll get there soon." He felt panicky about the safety of his wife and first child, and his anger grew with every stalled minute. He glanced around and realized that he couldn't even change lanes. They were boxed in on the left by a motor home, and on the right by a truck; in the front by a new Jaguar, and from behind by a red Nissan.

"Hey girl, how'ya doin'?" said Rooisha Jones, driving a red Nissan Altima, speaking into her cordless Bluetooth headset stuck in her ear. As she talked, she checked her eyeliner and lipstick in her lighted, sunvisor mirror. "I'm good too—frustrated with this traffic though. I'm on the 110, stopped and wedged between a huge damn truck and a big-ass motor home, and there's a crazy guy in front of me, leanin' into his backseat, swervin' all over the road. But hey, I have excitin' news. I'm goin' on an audition for a new movie with—are you ready? Denzel! I know, way cool. I want this part so bad. It's a small part, but I need it. Besides, it's my turn. Rooisha's done paid her dues all these years doin' commercials and funky bit parts. Not only that, I got talent too. Mmhuh, and beauty. My agent always says that I got smooth, milk-chocolaty skin, hazelnut, brown eyes, perfect teeth, glossy black hair, and full, pooky lips, always on the verge of a kiss. Yeah, he calls 'em pooky. Crazy mofo. Oh, I wanted to tell you I had another argument with my dad. He always says I'm wastin' my time with my dream of being an actress. I told him that I'm not goin' to be a waitress down on the strip all my life, because someday I'll make it big. Only thing is—some other sister's goin' to get the part, provin' him right, while I'm sittin' on this no-good freeway starin' in my rearview mirror at this soccer-mom drivin' a minivan full of kids up my booty. It ain't right!"

"How's your toothache honey?" Jill Campbell asked her crying seven-year-old daughter.

"It hurts really bad mommy," the little girl answered between sobs.

Jill, a stay at home mom, dressed in loose sweat pants, sandals, and one of her husband's T-shirts, reached over to the passenger seat of her green Chevy minivan, stroked her daughter's forehead, and consoled, "Well, we'll be at the dentist soon, and he'll make you feel better." In the middle seat, her one-year-old little guy screamed and kicked, wanting out of his car seat. Her three-year-old boy, next to the one-year-old in the middle seat, screamed because her five-year-old son in the rear seat tormented him, tapping the back of his head with a plastic toy dolphin. No amount of animal crackers or boxes of juice would settle any of them down. She felt exhausted, staying up all night with her distraught daughter, then waiting all morning to hear from the dentist. Along with her concern for her daughter, and her frustration with her noisy, irritating boys, the vehicle idled poorly and had a tendency to stall, prompting her fear that it would break down in the middle lane of the 110 freeway.

As traffic came to a stop, she squeezed her face with both hands trying to quell her worsening headache and silently prayed that the engine wouldn't choke and die. She peered between her fingers into the cars in front of her. A young lady talked on her cell phone while doing her makeup. In front of the primping girl, all she could see was a man leaning over his front seat talking to a person in the back seat with her bare legs propped up on the back of the seats. To her left, the rear door of a huge motor home. To her right, the trailer of a semi-truck hauling metal barrels labeled *BioHazard*. In her review mirror, she saw an enraged driver beating his steering wheel.

"Damn traffic!" yelled Bob Shmidtz, pounding his fists on the steering wheel of his white 1993 Ford Taurus. He scooched back in the seat so his protruding stomach roll wouldn't restrict his steering. He wore a tight, short-sleeve, lemon-yellow dress shirt with its buttons bulging, a morose green tie, stretchy-waist, tan slacks, and black shoes with such a high gloss they looked plastic. For the third time, he reached over and cranked the air conditioner knob up as far as it would go just to make sure that it was blowing at its maximum capacity. He rubbed his chest, trying to alleviate a severe case of heartburn. He felt aggravated, not only because of the stifling heat and smog, the traffic, two glazed donuts, and three cups of coffee, but because he was worried about getting to a scheduled appointment.

Earlier in the day, inside his boss's office with the door closed, his sales-data-obsessed boss, Brad Overhue, had barked, "Bob, your sales have been down for the last three months. You're not even close to the quota we set for you. Consider this an official warning. If you can't run the ball into the end zone, then I'll have to find someone else to score the three pointers." Bob wanted to tell his ignorant boss that a touchdown is six points and in basketball, there's a three-point basket. Instead, he tried to explain, "I'm sorry Brad, but my crappy car keeps breaking down, and the auto-expense isn't enough to..." Before Bob could finish, Brad's cell phone rang with a catchy Reggae ringtone. Brad held his index finger in the air silencing Bob, and then with the same finger he answered his phone, speaking in his low and serious boss voice. "Brad Overhue. Hello Jim, I'm good. What's your problem? I see. Uh-huh. I see that you're a whussy, and that you're tryin' to make a sale by givin' away the farm. You hold our margin or you walk away from the deal. Listen up. I lose my cut if you drop any lower, so make it happen Jim or I'll send someone else in with some muscle to close the deal, and you'll lose *your* commission." Brad snapped his phone shut, clipped it back onto his belt, then focused again on Bob, who stared down at the floor. "No loser excuses Bob," continued Brad, "get the sales up! Got it Bob? Up, not down! Here's a sympathy lead for you. Go see them, and Bob—don't screw up, it could be big profit. We're done here. Hit the streets, and make it happen!"

As Bob drove on the 110, he fretted about losing the deal and his job. He was the sole supporter for his wife and three kids and they lived from payday—to no pay—to payday, never getting ahead. Every minute that he sat in stalled traffic fueled his desperation. He felt trapped by not only the big motor home on his left obstructing his view, and the rear of the truck and trailer rig crowding him on the right, but by his needy wife and kids, and his barbaric boss. He peered out and over the orange *Biohazard* drums on the back of the trailer at an eye-catching billboard that diverted his thoughts for a moment.

As traffic inched by an outdoor advertisement, all the motorists gawked up at it, for it was a welcomed bit of entertainment on the dismal freeway. The enormous sign, divided into four sections, advertised Howl, a stout new beer.

The first skinny panel flaunted a frothy bottle of Howl beer with a howling man-wolf on its label.

The second section depicted a scowling, pissed-off-at-the-world, clean shaven, handsome man dressed in slacks and a black leather belt, a long-sleeve, white shirt and bold red tie; his short styled hair combed straight back. He held an icy bottle of Howl beer, and was in the middle of twisting off its cap.

The third column portrayed the man as wolf-like: hairy, with half-pointy ears, and a half-extended snout. With his tie gone, and his shirt buttons ripped off down to his belt buckle, a thicket of coarse black hair jutted out from his chest. With his fuzzy head tilted back, and his bristly arm in the air, he chugged an upside down bottle of Howl beer pressed to his beastly mouth.

The fourth division showed the bushy, bare chested man completely transformed into a man-wolf. Its outstretched, clawed, furry hand gripped an empty bottle of Howl, and with its head thrust back and its snout in the air—it howled.

At the bottom of the advertisement, stretched across all four panels, the ad's slogan: SATISFY THE BEAST!

Past the Howl sign traffic picked up speed. All the relieved motorists stomped on their accelerator and zoomed up to sixty-five. As usual, there was no indication as to why traffic had stalled.

"It's about flippin' damn time!" grumbled Ben, as his frowning wife, with her arms crossed, sat silently on the sofa behind the front passenger seat.

"Whoooweeee," whooped Cody, slamming his truck through the gears, "I'm homeward bound to beers and booty!"

"All right now," said Bupinder, "before I lose this sweet baby, I will see what she can do!"

"Yolanda," yelled Carlos above the sounds of accelerating traffic, "we're moving now. We'll be at the hospital soon!"

"Huuuurrry, Carlos!" shouted Yolanda. "The baby's head—it's—it's crowning!"

"Thank you, God," whispered Jill. Her distressed daughter whimpered. Her bratty boys acted out and screamed.

"Mmmhm. Now that's what I'm talkin' about," piped Rooisha, still on the phone with her girlfriend. "We're jammin' now, and sister—I'm on my way to stardom!"

"The sales machine," stated Bob, trying to act confident, drumming on the steering wheel with his hands, "is on the roll again."

Speeding along, traffic approached a tunnel underpass

leading to the northbound I-5. The freeway narrowed from five lanes to three.

Entering the arch shaped, concrete tunnel, the semi-truck driven by Cody hugged the cement curb along the white tiled wall on the right. The motor home with Ben and Eileen crowded the curb and tile on the left. The vehicles, driven by Bupinder, Carlos, Rooisha, Jill, and Bob, sped down the middle lane, bumper to bumper, sandwiched between the truck and the motor home. Two strings of dim ceiling lights ran the hundred-yard length of the three-lane tunnel, with sunlit, smoggy haze glowing at each end.

Bupinder, still bummed, but trying to smile again, sang along with a CD in his native Punjabi, "*Hai hai ni legeya sada dil mirza; oye oye ni legeya sada dil mirza.*" Singing exuberantly, while focusing his eyes on the knobs that adjusted the bass and treble on his CD player, his car drifted out of the middle lane toward the semi hauling hazardous waste.

As Bupinder's car veered, all the drivers around him, simultaneously diverted their eyes from the road.

Cody looked down in his passenger seat for his AC/DC disc.

Ben engaged the motor home's cruise control, then with one hand on the steering wheel, he spun in his swiveling captain's chair, and with a pallid face, peered at Eileen sitting on the couch, and groaned, "We need to pull over so I can use the toilet, or I'm going to blow it out my pants."

"I tried to warn you," Eileen replied curtly.

Carlos twisted in his seat and checked on Yolanda. With the windows down, and the air circulating again, she seemed a little better, until she moaned, "Ohhh—Carlos—another contraction. I have to push, I have to push," then she shrieked, "I'm going to have the baby!"

Rooisha resumed checking her makeup and hair in the mirror of the sunvisor, and continued jabbering to her girlfriend, "A movie with Denzel. Can you believe it? This is my chance and I'm so on it sister."

"Were almost there sweetie," Jill said compassionately to her daughter, then rotated to face her boys and screeched, "Stop it! All three of you, just stop it, now!"

Bob took out his cell phone, and began punching in numbers, intending to call his potential client and apologize for his tardiness. All the while, mumbling, "I've got to make this sale. I've got to make this sale."

With all the drivers distracted, Bupinder's shiny new, well-built car drifted expensively and smoothly out of his lane. With no warning honks or screeching tires, he crashed into the truck, with the Jag's gleaming silver hood lodging up under the dirt caked wheel well of the truck's front left tire. The jarring impact instantly changed his voice from belting out in song to screaming in horror. The harrowing discord of the huge revolving tire grinding and shredding the car's metal hood echoed throughout the tunnel.

"What the hell?" yelled Cody, swerving his eighteen-wheeler up and over the cement curb, slamming into and gouging off the tunnel's right side tile lining, causing his trailer, hauling the drums of waste, to bounce and rock violently. He gritted his teeth, as his slithering snake biceps bulged, trying to steer the big rig. He stomped on the brakes, filling the tunnel with thick tire smoke. Two of the drums broke their slack strapping, somersaulted off the truck, and banged onto the asphalt.

"What the hell?" mumbled Carlos, cranking his Toyota, barely missing the tailend of the Jag and the bouncing orange barrels, but colliding with the motor home to his left.

"Carlos," screamed Yolanda, "what the hell is happening?"

"What in the Sam Hell," grunted Ben, as the motor home clobbered the left tiled wall, popping pieces of tile off like popcorn. Eileen gasped as she tumbled to the floor, knocking her sunglasses off. Ben glanced in his right rearview mirror at the sideswiping Toyota.

"What the hell?" Rooisha said clearly, then smacked her Nissan into one of the metal barrels, shoving it ahead of her, then crushing it between her car and the Toyota in front of her. The impact ripped open its welded side seam, vomiting out all of its glowing contents.

"What the heck?" Jill murmured under her breath, as her minivan, a car length behind a red Nissan, hit the second bouncing drum, kicking it airborne and causing it to spin, and spray its contents out a gaping open seam around its rim. As the putrid slime showered the vehicles, Jill rear-ended the Nissan, then ricocheted off, crunching into the trunk of the Jag. The spouting drum shot backward over Jill's minivan, and then punched the roof of a Taurus.

"What the...?" Bob shouted, as he piled his Taurus into the back-end of the Nissan, ripping open his car's hood and puncturing his radiator, spraying steam. With the blow between his gut and the steering wheel, the horn of his Taurus stuck on.

The damaged, empty barrel flipped off Bob's vehicle, hit the roadway, rolled across the asphalt, and then stopped against the chrome bumper of a white Honda, halted in the middle lane, uninvolved in the accident.

Motorist Peter Chang, a tax preparer, sat unscathed, yet mortified, watching out the bug spattered windshield of his white Honda Civic, as the careening, crashing vehicles in front of him banged to a stop in a mass of metal, blocking all three lanes, with the semi-truck and the motor home flanking the cars piled up at the center. Stopping his own car five car lengths behind the pileup, he peered out at a dented, orange barrel with an open rim rolling out of the vehicular chaos. He mumbled in disbelief, "What the hell?" and watched it as it loped up to his car and came to a stop nudging his bumper. Trembling, he called 9-1-1 on his cell phone, as other motorists also reported the accident. His vehicle, the two in the other lanes, and the rest of the traffic behind the accident all screeched to a stop without incident.

A few motorists behind the accident climbed out of their vehicles with the intention of helping the accident victims. They took a few steps, stopped, and looked at the threat of the metal mayhem, the caustic spill, and the steamy gases, and pondered whether to risk venturing into it or not. While they stood there surmising, the trenchant vapors began burning their nostrils, and they ran to safety out the back of the tunnel.

Three miles back, on the southbound shoulder of the freeway, CHP officer Mike Rhodes had just finished writing a speeding motorist a ticket. In contrast to the crawling stop and go traffic on the northbound lanes, traffic heading south was overzealous. While stashing away his ticket book in a compartment on his motorcycle, he received an emergency call about a multi-vehicle accident involving hazardous waste. He cinched down his helmet, adjusted his mirror sunglasses, swung his leg over his motorcycle seat, and fired up his machine. He flipped on its lights and siren, charged into traffic, raced up an exit ramp, crossed the overpass, and accelerated down the onramp. As he sped down the dotted white line between two lanes of creeping traffic, he received a second call. Not only was there a multiple vehicle accident and a hazard waste spill, but there were unrestrained wild animals. He wondered: *What sort of wild animals?*

Road rage. If acted out: dangerous and against the law. People are trying like hell to get somewhere. They're strapped behind the steering wheel, burdened with everyday worries, fears, and frustrations; laden with responsibilities, accountabilities, and schedules. Plans, goals, and dreams, all thwarted—for now—by snarled traffic. Frustrated, impatient, and angry; migraines, high blood pressure, and irritable bowels. Stop and go traffic—not just an inconvenience—not just a jacked up schedule—but a spoiled vacation for retirees after forty tedious years of toil; jealousy for an insecure tough guy beating home to his cheatin' ol' lady; a failed escrow for an overdrawn realtor; a horrific ride for a husband and wife on the way to the hospital to birth their first baby; a headache for a worried mom taking her sobbing little girl to the dentist, and a lost job for a salesman barely providing for his family.

Red brake lights, flashing on—off—on—off—for miles and miles. Smog—heat—idling engines. No lane changes. Trapped in a herd of grazing asphalt cattle. Vehicles, jamming the vital causeway like cholesterol clogging an aortic artery. Drivers try to stay calm. Their rage is mostly caged—until a roadside message goads, "Angry? Enjoy a cold beer—satisfy *your* beast—and howl." As motorists drive by the Howl advertisement, some crave a cold beer, but all subconsciously or even consciously desire to uncage their rage and howl—howl out of frustration—howl with worry—howl in fear—howl in pain—just howl and howl. It would feel so damn good.

Inside the crypt-like tunnel, a spooky stew of wicked ingredients simmered in the torrid summer heat, cooking into a psycho-physiological goulash of strained human emotions, toxic chemical vapors, choking exhaust emissions, and scalding radiator steam. Toss in a blaring horn, idling engines, and wailing sirens, and then add a powerful visual of a howling man-wolf, along with a command to 'SATISFY THE BEAST,' and the pot boiled over. In the eerie ambience of the tunnel's confinement, each victim partook of it—all of it—all at once.

With each accident victim's first vaporous breath, the reactive concoction invaded their lungs, infiltrated their blood, and then penetrated down to the protoplasmic core of their molecular composition. It then corkscrewed beyond matter into the primal nucleus—the very genesis and sustaining source of life—the unseen energy where an infinite number of infinitesimal suns infinitely burn. With this alien invasion of pollutants, a spontaneous barrage of collisions occurred between the toxic invaders, and the identity-antibodies of each human. This generated combustion, fusing the green slime's atomic compounds: radium, cesium, and iridium with each victim's crystallized anthropomorphic bio-salts. With this radical effect jolted with life force, and then linked with the fresh and striking imprint of a howling man-wolf, the DNA—the chromosomal codes determining species—transmuted. Simply put, the Homo sapiens blueprint detoured into the inconceivable—howling, hairy beasts.

Inside the tunnel, as the tangled vehicles came to a stop, Cody clambered out of his truck, still wearing his cowboy hat, and maneuvered down onto the trunk lid of the Jaguar protruding out from under his truck's front left wheel well. He cradled his throbbing left elbow that had banged against the inside door handle during the crash. He was relieved that he wasn't hurt much, but he felt angry over his wrecked truck and the fact that he wouldn't make it home before Regina hit the bar. Unaware of any biological danger, he inhaled the gaseous amalgam of vapors and coughed. Immediately, he felt dizzy; his eyes teared; his vision blurred; his fingers tingled. A blaring horn echoed inside his head, rattling his nerves. He breathed in again; his nostrils burned, then his throat, and then a sharp pain stabbed his lungs. Clutching his chest, he turned and peered at his damaged truck. Blinking his eyes, regaining his focus, he scrutinized the load, and saw straps dangling and barrels missing. He coughed again; a deep hack that made him gag. Sweat drizzled down his face and beaded on his arms. His eyes searched the tunnel, and in the dim, artificial light, through the escaping radiator steam, thick carbon dioxide and a grimy, green effluvium rising from the hazardous goo, he saw one barrel crushed between two cars, and the other empty barrel behind the accident resting against another car, and with dread, he spotted the barrel's nasty, slimy entrails splashed everywhere. The snot-like gunk oozed off the cars and accumulated into percolating pools on the road. From one slick, a slimy bubble swelled, and then, when it was nearly translucent, it burst, sneezing out a puff of vapors that rose to join the rank cloud creeping along the tunnel's curved ceiling and out the hazy sunlit openings.

He coughed again and then choked. His body temperature rose to a feverish 106. Instead of breathing, he panted. His skin stung, then burned, then welted with blotchy, red patches. He peered down at his distending arms, and aghast, he saw dark, coarse hair follicles sprouting, then before his eyes, the hair grew one—two—three inches long. His face itched, so he reached to scratch it, and realized, his nails had grown three-quarters of an inch, and his face was also budding hair, not only from his chin and under his nose, but across his forehead and cheeks. His muscles, ligaments, and joints screamed in pain, and every bone in his skeleton hurt, especially his teeth. He felt hot, ripped his sleeveless T-shirt off, and then yanked his boots and socks off of his cramped feet. Now, wearing only his jeans and his cowboy hat, and still on top of the Jag's trunk, he stood up, only to drop back down to his hands and knees in convulsions, snarling and foaming at the mouth like a rabid dog.

Below him, the driver's door on the Jaguar popped open and a smartly dressed man in a three-piece suit tumbled out onto the pavement. He rolled back and forth like a man on fire, screaming, struggling to remove his clothes and put out the inferno cooking his skin.

Cody, on all fours, and frothing at the mouth, turned his head, glanced at the minivan scrunched up against the Jag, and saw a lady stepping out of it and closing the door behind her. Peering in through her van's windshield, he saw her four terrified children and heard their cries, "Mommy, please don't leave us! Mommy pleeease." As soon as the woman's lungs drew in the vapors, she collapsed to the asphalt alongside her van, out of sight of her children. She writhed in agony in a tumultuous furor of metabolic upheaval.

Her horrified kids watched their mother get out of the car, then disappear next to it. They gawked out the windshield at the lamenting, mutating man on top of the car, directly in front of them.

"Mommy, mommy!" they wailed, without a response from her. Wide-eyed and aghast, they continued watching the truck driver in the blue jeans as his jowls extended, his teeth grew, his ears stretched out, his eyes turned yellow, and his muscular arms and legs elongated into hairy, bony appendages.

Before the children's eyes, Cody mutated into a man-wolf, just like the one he had seen in the Howl advertisement. Still on top of the trunk, he stood up, thrust back his head, and howled.

Prostrate on the asphalt, Jill quickly, yet tortuously changed into a she-wolf. Under her shirt, her breasts became flat with prominent nipples. Her rib cage, hips, legs and arms became bonier. Brown matted fur covered her entire body. Using the van's door handle, she pulled herself up. Her motherly instinct kicked in, and in her abominable appearance, she popped open the van's door, thrust her head in, and peered with her large yellow eyes at her children.

At the sight of their mommy-monster inside the van, the kids screamed and cried hysterically, "Mommy, no, mommy!" They all kicked their legs, as though trying to escape, but their seatbelts held them snug. Jill stared at her daughter with compassion, as a mother wolf to her injured pup. She then snapped her head, facing her bratty boys, and glared at them. The boys froze in terror. The littlest guy put his snuggle-blanky over his head. The middle son covered his face with his small hands. The oldest boy in the back seat threw his plastic dolphin at her, bouncing it off of her head. She began with a low, snarling growl, baring her prolific canine teeth, and then burst into barking, which prompted the scared boys to shriek hysterically. She then withdrew from the van, slammed the door, thrust back her head, and howled.

Bupinder, still on the asphalt, tore off his jacket, vest, and shirt; kicked off his loafers; and then in violent spasms of torment, he altered from man to beast. Dressed only in slacks and a tie dangling upon his hairy chest, he sprung to his socked feet. He then peered at his lavish yet destroyed car, thrust back his head, and howled.

On the other side of the pileup, Ben yanked open the motor home's door, only to find his exit blocked by a twisted Toyota, so he shut it, and stomped through the trailer to its back door.

"Please, Ben," Eileen urged, "Stay in here until the authorities arrive."

Ben ignored her, pushed the button to lower the automatic steps, ripped open the door, and stepped outside, slamming the door shut behind him. He felt furious over his brand new, wrecked motor home, and bothered that his underwear beneath his jumpsuit felt squishy from a little accident he had had when the big accident had occurred. He stood on the road, surmising the situation, still wearing his BlueBlocker sunglasses. Immediately his lungs ached, and his head pounded. He felt faint, turned, and shuffled a few steps, endeavoring to reach the safety of his motor home, but paralysis seized his muscles and he dropped to the ground.

His petrified wife, her hand over her mouth in disbelief, watched out the window in horror as her husband jerked on the ground, changing into a hairy beast. She shifted her focus from Ben and peered out across the scene. Through the steamy green gloom, she saw a howling truck driver in tight jeans, wearing a cowboy hat, and standing atop a car. She saw a howling woman in a T-shirt next to a van, and another howling man in a tie and slacks next to his car. Catching her attention closer to her, another car door opened, and she saw a stylish African-American woman shove back an airbag and topple out holding her face with both hands. Within seconds, the attractive girl collapsed to the ground in a pain-racked fit and changed into a she-wolf in a red sexy dress.

Behind that girl's car, Eileen watched another car door open and a chubby man stagger out, covering his ears with his hands, trying to muffle the sound of his car's, incessant, blaring horn. He wore a yellow shirt and a green tie matching the color of the goo slathered on the cars and covering the ground. He immediately slipped in a slick of spillage and flipped to the asphalt with his shiny, plastic shoes in the air. After wrenching and rolling around, changing into a chunky, furry wolf, he gained his footing, stood up, ripped off his tight shirt, wrestled his tie off over his head, raised his jowls into the air, and howled.

The she-wolf in the pretty dress raised her snout and howled, and then Ben, a man-wolf in a blue jumpsuit and sunglasses, howled.

Eileen looked down, right next to their motor home, and saw through a car's windshield a man climb over its front seat to assist a woman in the back seat with her legs in the air.

Carlos, suffering whiplash, but otherwise okay, climbed into the back seat with his wife. He lay on the floorboard next to her sprawled out on the seat. The vapors, like a viper searching for prey, had slithered silently in through the open windows. They both breathed it in, then coughed violently.

"Carlos," screamed Yolanda, "what is happening?"

"I don't know," yelled Carlos, "but I feel very sick!"

"Me too," she moaned, "I'm worried about the baby."

They embraced, hugging each other in close, and while still in each other's arms, and both convulsing, they changed into wild, canine beasts.

Yolanda shoved Carlos away from her, and yowled hysterically in pain as a ball of fur pushed out between her bushy outstretched legs and plopped onto the seat. Her *canis lupus* permutation had transfused to her unborn child as well. She scooped up the whimpering wolf-pup-baby, still covered in afterbirth, and cradled it in her fuzzy, elongated limbs. Carlos jumped outside the vehicle, threw his head back, and howled. Yolanda and her baby howled in the backseat of their car.

Eileen, horrified, stared out of the motor home window, and the children, scared to death, gawked out of the minivan. They witnessed all of the beasts—amidst the fog of steamy, green vapor—strike a pose exactly like the man-wolf in the Howl billboard. With their heads thrust back and their snouts in the air, they each let out a riotous howl.

The news helicopter from the earlier traffic report arrived, whirring in the smoggy, gray sky above the tunnel. The same wisecracking newsman, Ty in the Sky, reported the news live. "Folks, we have an ugly accident inside the 110 tunnel at the I-5 interchange. A hazardous waste spill is pukin' green fumes out each end of the tunnel." He manipulated the camera, focusing on the span of the tunnel and the vapor escaping out each end, and then, while he continued reporting, he zoomed in on a close-up shot of the venting fumes, "9-1-1 calls from motorists fleeing the tunnel described the scene as a seven-vehicle accident, no deaths or major injuries, but there is a chemical spill, and some sort of wild animals on the loose. I knew L.A. was a zoo, but give me a break!" Zooming the camera out and panning along the multitude of vehicles stopped on the freeway, he quipped, "For a mile and maybe another smoggy mile, as far as this award winning reporter can see, cars and trucks are lined up grills to gas-holes, locked in a linear chain of exhaust pipes, but hey," he zoomed in for a close-up of a CHP officer on a motorcycle racing between traffic, "CHPs is on the way."

CHP officer, Mike Rhodes, sped between the stopped vehicles on the freeway, and hoped that all the motorists heard him coming and that none of them would open their car doors and get out of their vehicles. He passed the Howl billboard and glanced up at it. Its message penetrated deep into his mind.

He raced up, and stopped his bike just outside the entrance to the tunnel. He removed his sunglasses, stuffed them in his shirt pocket, and then scrutinized the green cloud. While keeping his eyes on the tunnel, he climbed off the bike, pulled off his helmet, and set it on the seat. He reached in a compartment of his saddlebags, yanked out a gas mask and slipped it on. He then strode a few steps into the tunnel. He heard eerie howling, stopped, drew his pistol, and then while pointing it in front of him, stepped cautiously underneath the wafting vapors and into gloomy uncertainty. He tread past a Honda Civic, as the terrified Chinese man inside yelled, "Help me! Please help me!" Mike stopped and stood behind the pile-up of vehicles. He breathed heavily inside the mask, while gawking out its plastic shield into the putrid mist, and saw, to his astonishment wolf-like beasts dressed in people clothes, standing on their hind legs growling, snarling, and howling. He shook his head, and slowly muttered, "What the hell?" One creature wore a cowboy hat, one a T-shirt, another a dress, others slacks and ties, and one of them in a blue jumpsuit even wore sunglasses. He had witnessed many unimaginable incidents and gory wrecks, but never anything like this. He aimed his weapon at the animals. His eyes searched the tunnel, and he spotted a distressed, gray haired lady peeking out a window in a RV. He heard children crying for help. He turned and saw four kids in a minivan. With his eyes on the growling man-wolf crouching on the back of a car, and on the rest of the animals that had now shifted between the cars and into a snarling pack, he maneuvered toward the kids with the intention of reassuring them that help was on the way. Just when he reached for the van's door handle, Cody—who had recently received a traffic ticket and had to attend Comedy Traffic School, which was enough to enrage any person, let alone a man-wolf—saw Mike, and with a burst of rage, leapt off of the Jaguar's trunk, and onto the officer. The flying tackle tore off the officer's mask, slammed both of them to the ground, and knocked the gun under the van. Cody sprung to his paws and joined the rest of the snarling pack.

Mike inhaled the steamy, toxic waste, coughed, gagged, itched, and ached. In a violent fit, as he flopped about the asphalt alongside the minivan, he transformed into a man-wolf. The pack howled with excitement. He stood—unaware of his mutation, but still concerned for the children—and peered up close into the window of the van. Again, like when their mom had popped up, the children screamed in horror at the grotesque monster. Mike noticed his own reflection in the window and growled, baring his deadly teeth at his horrific image, frightening the children worse. He spun around, facing the other wolves. His legs stiffened and his ears became erect and forward, as his hackles bristled. The other wolves cowered before his size and authority. He snarled, displaying his incisors, stared penetratingly at Cody, and approached him as prey.

Cody, with his ears down and his back arched in submission, backed up against Bob's Taurus. He tried to open the car door, but before he could, Mike leapt upon him, knocked his cowboy hat off, and locked his carnivorous jowls around Cody's left shoulder, sinking his teeth into the hairy tail of the rattlesnake tattoo. Cody yelped in pain as Mike tore into his flesh. The rest recoiled in fear, yapping in a high pitch. Mike let him go and Cody slinked away, whimpering in pain and embarrassment. Mike snapped back his head, and howled. The rest, even Cody, howled.

Two huge panel vans, orange with the black Haz Mat

symbol, sped down the shoulder of the freeway and screeched to a stop inside the tunnel. A white van full of animal control officers stopped right behind them. Eight men in orange body and head suits jumped out of the Haz Mat vans and began unloading pumps, fans, hoses, tanks, and other equipment. Four men, wearing gas masks and carrying rifles, clambered out of the white van, positioning themselves in front of the wild beasts. Ambulances and fire trucks arrived. An army of tow trucks—a couple of them huge for hauling RVs and semi-trucks—pulled up and parked outside the tunnel.

Ty in the Sky continued reporting, as he alternated his camera between aerial views and close-ups.

Inside the tunnel, all of the beasts, snarling and full of savagery, had maneuvered close together into a pack, facing the men in protective suits.

The animal control sharpshooters leveled their rifles and set their sites on the pack. Flying tranquilizers zipped through the air. Officer Mike Rhodes bolted for the opening behind the shooters.

Tranquilizers punctured them all, except Mike, who ducked and weaved toward freedom. The others yowled in pain and dropped to the asphalt. Yolanda climbed out of the car, and while cradling her baby, she knelt down next to Carlos. A dart found her neck, but the sharpshooters spared the baby snuggled in her hairy arms.

As the rest of them blacked out, Mike raced past the shooters, and then climbed up and over Peter Chang's car.

Peter screamed, covered his face with both hands, and laid down in the front seat.

The shooters spun, firing their guns.

Mike leapt off the car and back to the asphalt. Darts zinged by him, hitting vehicles and then ricocheting into other vehicles, one sticking in the tire of his own motorcycle. He dropped down to all fours to gain greater speed and dashed into the hazy sunlight amongst fire trucks, ambulances, tow trucks, and stopped traffic. All who saw him gasped.

The shooters charged out of the tunnel in pursuit, firing, reloading, and firing.

"Oh my golden awards!" remarked Ty in the Sky, still reporting live coverage of the scene. "One of the wild animals has burst out of the tunnel!" The helicopter moved in closer. "I can't believe my eyes—it—it looks like half man and half wolf. It's covered in hair, but wearing, what looks like a patrolman's uniform." The camera zoomed in on Mike, then the shooters, then Mike again. "Animal control officers are on his tail, maybe literally, because under that uniform, it may have a tail. It's running amuck in traffic, racing between the lanes, and zigzagging around vehicles. The shooters are chasing him, and firing at him, but missing."

Mike, now panting in the heat, stood up, looked down the rows of vehicles, and saw a garbage truck locked in traffic next to a large billboard. A dart zinged by. He glanced back at his hunters, then raced toward the garbage truck.

Motorists honked their horns, hoping to scare the creature away from them.

"He's quick and agile," continued the reporter, "and he's dodging the darts. He's jumped on the front grill of a city garbage truck."

The two stunned city workers inside the truck, shoved themselves backward against the seat, as Mike grasping the windshield wipers, climbed up the windshield directly in front of their faces. Darts bounced off the truck, one cracked the windshield, as he continued up and over the hydraulic lift arms, arriving at the top of the truck.

The huge Howl beer sign loomed next to the garbage truck. Mike stood up, stared at the sign, tossed back his head, and howled. Standing at his lofty position above the asphalt, the vehicles, and the motorists, he was at the pinnacle of his domain; his habitat, where everyday he is the alpha male, hunting, stalking, and capturing the idiotic motorists who break the laws of his sovereignty. His rage swelled and his snarls and howls multiplied as he thought about all of those uncivil motorists who tailgate and speed, who drive recklessly without regard for the weather or road conditions; without concern for the lives of fellow drivers. The imbeciles drive as though they own the highway, like they are free to make their own laws, but he—Mike laughed in the form of a howl with short, choppy, throaty sounds—stopped them in their tracks, and then put them in a cage. As his years of exasperation with highway stupidity erupted into a hostile fit of rage, he flailed his arms, and foamed at the mouth. He visualized stopping an erratic motorist, ripping him out of his car, lunging at his neck, and gnawing off his head, and then—guzzling down an ice cold bottle of Howl beer to satisfy his inner beast.

The camera zoomed in on Mike's snarling face as he spun in a three-hundred-and-sixty degree circle, growling and barking at the animal control officers, the noisy helicopter, and the honking traffic.

Ty in the Sky noticed the Howl billboard, and zoomed in for a close-up. "Hey, what's going on? The man-wolf on the garbage truck looks like the beer-beast in the billboard. Is this some kind of hoax? Whether it is or isn't, this superstar reporter could slam down a few frothy, cold ones right now too!"

Again, and for the last time, Mike peered up at the billboard, thrust back his head, and howled, beginning with a deep guttural sound that quickly slid up and into an earsplitting high-pitch. The sharpshooters chasing him stopped, took aim, and fired. A dart found Mike's neck, followed a split second later by another one striking his chest.

Mike reached up, yanked out the darts, flung them back at

the shooters, staggered backward a few steps, blacked out, and plummeted into the chute filled with garbage.

The helicopter's camera zoomed in on Mike lying motionless amidst the refuse, prompting the reporter to say, "Now, how symbolic is that? We clamber above the garbage in our lives, howl with rage, and then fall back into it."

Ben's wife, Eileen and Jill's children, as well as the drivers who had remained in their vehicles suffered some inhalation, and though their eyes burned and their skin tingled; they didn't breathe in enough pollutants, nor were they possessed of anxieties and anger great enough to cause them to transform.

As the crews carried away the anesthetized beasts, and began cleaning up the scene, a horde of CHP officers diverted traffic to the last exit before the tunnel. They closed the onramps to the 110-freeway all the way back to the 101 interchange. Cars directly behind the accident, one by one, were allowed to turn around and head in the wrong direction back to the last exit where they were finally on their way again.

Haz Mat Crews worked through the night sterilizing the accident site. Once they deemed the area safe, tow trucks separated and hauled away the wrecked vehicles. As the long night ended and the sun strained to shine through the sullied morning air, the authorities declared the tunnel open. Traffic again flowed like a river of metal, exhaust, and harried souls.

Each victim, with a mask over his or her face and breathing pure oxygen, lay in a hospital bed. Blood thinners, antibiotics, and immune-boosting drugs coursed through their bloodstreams fighting the effects of the contaminants. Throughout the long night, the chromosomal blueprint of their molecular composition reverted from hairy beast back to Homo sapiens, reinstating their human forms and features. Their bones still ached, and their skin, slathered with a healing ointment remained red, raw, and scaly. They suffered sore spots from the tranquilizer darts, bumps and bruises from the accident, and with every breath, there lingered a raspy congestion. All rested peacefully.

Eileen sat in a chair next to Ben, holding his hand. Cody's girlfriend, Regina, drove down from Bakersfield and snuck him a bottle of beer. Carlos and Yolanda hugged their baby, Jesse, now pink and cuddly. Bupinder talked on his cell phone desperately trying to convince his buyers back into escrow. Rooisha chatted on her cell phone with her friend. Jill's husband visited her with all four kids. Their daughter felt better after an emergency visit to the dentist. She and her rowdy little brothers—happily eating chocolate-chip cookies—appeared to have surpassed the terror. Bob's wife and kids were by his side. Mike's family and a few fellow officers gathered around him. A horde of news crews, their vehicles loaded with audio and video equipment, waited outside in the parking lot for an opportunity to interview the victims. Another CHP officer covered Mike's shift. Ty in the Sky reported traffic conditions.

On the 110 freeway, past the reflective glass skyscrapers, beyond the off ramp to Dodger stadium, and a quarter mile before the reopened tunnel, stop and go traffic inched along in the sweltering heat and noxious smog. As the motorists crept by the Howl beer sign, some of them merely craved an ice-cold beer, but others yearned to "SATISFY THE BEAST" and howl.

BLIND

A S THE ANESTHESIA began to wear off, Lance stirred in his hospital bed. The gentle touch and soft words of his wife, Becky, standing by his side roused his consciousness, and with a cloudy mind, and sluggish movements, he attempted to gain an orientation to his surroundings. He felt a plastic bendy straw touch his lips and he sipped cool water, urging him into greater alertness. As she whispered his name, "Lance, Lance," he turned his head to focus on her, slowly opened his eyes—blinked, then blinked again—and then wept bitterly. The brain surgery had been a success with the tumor removed, except now, he was blind.

Before the operation, Lance had 20/20 vision—seeing objects far away and up close crisp and clear. However, even then, his perception had been askew, seeing flaws, instead of beauty. In a garden teeming with flowers, he noticed the dandelion. On a freshly mowed lawn, he detected the lone, uncut blade of grass. In an immaculate house, he found the dust. On anything polished and gleaming, he saw a smudge.

He was worse with people, zeroing in on their wrinkles, creases and scars; their pimples, moles, and warts; their cold sores, chapped lips, and chipped teeth; their fat bodies, poor posture, bad hair, big ears, large nose, double chins, turkey necks, and bald heads. No matter who they were or what they looked like, he searched for and discovered their flaws. It wouldn't have mattered much if he had shut his mouth and kept his critical observations to himself. But, he didn't. They gushed out as constructive criticisms or as he called them, "helpful suggestions."

In the case of his loving and patient wife, he had recently made helpful suggestions. "Becky, maybe you should dye those few gray hairs. Let's hire a maid to help you clean this filthy house. It's okay if you buy a new pair of jeans that don't fit so tight." With each of his remarks, she acted as if she ignored him, but they hurt her feelings.

With his first-grade son, Keenan, he made helpful suggestions. "Son, you need to practice writing within the lines. You need to read faster. Don't worry that you're so much shorter than all the other boys—you'll grow someday." After Keenan heard the "you're so much shorter" comment, he acted out in class, and had to sit in a corner and miss recess.

With his four-year-old daughter, Stephanie, he made helpful suggestions. "Honey, try harder to color inside the lines. You need to use the correct colors because cats aren't purple. You need to stop with your silly giggles." After she heard the coloring advice, she colored a purple kitty on the living room wall.

With his coworkers, he made helpful suggestions. "The gym's got a sale going on new memberships. My dentist could fix that chipped tooth. I know a shop that could buff out that door ding on your car. Hey, here's a napkin to wipe the smudge off of your glasses. I'll show you an exercise to strengthen that sagging butt. If only you could lose thirty pounds, you'd be a total knockout. Have you ever considered hair restoration? Teeth whitening? Plastic surgery? A personal trainer? Liposuction?" The offended coworkers avoided him as much as possible.

His faultfinding scrutiny distressed his wife, children, and co-workers, but not his friends, because he had no friends. No one would choose to associate with such a hypercritical man. He brought into the open that which people wished to hide. They felt angry and embarrassed, and when some of them lashed out at him, he responded, "Jeez, I was only trying to help."

Although he was a twenty-nine-year-old, ordinary looking guy, with average height and weight, and with no obvious defects, he couldn't even look in a mirror. Why? He had a horrible self-image, so he turned his focus on others and their defects. Maybe he had neurotic parents—a worrisome mom and an overly strict dad. Who knows? Doesn't matter. He should have known to keep his judgment monster on a leash. But, he unleashed it, and it terrorized those around him.

He had perfectly seeing eyes, but abused them, and then lost them. It happens. There are life lessons to be learned. Sometimes they are harsh, and sometimes you don't get another chance. Now, physically blind, he couldn't see the imperfections. Like a thief without a gun, who can no longer threaten and rob, he was a hypercritical man without eyes, who could no longer see faults and criticize.

The sun shone, but he awoke to darkness, dressed in darkness, and ate in darkness. In darkness, he listened to his family and listened to the TV. In darkness he brushed his teeth and went to bed. When he awakened in the soundless dark of the night, he missed the glow of his nightlight. During the day's humdrum hours when his wife was at work, and his kids were at school, he sat alone in his blindness, or stumbled around the house afraid to leave. He missed seeing the world. He missed seeing the people. Whether he gazed upon an imperfect world or flawed people, it no longer mattered—he just wanted to see. In his memories, he saw the beauty. Why, when he could see, had he chosen to be blind to it? In his sadness, he cried. His tears poured out of his darkness and ran down his face. Every moment of everyday, he wished, hoped, and prayed that he could see again. All he knew was—regardless of why he had been critical—he felt remorseful for hurting those around him. Indeed, if he ever did see again, he would see—not the faults—but the splendid beauty of everything and everybody his eyes beheld. Never again would he make a "helpful suggestion."

Five months after the surgery, the swelling in his brain subsided, and he saw a faint light. A beautiful light. A perfect light. After several more weeks, his eyesight fully returned. Lance got another chance.

He walked with his family out into their backyard. He saw the sunlight's refraction all around him. He reached down, touched the plush green grass, and ran a blade of grass between his fingers. He smiled as though he could feel the color green. He walked over to a rose bush and drew a flower up to his nose. He smiled as though he could smell the color red. He turned and gazed at the angelic face of his wife with the sunlight glinting off her golden hair, and he saw that she was gorgeous, perfect, and his heart ached for her. He drew closer to her, cupped her lovely face in his hands and he kissed her softly on her lips.

"Becky, you look so heavenly, so beautiful," he complimented, "and I love you just as you are. I am so happy to see you again." She grinned, as her eyes moistened with tears.

He looked at his son and saw his little boy's ruddy face and his cheerful twinkling eyes, and he told him, "Son, you're a really cool kid. You're handsome and you're smart. I want you to know that I'm proud of you." Keenan laughed, jumped up and down, and clapped his hands.

Lance lifted up his precious daughter into his arms, and he kissed her on her soft little cheek. "Sweetie," he said, "I love your milk-chocolaty smiles and your happy, silly giggles, and the little pictures you color for me. You are a beautiful little girl, and a wonderful artist. I love you, and your brother, and mommy very much." She smiled, kissed him on his cheek, hugged his neck, and then laid her head on his shoulder.

Later that day he looked at himself in his bathroom mirror. For a long while he just stared. Finally, he pointed a finger at himself and said, "Hey man, you're not perfect—but you're okay."

Three weeks later he returned to work. During lunch, his

co-workers threw him a "welcome back" pizza party, and he thanked them for their kindness. He found something remarkable in each one of them, and he complimented them. They smiled, and over time, some of them became his close friends.

Lance's normal 20/20 vision had returned, however, his perception had changed. He never again saw a smudge.

JUST A HAND

9 -1-1 EMERGENCY, BAKERSFIELD," answered the woman.
"Hi, uh—this is Travis Bonner," the caller drawled, "and I'm a pumpin' unit mechanic out at the Poso Creek oilfields."

"How can I assist you Mr. Bonner?"

"Well—I found somethin' strange out here. It's a hand—nothin' else—just a hand."

A red-tailed hawk soared above the desolate oilfields in the bleary summer heat. A web of dirt roads crisscrossed the dismal landscape strewn with hundreds of oil pumping units, power poles, pipelines, and storage tanks. The pumping rigs resembled giant grasshoppers as they dipped, endlessly sucking crude oil out of the ground.

The circling hawk's keen eyes scanned the hilly terrain, searching for a furry movement amongst the sun-scorched weeds and the weathered equipment. It locked its eyes on a hapless ground squirrel, then swooped down and snatched it up with its piercing talons. The small creature twisted and squeaked as the raptor carried it up to its perch at the top of a pole.

The oilfields encompassed about five square miles around where the Lerdo Highway ended at highway 65, just south of Poso Creek: a dry, sandy creek bed that snaked its way down through the Sierra foothills and into the heart of Kern County. It trudged through cattle ranches, under country roads, and cut a swath through the California grasslands. As the creek approached highway 65, it coursed just north of

Oildale, a small town that latched on to the northeast side of Bakersfield.

A quarter-mile east of the oilfields, the hot sun was stabbing rays of light through the olive-green foliage of a large manzanita bush, exposing its red bark, and a corner of a plastic garbage bag sticking out of the loose dirt.

An approaching noise engulfed in a blur of dust caused the hawk to stop feeding and peer down. Sensing a threat, it gripped the dead animal in its talons and flew to another power pole a short distance away.

The white Chevy pick-up barreled down the dirt road toward the far end of the petroleum fields. It was loaded with Douglass utility boxes on both sides of its bed, along with a crane hoist and a 3-gallon Igloo water container.

Travis Bonner bounced in the truck's cab as he neared pumping unit # 31, section 9-27-32. He craned his head and looked out the windshield to see a red-tailed hawk fly overhead with a dead squirrel dangling from its talons. A startled coyote loped away from the sheltering shade of pumping unit # 31.

With one hand, Travis gripped the steering wheel, and with the other he grabbed his clipboard and double-checked his location on the field map. The truck's radio played country songs on station KUZZ 107.9, beaming out of Buck Owen's Crystal Palace in Bakersfield.

Travis pulled his truck up behind a Lufkin pumping unit, a conventional crank type known as the "work horse" of the oil patch. As his vehicle slid to a stop, the dust cloud chasing the pick-up overtook it, then floated past, drifting back into the oilfield. As the dust settled, he reviewed his work order, which directed him to change the "V" belt on the rig's drive motor. He grabbed his red can of Grizzly smokeless tobacco out of the cup holder, twisted off the top, and packed a large pinch between his lower lip and gum. As he stepped out of the truck, the 105°

temperature slugged him in the face. To shield his skin from the burning sun, he wore a company issued blue hardhat and a blue long-sleeve coverall.

He unlocked a toolbox, grabbed a one-inch combination wrench, walked over to the pumping unit, inspected it for a moment, and then shut off its power.

He placed the wrench on the rusted bolt head that fastened down the belt cover and tried unsuccessfully to loosen it. He positioned himself behind the tool, sucked in a deep breath, spit a brown wad of tobacco juice on the ground, and pushed the wrench as hard as he could. The bolt head stripped and his wrench slipped, causing it to bounce off the motor mount, then the brake lever handle, and land in the dust near the base of the pumping unit. As he walked around to the backside of the motor, he fired off a barrage of cuss words, like a coach after a bad call.

As he bent down to pick up the wrench, something lying next to it caught his attention. He stopped, instinctively recoiled with alarm, and shuffled a step backward. He took a step closer, leaned in, and studied it with curiosity. He then gagged and spit out his entire wad of chew. There, in the dust, was a human hand, palm down, detached from the rest of its body. Some of the curled fingers had bones exposed, as well as some sinew. A greenish necrotic flesh covered the rest of the hand. Flies swarmed around it and crawled on top of it. He gawked for a long moment while he thought about what to do. He then returned to the truck, snatched up his cell phone, and called 9-1-1.

Boom! The rifle fired. The 22-caliber bullet struck Jerry "Spider" Zeeder point-blank in the face, below his left eye, lodging in his brain.

David Kell jerked, gasped, then sat up in bed. His eyes were open, yet his mind lingered in the nightmare of Spider's murder. As he swung his feet onto the floor, he choked out a ragged cough, then drew in a deep breath. Still half asleep, he sat motionless on the edge of the bed. As the shocking images of his dream played out, he visualized the flash of the gun and Spider's head snapping back. He saw him raise his hands to his face, stumble back a step, then collapse on the living room floor. The blaring horn of a nearby freight train roused David. He scratched his scalp, then rubbed his eyes as the dream faded and he fully awoke. He felt clammy and ran his hand under the wet collar of his T-shirt. He yawned, stroked his facial stubble, and shoved back his sweaty hair with both hands.

The only light in the dark room was the glow from an octagon fish tank and the red numbers 5:13 a.m. on a digital alarm clock. The aquarium sat atop a beat-up dresser. The clock rested on the nightstand alongside a pack of generic cigarettes, a Bic lighter, and a white plastic ashtray. A filthy cotton sheet and a tattered wool blanket lay wadded up on the floor off the end of the bed. A pile of dirty clothes lay in the corner. The smoke-stained curtains stirred as a breeze crept in through the open window. Only the humming of the fish tank's small aerator and its popping air bubbles rippled the silence.

Sitting groggy on the edge of the bed, he reached over to the nightstand and groped for his cigarettes and lighter. He tapped a cigarette out of the pack, lit it, sucked on it hard, held the smoke in for a couple of seconds, then slowly exhaled. He sniffed his runny nose, wiped it with the back of his hand, and then inhaled another long drag.

It was the morning of the fourth day after the murder. He stood up, stretched, and scratched the heat rash around his crotch. He had fallen asleep still wearing his jeans. He took a few steps over to the fish tank, opened the cover, and then sprinkled some food onto the surface of the water. He sat down at the end of the bed and stared at the three tropical fish. Two of the guppies gorged on the floating flakes. The third floated belly up, dead and bloated. His thoughts reeled back to Spider.

He recalled how his roommate had collapsed from the gunshot, quivered for a moment, and then dropped his arms to the floor. Blood had streamed out of the bullet hole and trickled down his cheek, as he had stared with a confused look up at the ceiling fan, swallowed hard, and then drew in one, last, shallow breath.

Panic had engulfed David as he realized the horrific circumstances. He had two felonies against him: One strike for drugs, and a second for burglary. California law said three strikes and you're out—no parole. He had shot and killed a man—his third strike. He knew the law would grant him no mercy.

He had done time—five years up at Tehachapi—but never again. He took a long fidgety drag on his cigarette. He would never confess. He stood up, inhaled the rest of his cigarette down to its filter, and then snuffed it out in the ashtray. His two-day high on crystal meth had left him dehydrated, and he felt an aching thirst. He left the bedroom and went to the kitchen. His eyes were sensitive to light, so he moved about the house without turning on any switches. In the small kitchen, he opened the refrigerator, grabbed a carton of orange juice, and chugged half of it down. He believed that drinking the juice would boost his drug-damaged immune system. He looked at the microwave and saw the time—5:35 a.m. He was anxious to watch the early news at six and see if anyone had discovered the body.

He left the kitchen and headed down the hall to the bathroom, where a night-light illuminated the toilet. He took a long leak, so long that he almost smiled but didn't. He zipped up his jeans, then leaned on the sink, and stared at himself in the mirror.

His bloodshot brown eyes were gaunt, surrounded by dark circles. He picked up a plastic comb and raked back his shoulder length, oily black hair. He scrutinized the wrinkles etched in his face, and thought he looked older than his twenty-four years.

As he gawked at himself in the eerie light, his face seemed to transform into that of Spider's.

Spider's contorted look and the expression of shock in his eyes as the bullet tore into his brain had seared itself into David's memory. He had waited for him to breathe, blink, or twitch, but he didn't move.

With David's status as an ex-con, there was no way he could have called the cops. He'd watched enough episodes of CSI to know about crime scene forensics. Acting quickly, he had grabbed an empty pizza box on the couch and slid it under Spider's injured head so the blood wouldn't stain the floor. He then stepped outside to the street, where he checked for any response to the gun blast.

David's two-bedroom home sat in an old industrial area on the cuff of Oildale. Patches of bare wood surrounded by curled and peeling flakes of off-white paint looked like open wounds on the weathered structure. The dead grass and weeds that encircled the house had two dirt tire tracks that lead up from the street to the carport.

Beyond the dried-up backyard was a street, and just past that were the tracks of the Southern Pacific Railroad. At any given hour, Amtrak or freight trains rolled by blowing their horns as they approached the busy intersection a half mile away. A large vacant warehouse sat on one side of the house, and an empty lot adjoined the property on its other side. Across the street loomed another distribution center. His home was the only residence that had remained in the commercial zone. He was lucky to have the place. It had been his stepdad's widowed mother, Grandma Patty's place. After she passed away, his stepfather had rented it to him. He'd also sold him her 1975 Dodge Dart for $300. The ugly yellow car had extensive dents and chalky, oxidized paint, but it ran.

Standing at the curb, David looked up and the down the

block. With no response to the gunfire, he raced over to the carport and pulled two plastic garbage bags off a roll. He ran back into the house, slid a bag around Spider's upper torso, and then pulled another bag over his legs up to his waist. He grabbed a roll of duct tape from a kitchen drawer, and bound the bags together where they overlapped. He then gathered up Spider's few belongings and stuffed them in the sports bag. He hurried back out to the carport, jumped in his car, and backed it up to the front door. He then dragged Spider's lifeless body, clad in plastic and tape, over to the car, and heaved it into the trunk. The sports bag followed, along with the bloody pizza box.

With utmost respect, he obeyed all the traffic laws as he drove north on highway 65, the few miles to Poso Creek. He then turned east down a dirt road that the repairmen used to service the rigs. A half-mile past the oilfields, he backed up the Dodge to a large manzanita bush. He popped the car's trunk, looked all around, heaved Spider's body into a hollow under the bush, and buried it by shoving and kicking loose dirt on it. On his way back into town, he disposed of Spider's sports bag and the pizza box in a dumpster behind a corner mini-mart. Once back at the house, in a fear and drug induced frenzy, he meticulously vacuumed, cleaned, and polished away all the inhabitance of Spider from the house. Lastly, he wrapped his rifle in a plastic bag, then stowed it deep within a crawl space under the house.

The murder had happened on Saturday afternoon. It was still Wednesday morning, four days later. He left the bathroom and sat on the couch in the living room, anxiously watching the news on his 14-inch portable TV.

Over the past year, David had worked as a machine operator, loading and unloading brass parts destined to become plumbing for bathroom urinals. Two workdays had passed, and now, on the third day, he had still not notified his boss about his absence.

The telephone rang, startling David. He glanced at the clock on the wall and saw that it was 8:17 a.m. He knew who it was, but let it ring until his answering machine picked it up.

"Hey David, it's Mike. Again, you're not at work, and no word from you. In the past, I've let you slide, but you haven't called me in three days. You leave me no choice." Mike paused, took a deep breath, and said, "I'm going to have to let you go. Your last paycheck will be mailed out today."

David dropped his head into his hands and sighed. He did not bother to pick up the phone; he knew Mike had made up his mind.

"Oh, and one last thing David, everybody knows you're strung out on something. Go get some help. Goodbye."

Add another "un" to the tragedies of his drugged-out unlife. He was now unemployed, unhealthy, unhappy, and, ever since his girlfriend had left him—unloved.

It all started with his addiction to methamphetamine. His drug use cycled from a three-day high during which he would feel an increased alertness and sense of well being until his inevitable crash. Upon awaking, he would feel depressed and restless until his next high. Over the last eight months, the thrill of the drug and the fatigue that followed had caused him to miss many workdays. He had lost pay, which had compounded his financial woes and prompted him to seek out a roommate.

The Wednesday preceding the murder that occurred on Saturday, David arrived home from work at 5:17 p.m., his usual time. Popping open a cold beer, he heard a knock on the door. He peeked out between the curtains of the kitchen window and saw a man he did not recognize. The man, five-and-a-half-feet tall and thin, sported a shaved head and wore a sleeveless, white T-shirt, and blue jeans. Wrapped around the bicep of his left arm was a realistic tattoo of a black tarantula. A cigarette dangled out of his mouth and he carried a gray sports bag.

"What do you want?" David yelled.

The stranger snatched the cigarette out of his mouth and looked over at the window. "I heard you need a roommate."

"Yeah, how'd you know?"

"A friend of mine, Matt, at your work, told me."

"All right, okay dude, hold on." David opened the door, and said, "I'm David, and yeah, I do need a roommate."

They shook hands and the stranger said, "I'm Jerry Zeeder, but people call me 'Spider'." He turned proudly sideways so David could get a good look at his tattoo.

David studied it closely. The painstaking rendering of all the minute hairs impressed him. "It looks real, man, that's for sure."

"Yeah, thanks dude, my tat man just finished its eyes and fangs a couple of days ago. It took a lot of sessions, but it's all done and paid for now." He took a long drag on his cigarette, then said, "Anyway, I've been crashed over at my brother's house for awhile until his wife started bitchin' that 'I was crowdin' them,' so I decided to split. Matt told me that you were lookin' for a room-mate, so I caught a bus and rode over."

"Cool," said David, "I'll show you around, then we'll talk about it."

After Spider checked out the place, they sat at a table in a small dining area next to the kitchen. The stove and oven formed a partition separating the rooms. They drank beers while discussing rent and utilities.

"Okay, you can move in," said David, "but one last thing, I need the first month's rent up front."

"I'd like to move in, but the only thing is, I used to work for a painting contractor, who still owes me some cash. When he gets paid, he'll pay me, and then I'll pay you. How's that sound?"

"I need the money now, dude." David demanded. He knew he had one last snort of "go," before he ran out. He needed to buy more.

"Well, I should get paid Saturday. I'll pay you then. Then, next week, I'm supposed to start painting with another company."

"That'll work. You need some help gettin' your stuff moved in?"

"I'm already moved in, all I got is what's in that bag."

"Okay man, but on Saturday you'd better pay me. Don't jack with me, I mean it."

Three days later, on midday Saturday, Spider sat on the couch in the living room and watched a fishing show on TV. He munched on the last piece of Friday night's leftover pizza. The empty box sat on the couch. He muted the sound on the TV, picked up the phone, and called his brother, letting him know he had found a place. After a few minutes of conversation—in between bites of pizza—he hung up and turned the volume back up.

David sat on his bed in his room with the door shut. He took out a cigar box from under the bed and opened it, removing a small pharmaceutical vile. He poured out the last of the meth, a small white rock the size of a green pea, onto the smooth surface of a small mirror. He used a cancelled credit card to chop the compressed chemical into a powder and form it into a line. He then placed a rolled up one-dollar bill up to his right nostril and snorted the white dust. The high was not as immediate as in the past when he had slammed it into his vein with a needle. Nevertheless, within five minutes, he started to feel good.

As the drug took affect, paranoia set in. He was now out of meth. He needed money—Spider's rent money—to buy more. He marched out to the living room and confronted him.

"Hey Spider! Where's the rent money you promised me today?" David fired off the words like an M-16.

Spider glanced at him and recognized David's accelerated speech and gestures. He knew he was tweakin. "Just hang in there man, you'll get it. Go and enjoy your high." He resumed watching TV and changed the channel.

"Come on dude, you can't just crash here for free. I need that money!"

"I said," replied Spider, annoyed, and raising his voice, "you'll get it when I get it, so chill! Okay?"

"Chill? You want me to chill. You're sittin' on my couch, watchin' my TV, in my house for free, and you want me to chill? Dude, you need to cough up some rent money!"

"Listen, I can see your ampin' man. I guess you didn't want to share your high, but dude, I've got a job lined up, and once I get my first paycheck, I'll pay you."

"Yeah, right!" He yelled, trembling. "That's B.S. man! You're jackin' with me. So, you need to hit the road!"

Spider stood up and got toe to toe with David, and shouted, "I'm not leavin'! Just wait a couple of days and you'll get your damn rent money."

"You lay down some cash right now Spider, or get your crap and leave!"

"Oh, come on man, you're spun, that's all," said Spider calmly. "I'll pay you next week sometime, so just relax." He then sat back down on the couch, pointed the remote at the TV, and started flipping through the channels again.

David stomped back to his bedroom and returned with a loaded 22-caliber rifle. He pointed it at Spider's face, and ordered, "You need to leave! Now!"

Spider stood up and backed away from the couch, toward the middle of the room. He stared down the long, dark barrel of the rifle. The gun site was only inches away from his face. He noticed the wild-eyed look on David's face and realized that he could die at the hand of this irrational drug addict.

David followed with the end of the gun six inches from Spider's face. For once, he felt in control. The infusing power of the rifle swelled, as he resolved not to let up on him.

In a calm, low tone, Spider said, "Okay, okay, man, just get the gun out of my face. You're over-amped man, just calm down."

"As soon as you hit the road, I will," snarled David, shoving the barrel within an inch of Spider's face.

Spider became angry and shoved the gun barrel away from his face, and shouted, "You're the biggest jerk, I've ever met! Stop pointing that gun at me!"

David raised the rifle and again, aimed it at his face. Spider's fear tasted good to him, like a cold beer on a hot day.

"Get the gun out of my face!" screamed Spider, reaching out with his right hand and grabbing the metal barrel of the gun.

"Get your hand off of it, Spider!" demanded David.

"Get it out of my face!" he fired back.

"Let go!" growled David. "Don't make me shoot you!"

"Give me the rifle!" bellowed Spider, yanking the rifle toward him, attempting to wrest it from David's grip. His move forced David's finger to squeeze the trigger.

The rifle fired a bullet into Spider's face. He staggered back a step, dropped, and hit the floor.

David's eyes grew wide with the realization of what had just happened. He screamed and pointed down at Spider, "You should of let go! I was just trying to scare you man. I wasn't going to shoot you! It was all that grabbin' you did. You died by your own hand, not mine. Dude, it was your hand!" David moved quickly to cover up what had happened.

The day after David had lost his job, his paycheck arrived in the mail. It was the afternoon of the fifth day after David had murdered Spider, hid his body, disposed of the sports bag, and stashed the gun. He drove down to the liquor store for cigarettes, beer, and orange juice, and then stopped by his supplier to buy more crank. He returned within an hour, wrapped a hot dog with stale white bread, smeared it with mustard, popped open a beer, and watched TV.

He watched each newscast throughout the day, waiting fearfully for them to report a body discovered out at Poso Creek. As he watched, he drank four more beers and smoked two packs of cigarettes. The news never reported it; the decomposing body and his secret remained undetected. Since he'd buried Spider where nobody goes, and had cleaned up the crime scene, he thought he might just get away with it. He decided to relax and get high.

He went to the bedroom, opened the cigar box, took out his paraphernalia, and snorted a fat line of meth. He then went back into the living room, kicked back on the couch, and welcomed the oncoming euphoria. After a few minutes, his dry mouth reminded him that he had left the carton of orange juice in the car. He pushed himself up and walked over to the front door.

Just as he turned the knob and pulled open the door to the front porch, he heard two voices simultaneously—a woman newscaster on the 5:00 p.m. news reporting, "A body was found today near the Poso Creek oilfields, the victim of a gunshot wound," and the deep voice of a man standing right outside the opened door, asking, "Are you David Kell?"

David caught a glimpse of the breaking news on TV, and saw an aerial shot zooming in on a manzanita bush sectioned off with the yellow tape of a crime scene. He then snapped his head around to the front porch to see the two men in suits standing in front of him. He gasped and shuffled backwards a step. His face turned white with horror as his narcotized mind tried to process it all. His heart raced, his breathing became shallow, and sweat beaded immediately on his forehead.

"Authorities located the body," the TV news anchor continued in the living room, "after a mechanic, Travis Bonner, found a detached hand lying next to a pumping unit." As the woman reported the news, the man at the front door repeated himself, "Are you David Kell?" Then added, "We're with the Bakersfield Police Department—Homicide."

David felt a drug and anxiety-induced panic attack rushing in on him, but he managed to stammer, "Yes, yes, I'm David Kell."

As both men flashed him their badges, the taller man with a barrel chest said, "Mr. Kell, I'm Detective Stedman, and this is Detective Sanchez."

David tried to show composure, although he wanted to scream hysterically and make a run for it. "Man, you guys startled me," he replied calmly, with a slight chuckle, "how can I help you?"

"Well, Mr. Kell," said Sanchez, "earlier this afternoon, a pumping unit mechanic out at the Poso Creek oilfields found a decomposing hand lying next to a rig. He made a call to 9-1-1 and our department's forensic team responded immediately with a cadaver dog. The stench was so strong, they located the body quickly. There was no identification on the victim, but there was an interesting tattoo on his left arm."

David tried to act attentive, without appearing guilty. In his mind he pictured the creepy tattoo he had seen on Spider's arm, and then he visualized the jail cell up in Tehachapi that had been his home for five years. He nodded as Sanchez spoke, then interjected, "What does all that have to do with me?"

"You see Mr. Kell," said Stedman, "we were able to identify the victim within a couple of hours. The tattoo was very unique; a black hairy tarantula. Our lab confirmed that it was recently completed, so, after a few phone calls to local tattoo parlors, we got lucky. We found the artist who not only did the tattoo, but who was also a friend of the victim. He gave us his name, Jerry Zeeder."

"Why are you talking to me?" David questioned, speaking fast, as his hands trembled due to the meth.

Sanchez glared at David, then remarked, "Mr. Kell, are you high on something?"

David's heart pounded as his mind screamed: *Keep cool!*

Keep cool man! They know you're high! "No, no," he nervously responded, "I've always been a little high strung. I'm not tweakin' man."

Both detectives eyed David closely as Stedman continued, "So, we contacted the victim's brother, Paul, who said that Jerry had recently moved. He didn't know the address, but Jerry had called him and told him it was in Oildale, and the only home in the middle of a bunch of warehouses. Jerry, also told his brother, he was living with a guy named David Kell."

David still played innocent and said, "So what's your point, detective?"

"The point, Mr. Kell, is that you are an obvious drug user and an ex-con with two strikes. Jerry Zeeder lived here for a few days, and now he's dead!"

"You can't prove he lived here!"

"Come on, David," Sanchez replied with certainty, "all we need is one single hair, a finger print, or a drop of blood. Maybe we'll find that hair in the shower drain, or the fingerprint on a beer can out in the trash, or the drop of blood in the trunk of the car. It's nearly impossible to erase someone's presence from a place he's been. We've got a warrant to search your house and property from top to bottom, inside and out, as well as your car from front to back. We'll find something, oh yeah, we'll find it."

"Even if you could prove he was here, that doesn't mean I killed him." David fired off confidently.

"If not you, David, then who, huh?" said Sanchez.

"That's your job Detective, not mine!" David felt like he was holding his own with the two of them.

"Well, we've found out who," jumped in Stedman, "and it's you, David, and we'll prove it. There's no doubt you did it. Now David—did you really think you could get away with murder?"

David became silent as he pondered how to answer the

question. It was easy, but seemed difficult. He could not answer yes, or no, for both would be a confession.

"Well, David, what's your answer?" pressed Stedman.

Not knowing how to respond, David simply stammered, "I—I—didn't do it."

The two detectives just stood with their arms crossed and stared at him.

Their scowling silence intimidated David. A sickening feeling crept over him. He knew they would prove it, and prison would be his home for the rest of his life. They would find a follicle of hair, a fingerprint, or a stain of blood, along with the rifle under the house. The ballistics would match. As the combination of meth and fear continued to jolt his mind and body, he tried hard to stay in control, but the intimidation of the two detectives weakened his struggle. He didn't know what to say. He thought the truth was just crazy enough to work. After all, it was an accident, of sorts. So he blurted out, "I didn't do it, I tell you. You got to believe me. He did it. Spider reached out with his hand and yanked on the gun, making me squeeze the trigger. It was by his hand, not mine. His hand! I tell you!"

"Sure, David," Sanchez said calmly, "we believe you, just like we believe it was an accident that he wound up buried out at Poso. He was hiking out in the middle of the heat and hills, then accidentally shot himself, fell into a garbage bag, and rolled under a bush."

"I didn't do it!" yelled David hysterically. "I swear, I didn't do it! He did it! He shouldn't have grabbed the gun!"

Sanchez spun David around, shoved him against the entry wall, and ordered, "Put your hands behind your back, you're under arrest for the murder of Jerry Zeeder."

Stedman slapped the cold steel handcuffs around David's wrists. He then read him his rights, as the newscaster on the living room TV reported, "With the summer heat on high, swimming lessons for kids, five to twelve years old, will be starting up at the following locations...."

As the detectives led David out to the patrol car, he hung his head and sobbed, mumbling, "He died by his own hand, not mine. I didn't pull the trigger. He did. It was his fault. I remember clearly, he died by his own hand."

David continued to cry and mutter as the detectives pressed his head down and shoved him into the back seat of the unmarked police car.

Earlier that day, at the same time that David had driven down to an Oildale liquor store, a hungry coyote had trotted along the eastern fringe of the Poso Creek oilfields.

The afternoon sun baked the stark hills as a hot breeze kicked up a whirling dust devil that dissipated shortly after it appeared. A small lizard zipped across the parched ground to hide in a crevice between two rocks.

The coyote stopped abruptly and raised its pointed nose into the air, sniffing a scent. It zeroed in on the potent odor, then tracked it less than a hundred yards to a large manzanita bush. It dug around the roots and loose dirt of the plant to discover a buried plastic bag. As the animal chewed through the duct tape and plastic, a human arm sprung out. The coyote gnawed through the wrist bones, releasing the hand. As it chewed, a larger, more aggressive coyote showed up, growled, and nipped at the first. The first coyote gripped the hand in its jowls and ran west towards the oilfields where it came to rest in the shade of a pumping unit.

As the coyote dropped the hand and panted from its run, it heard a loud rumbling noise and peered around the back of the pumping unit to see a truck charging straight for it. Frightened, it fled, and abandoned the hand. As it loped away, it saw the shadow of a large bird sweeping across the ground. It looked up to see a red-tailed hawk flying overhead with its prey hanging from its talons.

The truck stopped amidst a cloud of dust, and Travis Bonner stepped out into the blistering heat. He grabbed a wrench and shut the off the pump's power. In the dust, lying next to pumping unit #31—was just a hand.

SUCH GRIEF

As the sun burst over the Pickwick Dam, beaming down upon the historic battlefield of Shiloh and the small town of Savannah, Tennessee, the telephone in the motel room rang, awakening the son from a fitful sleep.

"Hello," the son muttered, emotionally bracing for what he expected to hear.

"I'm so sorry," said a hospice nurse, speaking compassionately in her hill-country drawl, "but your daddy—he passed away early this mornin'. The doctor's on his way to make a legal pronouncement, and we've contacted the funeral home. You'll need to come on down and sign some papers please."

"Okay. I'll be there shortly," he replied, then hung up the phone. He sat on the edge of the bed expecting to sob; but not a tear. As he dressed, and as he drove over to the hospice he felt like weeping; but not a tear. As he signed papers, as he talked to the man at the funeral home, and as he called family members, he thought he would cry; but not a tear.

The day before his father died, the son had flown across the country, racing, desperately hoping to reach him before death's eager undertaking. After multiple flights, fraught with layovers and delays, and a weary, dark drive down the lonely, backcountry roads of Tennessee, he stood aghast at the end of the sterile bed, peering down at the pale, dehydrated rogue posing as his seventy-five year old father. Calming music played in the hallway, but in the small room, the liver disease chose the swan song, playing out a pitiless, languorous strain upon each labored breath of the perishing soul.

The son, overcome with sympathy, drew close, bent down, and kissed his father on the forehead. "I love you, Dad," he whispered, stroking back the worn-out man's matted white hair. "I'm so sorry you're laying here like this. I wanted to tell you that I forgive you for not being there when I needed you. On those few holidays that you did drop in, you could've stayed longer than a quick cup of coffee. I'm fifty years old now, and over all these years, well—Dad, I just missed you." He paused, silently wishing his unconscious father would open his eyes and sincerely apologize for causing such grief. Not for the grief of the moment—which held more pity than sadness—but for the lifelong sorrow; a raw pain that had clutched his life. He drew in a deep breath, exhaled slowly, then continued, "Please forgive me for feeling hurt, and for being so angry at you. I just wanted to spend more time with you; to be father and son."

His father didn't respond; his eyes remained shut; he didn't stir or utter a word. In the past, the son had felt exasperated over his father's lack of response. But not this time. This time, his father couldn't respond, compared to the times when he could, but didn't.

The son lingered, staring down at the dying patriarch. Something tugged at his soul, something pleaded within—it was a longing, parched and famished; a hunger for just a morsel; for just those few fond words of sustenance: "Son—I'm proud of you." If only his father would have spoken those bountiful words, his boy's starving soul would be satisfied, but with his father's death imminent, the son's ache would live on. The son hung his head in defeat, and then sighed, "I'm sorry, Dad, that we weren't closer. Goodbye."

It was after midnight, and the exhausted son had said all that he needed to say, so he left his father's side, the antiseptic room, and the hospice. Hours later, at sunrise, the son received the nurse's call notifying him of his dad's death. Filled with grief, he wanted to cry; he needed to cry; but not a tear.

According to his father's wishes, his earthly remains were cremated, sent to California, and buried in the cemetery in the small town of Clovis. The tombstone already stood at the gravesite from fifteen years before, when brain cancer had taken his wife. Engraved into the granite marker was her name and life years, and his name and date of birth; his date of death soon to be added.

Family and friends gathered at the cemetery for a graveside memorial, and then met at the home of the eldest son. They ate, talked, and comforted one another. In remembrance, some watched home videos portraying decades of the man and his family.

Once everyone had left his home, the bereaved son sat on the couch and clicked on the family videos. After a few minutes, he shifted to a wooden rocking chair and scooted closer to the screen, scrutinizing—clicking rewind and pause—the captured images of his father.

When his dad was a young man, he was right there, having fun, interacting with his four kids as they made wishes and blew out birthday candles, sang carols in front of the Christmas tree, and dressed absurdly for Halloween. Then 'Nam, and three tours of duty. His kids missed him terribly. "Where's Dad? When will he come home? Is he going to die?" His wife needed him desperately. He finally returned home, but he looked tired and troubled, with deeper lines and creases upon his face. The war had consumed his vitality—in Saigon, at the Airforce personnel office, on the second floor above the morgue.

His son continued examining the videos, and saw diplomas, wedding cakes, and new homes. His father—heavier, with salt and pepper hair—was there, standing in the background, aloof, but there, grimacing, as though he suffered a ceaseless stomachache. The son remembered that during that time his grandparents had passed away. His dad's mother, plagued with cancer, died first, followed three months later by the sudden death of his dad's father.

Years passed by as minutes while the son analyzed the videos. There were newborn babies wearing tiny pink or blue knitted caps, excited tots ripping through Christmas presents, and bigger, golden-roasted turkeys surrounded by a growing throng of family. In their midst, in a wheelchair, sat the son's mother, the wife of the then sixty-year-old man. She wore a colorful scarf to hide the humiliating effects of chemo. She dearly loved her precious children and grandchildren, and they dearly loved her. The aging, somber man, her husband of thirty-five years, stood behind her wheelchair, holding on to its handles. After her slow, agonizing death—at a young fifty-seven years old—she disappeared from the family videos. The gray haired man vanished as well, except for a few brief appearances of him holding a cup of coffee.

The son pushed pause on the remote, and sat alone—in the soft glow of the lamplight, and in the hush of the early a.m.—contemplating.

He understood why his father had carried such grief; a sadness, so tormenting, so debilitating, that he could hardly shoulder the responsibilities of family. The meaningless atrocities of war, and the cruel deaths of those dear to him created a sorrow in the man that intensified to the point, that in his final years, he just showed up for a cup of coffee.

The son clicked play, and watched the end of the last video. He saw himself six months earlier, celebrating his own fiftieth birthday. Immediately after the guests sang the birthday song, and he blew out the candles, he heard the words. Not at the time of the party, because of the noise surrounding him, but the camera had picked up the audio of those standing close by.

He clearly heard the raspy, cigarette ruined voice of his dad's best friend, "Man, your son has sure done well."

"Yes, he has," his father replied in his sergeant's voice, bold amongst the clamor, "I've always been proud of my boy."

There it was! The son heard it! He excitedly pushed rewind, and then play. He listened again. "I've always been proud of my boy."

The son's famished soul gobbled up the words. He played the affirmation over and over again, until his spirit swelled with esteem. He then clicked off the TV, leaned back in his rocking chair, and smiled. What had taken decades to record, hours to watch, and a moment of reflection upon, all flashed before his eyes as compassion for his dad. Overcome with loss and his eyes filled with tears, the son buried his face in his hands and sobbed.

Yoohoo

"YOUR FIRST HOMEWORK assignment," said the young and pretty teacher to her fifth grade class, "is to write a story about your summer vacation."

The students sat at their wooden desks lined up in rows, as the teacher stood at the front of the class. She wore a short, flowered sundress and a bouffant hairdo, as a lot of woman did in 1966. Most of the boys sported plaid shirts, blue jeans, and short haircuts, while most of the girls dressed in bright, solid-colored dresses, and modeled long straight hair parted down the middle. Edison Elementary was mostly just a big, rectangular, two-story brick box full of kids. End-of-summer sunshine beamed down upon Tampa and in through the open windows of the school house, as two overworked, oscillating fans tried to blow the lazy humidity back outside. The trees in the schoolyard were huge, and though their foliage was sparse, their moss was thick, so they covered the grounds with lots of shade.

"The assignment is due at the end of this week, on Friday," stated the teacher, "and each one of you will be asked to read your story to the rest of the class."

All of the kids grimaced and moaned at the assignment. Not Kerby; he smiled. He liked to write stories.

On Friday, following the afternoon recess, and after Matt talked about his family's trip to Disney World, and after Jill's tale about camping at Lake Kissimmee, and after Bobby's story about the Kennedy Space Center, Kerby stood up and scampered to the front of the class, eager to read his story. He gazed out at his classmates, cleared his throat, and then loudly cleared it again, making the kids laugh. Then he began, with his pronounced southern accent to read his story.

"My Summer, by me—Kerby Speck," he started. "There are three things that I like to do, and mostly did all summer: play baseball," he held his thumb up counting, "climb trees," out came his index finger followed by his middle finger, "and write stories. My dad's in Vietnam, so we didn't take any fun family trips. So, nearly everyday, I played down at Gidden's Park. It's got swings, seesaws, and a slide, and a baseball diamond with a backstop. It's also got lots of climbin' trees, and the best part is, the park's only two blocks from my house. One muggy day—I remembered it was muggy 'cause I sweated a lot and my T-shirt stuck to me—I was playin' third base in a pick-up game at the ball field, when I caught this high pop-fly hit by this big and mean junior high kid. It went straight up twelve-o-clock high, and it was noon, so after the catch, I saw a bright round dot in my eyeballs for a while. The mean kid got mad that he popped out, and then when it was his turn to bat again, he smacked a line drive into my left foot. I made a shoestring catch, and since he was out again, he got worse mad. When it was my turn to bat, I smacked a home run out in left field, just over his head. When I ran the bases, I made fun of'im, reachin' up into the air all sissy-like, like he'd done when he'd missed the ball. So, he got all crazy mad, threw down his mitt, and chased after me down the third base line. Right after I stepped on home plate, he slugged me real hard in this arm." Kerby rubbed his left arm, wincing at the memory, saying, "It still kind of hurts. After playin' ball most of the afternoon, without keepin' track of runs, everybody went home, includin' the mean kid. I decided to climb my favorite tree at the park. I don't know what kind it is, but it's real, real tall and it's got lots of leaves to hide in. From the top of it, you can see a long ways off: the ball diamond, the playground, and even over some rooftops to the traffic light at Nebraska and Hillsborough. When you're climbin' the trees, you've got to be careful that you don't get into the moss, 'cause it's got no-see'em bugs crawlin' in it. Some people call'em red bugs, and other people call'em chiggers, but since they're tiny, and I can't see'em, I call'em no-see'em bugs."

Most of the kids in the class called them no-see'em bugs, so they snickered.

"When I had climbed half way up the tree, I looked down to see how high I was, and I saw Yoohoo—he's a small kid our age, but goes to a special school for kids that can't hear or speak. Another kid told me that Yoohoo was borned deaf, and that his speech box had to be taken out 'cause of cancer. Anyway, I call'im Yoohoo 'cause I don't know his name, and he can't speak to tell me, so, 'cause I'd seen'im a couple of times, drinkin' a Yoohoo choc'laty drink in a bottle, I call'im Yoohoo. He don't seem to mind."

Some of the students in the class moaned, "Mmmm, Yoohoo," thinking about the cold, chocolate drinks in a bottle, prompting the teacher to "shush" them.

"Well," continued Kerby, "Yoohoo waved his hands and jumped up and down. I hollered: What do you want? And then I remembered he couldn't hear me, nor holler back, so I climbed back down, and with my face real close to his—so he could read my lips—I asked him: What do you want? He pointed up in the tree. So, I showed'im what limbs were good to hang onto and to step on, to get to the top. He climbed like a monkey, right behind me all the way to the tippy-top, where we sat on a limb together spyin' out over the park and our neighborhood. We saw what looked like a bird flyin' toward us, but it flew in a weird way, and sounded funny too. It flew right at us, causin' me to yell and Yoohoo too, but no sound came out of his mouth. The creature landed on the tree trunk right next to us, almost causin' us to fall out of the tree. Lookin' at it close, we saw that it was a giant grasshopper, all ugly, green and orange, with long legs, and big eyes. I whipped off this shoe," Kerby pointed down to his Ked's All-Stars right sneaker, "and I whacked it hard! It dropped like a stone to the ground, where after a couple of minutes, we saw it flutter to another tree. I had some candy in my pocket—small jawbreakers, not the big ones. I got the candy by pickin' up and redeemin' Co-cola and Nehi bottles lyin' alongside the road. So, I put a jawbreaker in my mouth and asked Yoohoo if he wanted one too. He nodded yes. It was gettin' late so I started to climb down and go home for supper. I asked Yoohoo: Do you need some help gettin' down? He read my lips, and shook his head no. I tried to talk'im into to goin' down with me, but he frowned, shook his head no, and moved out on the limb away from me. I said, okay, and climbed down the tree and onto my sister's girly bike, because my bike was broken, and then I rode home for supper."

"Uh, Kerby," interrupted the teacher, "it's really nice that you made friends with Yoohoo, and your story is simply fascinating, but is it much longer?"

"No, not much, but I'm gettin' to the really good part now. After dinner when the sun was settin', I was bouncin' on my Pogo stick in front of my house, when my friend, Chucky Fried showed up. He's in seventh grade over at Memorial. I call'im Chucky Fried 'cause it's short for the very first name I gave'im, Ken-Chucky Fried Chicken, 'cause his name's Chucky, and his family's always eatin' out of those big, red buckets of Kentucky Fried Chicken. Well, he said, 'Hey Kerb, there's cop cars down at the park. Let's go!' We raced down there and sure enough, there were two cop cars at the park askin' kids if they'd seen a deaf-mute kid. I figured the kid was Yoohoo, so I went straight over to the tree, looked up, and saw him way at the top still sittin' on a limb, with his legs danglin', but huggin' the trunk, scared to come down. He was cryin', but with no sound. I climbed up to him and asked: You been up here all this time? He nodded, yes. Then I told'im: I'm sorry you got stuck up here, but you should've come down with me. He then made hand signals for me to help him down. I helped'im all the way to the ground, stayin' underneath'im the whole way in case he fell. Once on the ground, he smiled and gave me a high-five-hand-slap. We walked up to the policemen lookin' at a map, as one told the other, 'You cover those blocks, and I'll cover these. Hopefully, the poor kid wasn't kidnapped.' I said to the police: Here's Yoohoo, I found'im stuck up that tree. They shook my hand, and thanked me, and then one policeman took'im home to his worried mama, while the other gave me and Chucky Fried a ride home. Since we weren't criminals, but I was a hero, ridin' in a police car was really cool. All the other days durin' my summer were all about the same. I played baseball and climbed trees. I also wrote lots of stories, because some day I'm gonna be a famous author. The end."

The kids clapped as Kerby bowed over and over again all the way back to his desk.

"My goodness!" exclaimed the teacher. "Thank you, Kerby. What a story!"

QUEEN BEA

KURT STERLING, QUARTERBACK for the Porterville Panthers, glanced up and down the line at his teammates and at the Monache Marauders squared off against them. He shouted out the commands and as the center, big Tommy Wheeler snapped him the ball, both teams exploded into action, followed by the grunts and groans of the crashing linemen. Cory Lawson, the Panther's tight end, faked in and out, then blasted past his Marauders defender.

The loud speakers squawked with the announcer's rapid call of the play.

"Sterling drops back—Ohhh, great block by Wheeler—Sterling, in the pocket, looks down field—Lawson's wide open at the ten—Sterling to pass—Nooo, I can't believe it! He held onto the ball—He's scrambling! Ohhh, the Marauders Kragg and Ramos plant him into the turf!" The announcer pauses as the crowd on one side of the field roars, while the other groans, he then resumes, "Wheeler gives him a hand back to his feet. Sterling's shaken—but seems okay. That was a brutal sack. It's only the third this season for Sterling. With a loss of six yards, it's third down, and twelve yards for the first."

The Panther's coach, Jack Baier held his hands in the air in a T, yelling, "Time out! Time out!" As the referee blew his whistle, the coach hollered, "Sterling! Hit the sideline!"

It was Friday night, late October, and just cool enough to wear long-sleeves. The stadium lights glared down upon the players, the trodden grass field, and the white chalked lines of the high school football field.

The excited spectators packed the bleachers to watch the two local teams play out their intense rivalry. The contest—dubbed the Porter Bowl, named after Royal "Porter" Putnam the founding father of Porterville—was the biggest game of the season. Although the Marauders had won it the last two years and were the favorites to win it again, the Panthers, up by seven points in the third quarter, had a loose grip on victory. Tension mounted as the game clock ticked.

Beatrix Payne, eighteen, and a senior at Porterville high, sat impassively amongst the green and orange dressed throng of screaming, flag waving supporters. She looked as she usually did; dark clothes, morose shades of heavy make-up; and jet-black hair, short and spiked; and as always, she chewed bubble gum. The school band played the fight song, while the cheerleaders performed dance and acrobatic routines while shaking their pompoms. The school mascot hammed it up. All around Beatrix, the onlookers sang and clapped, cheering on their team. She couldn't care less about football and school spirit, even if it was the Porter Bowl. She was there watching Kurt.

Kurt's dad, Kendall Sterling, Porterville's district attorney, sat front-row-center, directly behind the team. Jim Lawson, Cory's dad, and Bob Wheeler, Tommy's dad sat with him. Jim was a deputy sheriff. Bob was a member of the city council with aspirations of running for mayor. All three dads had driven their sons hard to be the best.

Kurt dashed off the field over to Coach Baier. The coach grabbed Kurt's facemask, jerking him in close, and screamed, "What the hell is wrong with you? Didn't you see Lawson open?"

From the bleachers, Kendall Sterling cupped his hands

around his mouth, and yelled, "Come on Kurt, you can do better than that!"

The coach released Kurt, shoving him back a step. Kurt glanced at his dad, frowned, then answered the coach. "Sorry coach, I saw him, but—but…" he stammered fearing his excuse would sound ridiculous, "a bee flew into my helmet, messin' me up."

"A what?"

"A bee!"

"You're kiddin' right? Now, get out there! Stay focused! Be the hero everyone expects you to be!"

Kurt raced out to the huddle to call the next play. Inside the tight ring, their helmets nearly touching, Cory Lawson grumbled, "What's up with you Kurt? I could've scored on that last play! Share some glory, and pass me the ball."

The players, breathing heavily from the last play, rested their hands on their knees, and focused on Kurt.

Kurt replied, "I know, Cory, this play, I swear, it's comin' to you man! J26, L20 on six! Break!"

Disbanding the huddle, they clapped once, shouting, "Win!" then scrambled to the line, where both teams sneered, growled, and spewed profanities at each other. A Marauders lineman, Rudy Ramos, stood up out of position, pointed at Kurt, and blasted, "You're gonna' die dude!"

Kurt ignored him, and barked out the commands.

A scant cloud blew in from the southeast, hovering in the dark above the field.

Tommy hiked the football into Kurt's hands.

The cloud dropped from the night sky into the brilliance of the lights.

Kurt scrambled back to pass. Wheeler blocked the rush. Lawson ran a pass pattern, twenty yards down and out.

The spectators looked curiously at the odd, shape-changing cloud, then watched it veer toward the unaware players.

The announcer narrated the action. "Sterling is dropping back. He's going to…" bewildered by the cloud, his blaring voice paused in mid-sentence, and then began again, "Some sort of strange cloud has dropped into the stadium—it's clustering around Sterling—oh my word! He's fumbled! Both teams are diving on the loose ball! Sterling is running toward the Marauder's goal! He's in trouble!"

The surprised crowd gasped, then fell silent, as all eyes watched Kurt running in the thick of the cloud, flailing his arms, and screaming in terror.

The announcer continued, "The Marauders have recovered the ball! Sterling's in the Marauders end zone—I can barely see him in the cloud—he's on the ground! He's rolling back and forth—he's curled into a ball—he's not moving! Oh my word! What's going on?"

Coach Jack Baier, Kendall Sterling, and Tommy Wheeler bolted to Kurt's aid. Sheriff Jim Lawson called for assistance on his radio.

City Councilman Bob Wheeler jumped up and shouted on the cheer squad's microphone. "Everyone—please stay calm and remain in your seats!"

As the men approached the cloud, they realized it was not due to weather or chemicals, but a dense swarm of bees. Trying to get to Kurt, the rescuers frantically waved their hands swatting at the agitated, stinging bees. Bill Wood, the Panthers assistant coach, rushed out with a fire extinguisher, and blasted the insects swarming on and around Kurt. The bees scattered, clustered back into a swarm, then buzzed past the lights and into the starry sky.

Kurt lay on the ground moaning. An ambulance with its red light flashing drove silently onto the field. The crowd murmured. The players paced. The cheerleaders cried.

After considerable effort, the two paramedics tugged off Kurt's helmet. His hideous appearance stunned those close enough to see him. Scarlet, swollen flesh masked his once chiseled face. Bulging red eyelids shrouded his striking blue eyes. The sleeves of his jersey pinched his distended arms— double their normal size.

Beatrix watched without expression as the ambulance cut across the field and drove out of the gate. With its siren wailing, it sped Kurt to the hospital. Kurt's girlfriend, Ashley, a cheerleader, along with two other cheerleaders, Amber and Allison, left with his dad and mom in their car on the way to the hospital.

Beatrix pulled her purple bubble gum out of her mouth, stretching it out like saltwater taffy, then wrapped it in her twirling index finger all the way back into her mouth, raked it off with her front teeth, and started chewing again. She stood up, smirked, and casually walked down the bleacher's steps, and left the stadium.

The game resumed, but the Panthers had lost their star quarterback, and their spirit to win. The Marauders won the Porter Bowl for the third year in a row.

Immediately after the game, most of the football players, a crowd of students, the coaches, and several faculty rushed to the hospital. Some waited in the hospital's waiting room, while the rest held a vigil in the parking lot.

At 10:36 p.m., Kurt died from the toxic shock of over five hundred bee stings.

That night, Tommy Wheeler could not sleep. He thrashed around in his bed feeling awful. He thought about Kurt, one of his two best friends since kindergarten. One minute, he had snapped Kurt the football, the next, they sped Kurt off. No last words—gone. Adding to his grief, he felt the disappointment and embarrassment of losing the Porter Bowl—for the third time. He rolled over in bed, trying to get comfortable, but his bulky, six-foot-six body ached from bee stings, and crashing into

Marauders. Underlying all that, his conscience haunted him. He felt horrible guilt over what they had done to Beatrix Payne. Finally, overwhelmed by physical and emotional exhaustion, he fell asleep.

The next day, mid-morning, Tommy climbed into his fully restored, torch-red 1970 Plymouth Barracuda convertible—a gift from his parents on his eighteenth birthday. The steering wheel felt sticky, probably from fast food he thought. He'd deal with it later. It was a bright day, and unseasonably warm, so he lowered the car's top. He slipped on his sunglasses, cranked up a CD, and headed over to Ashley's house. Many of Kurt's friends were meeting there to comfort her and each other. Cory Lawson, his other best friend, would be there, and he was eager to see him. As he sped down rural roads toward her house, he thought again of Kurt. He still could not believe he was gone, or the way he died—bee stings. Playing football, going to school, and drinking beer would never be the same without Kurt. As he drove, the rushing air and the loud tunes felt comforting. He looked up into the sky and saw a red tailed hawk flying overhead, then watched, as it landed at the top of a telephone pole. Beyond the bird, in the sky, he spotted a strange cloud quickly approaching him—the same dark cloud that had descended into the high school stadium. Panic stricken, he shifted into high gear, smashed down the accelerator, and raced toward Ashley's.

He glanced in his rearview mirror, and saw the buzzing mass diving out of the sky. He was stricken with fear, but had hope; Ashley's house, and safety were only a couple of miles away. He thought about putting up the top, but couldn't, unless he reduced his speed. If he did, the swarm would overtake him. The Plymouth's rebuilt 383 purred as he accelerated to 110 mph.

He stared in his rearview mirror. To his relief, the swarm had disappeared. Twisting his body and cranking his head around, he searched the sky behind him, but saw no sign of the bees. He had out-raced them.

Hearing numerous splats on the windshield, he whipped back around and faced the road. His eyes grew wide with terror; his grip tightened on the steering wheel. He stared dead ahead into the black mass of bees. He stomped on the brake pedal, and frantically pushed the switch that raised the motorized top. The car's tires screeched, smoking across the asphalt. The top cranked slowly up and over. The glimmering guts of smashed bees painted the windshield. He flipped on the windshield wipers smearing them worse, blinding his view of the road. Just before the top covered the car, the swarm converged inside the vehicle, blanketing him. The top closed and locked, trapping the bees inside. He screamed, feeling the stings of hundreds of bees. The car drifted off the road casting up dust and gravel then hit an almond tree at fifty miles per hour.

Tommy's face smashed into the steering wheel. The car's doors flew open. Steam escaped from under the crumpled hood. In shock, and bleeding from a deep gash on his forehead, he unfastened his lap belt and rolled out of the car. The bees enveloped his body. The car's horn blared, but all he heard was a deafening buzz. With his face, neck, and arms red and puffy, and his eyes swollen shut from bee venom, he crawled blindly for a few yards, then fell unconscious.

Cory sat with the rest of the teens at Ashley's house. Ashley, still in state of severe shock over the death of her boyfriend, held a box of tissues in her lap and cried softly. Allison and Amber hugged her. Cory worried that Beatrix would show up and cause a scene in front of his girlfriend.

The grieving teens wondered why Tommy had not arrived. Allison flipped open her cell phone and called his house.

Tommy's mother, Sandy, answered, telling Allison that Tommy had left over an hour before. As Sandy hung up the telephone with Allison, there was a knock on her door. Her husband, Bob, opened it to greet their pastor, Rick Praly, standing there with a somber face. She moved close to Bob, her hand over her mouth, fearing the worst.

The pastor spoke compassionately, "Hello, Bob—Sandy—may I come in?" He stepped inside, stared down at the floor for a second, sighed from the weight of his burden, and then looked into their apprehensive eyes. "The Sheriff's department called me, and asked me to come over—I'm sorry—but Tommy was in an accident, and…."

Immediately after Allison had ended the call with Sandy, she looked out the window, and saw a sheriff's car pull into her driveway. Deputy Sheriff, Jim Lawson got out of it, and approached the door. She ran outside to meet him, followed by the others. Jim's son, Cory, wondering why his dad was there, stood next his girlfriend, Amber, who stood next to Allison. Jim glanced at his son, reached out, and squeezed his shoulder. All the other teens gathered around.

Jim furrowed his brow and looked straight into their eyes. In a soft, low tone, he said, "Kids, I got some bad news—and I'm just going to tell you like it is. Tommy Wheeler has died."

The teenagers just stared back. All were silent, until Allison shrieked, then started sobbing. Ashley, Amber, and some other girls, all with tear-filled eyes, gathered around and embraced her.

Jim took a deep breath, then continued, "A farmer driving out on Road 24, not far from here, saw Tommy's car smashed against an almond tree. When we arrived, we had to fight off a swarm of bees to get to him. We were too late. Tommy was covered with hundreds of bee stings, like what happened to Kurt Sterling." Jim paused, took his hat off, and wiped the sweat from his forehead with his shirtsleeve, then put his hat back on. "I'm sorry, really sorry. I knew you guys would be here, so I asked the department's chaplain, Mark Mercer, to come over. He's a good guy, talk to him, he can help. Cory, son, I'd like you to come on home." Cory didn't say a word. He just hung his head, walked over to his car, and got in. He glanced out at Amber and gave her the hand sign that he would call her later.

The Chaplain pulled into the driveway. Jim and Cory drove off in their cars, with Cory following his dad. As he drove, Cory angrily pounded the steering wheel with his fist, wailing, "No, no, no, not my best friends! They can't be dead!" He closed his eyes, blurring with tears and shook his head back and forth trying to dislodge the reality out of it. As he wept, his car tires edged off the pavement and onto the dusty shoulder of the road pitching his vehicle toward a wide, fast flowing irrigation canal.

His dad stared into his rearview mirror, and saw his son's car drift off the road in a huge swirl of dust. He pulled off the road, and watched with disbelief.

Just before Cory's car plunged into the cold water of the canal, he jerked the steering wheel. With its rear end fishtailing, the car bounced back onto the asphalt.

"I guess I'm next! Right?" Cory screamed. "What we did to Beatrix was wrong—but we don't deserve to die!"

His dad saw the recovery, sighed with relief, and they both drove on.

At home, Cory and his dad talked for awhile about the deaths of Kurt and Tommy. Cory wished his mom was there, but a year ago, she had left his dad, filed for divorce, and moved to Los Angeles. During football season, he didn't see her much.

"Son, I've got to go to the station and fill out reports," said his dad, "then I'm going over to see Bob and Sandy Wheeler, and then Kendall and Karen Sterling. Are you going to be okay?"

"Sure dad, I'll be alright. I'm just going to play a video game. It'll help keep my mind off of everything."

"Ok, son, just stay home for now. I mean it. Don't leave. I'll try to be back soon, and on the way home, I'll pick us up some dinner."

Cory sat in his bedroom and played a video game, but he couldn't concentrate on it. He kept losing players, and the game would say in its electronic voice, "You're dead!" His mind reeled from the deaths of Kurt and Tommy, his body ached from the Marauders pummeling, and his conscience bothered him about what Kurt, Tommy, and he had done to Beatrix. He leaned back in his chair, and gazed out the window at the glimmering water in the swimming pool. Seeing the hot tub next to the pool made him think that, maybe, a good hot soak would help sooth his mind and body. He went outside, searching the sky as he walked over to the hot tub. The sun shone, and there were a few fluffy clouds, but no dark, menacing ones. He looked out at the trees of the citrus grove that covered the hundred acres around the house. The oranges were still green. All was quiet. While the tub warmed up, he went inside and called Amber.

"Hello, Cory. Are you okay?" she asked in her valley-girl accent.

"Sure, I guess, well, no, not really," he stammered with his voice cracking, "are you?"

"No, not at all. I hurt for Ashley and Allison, and I am worried about you. Cory, what kind of trouble did you guys get into?"

Cory remained silent.

"Cory, are you there?"

"Yeah."

"What did you guys do? Answer me! I know you're in some kind of trouble. You've been acting strange since last week's party. What happened after we left?"

He sighed, then blurted out, "It wasn't me, it was Kurt and Tommy. I was just there with them."

"What did they do Cory. Tell me!"

"Well, after you girls left, we went back to the party. We drank a couple of more beers."

"Ooh, I knew you creeps would go back."

"When we were leaving, we saw that Beatrix's car wouldn't start. We gave her a ride home. She was acting all nasty with us, so the guys got a little nasty back."

"What do you mean by nasty? The A-Girls try to be nice to her, and then she stabs us in the back hittin' on our boyfriends?"

Cory felt like he was squealing on his dead friends. "I don't want to talk about it now. My best friends have just died; I'm not gonna snitch them out. I'm going out to sit in the hot tub and try to sort this all out." He looked out the window, and saw steam rising from the bubbling water. "It's all heated up, so I'll call you later."

"Talk to me now, Cory."

"No. We'll talk later, I promise. I love you."

"Okay. You'd better tell me what's going on. I love you too. Call me as soon as you're out of the hot tub."

They ended the call. He removed his clothes, wrapped a towel around his waist, walked out to the circular tub built into the ground, and eased down into it. He sighed, as the hot, steamy water comforted his body, but not his grief, nor his conscience.

He leaned back, resting his head on the deck, and reminisced about his best friends: Kurt, confident, commanding, and always strutting his muscles and good looks in front of the girls; and tall, bulky, rosy-red cheeks, baby face Tommy, forever loyal to Kurt for letting him copy his homework. They had all three grown up together, playing on the same soccer, baseball, and football teams, and had all gone together with their dads on camping and hunting trips. They had drank out of the same beer can, smoked the same bong, and made-out with some of the same girls. Together, they were uncontrollably rowdy, and over the years had gotten into a lot of trouble. Their influential dads had always bailed them out. Their mischief was well known within the community, and back in elementary school they had been nicknamed, Triple-Trouble.

He cupped his face with his wet, warm hands, and cried. He closed his eyes, and breathed deeply, trying to regain composure. He concentrated his thoughts on the next football season, at a university far away. Hopefully, Amber would attend the same school and they could get an apartment together.

He started to feel better when he felt an excruciating pain. He raised up, and slapped his arm, splashing water out of the tub. What he saw made him forget his emotional and physical pain. On the surface of the water floated hundreds of fidgeting bees. He looked up to see the dark swarm burst upon him. He sucked in a deep breath, then submerged under water. He opened his eyes and looked up through the bubbles. All was dark. The bees massing on the surface of the water blocked out the sunlight.

Running out of breath, his lungs burning, he punched his head out of the water and drew in a long breath, as well as bees into his mouth. They immediately stung his tongue. He plunged under water, spitting them out. A moment later, and out of breath again, he tensed his legs and thrust his nude body through the cluster of bees, soaring out of the tub, and onto the pool deck. The insects immediately covered his body, and he felt the stings of hundreds of bees. Feeling dizzy, he crawled toward the house. With his tongue swollen, he garbled, "Dad! Dad!" The bees kept stinging, and stinging, from the bottoms of his feet, up his naked body, to his face. He groaned in agony, then passed out.

Later that afternoon, his dad returned home with dinner. Jim felt devastated. Kendall and Bob were his best friends, and he felt their sorrow deeply. Their sons, Kurt and Tommy, were like sons to him. He walked in the house and hollered for Cory. No answer. He walked out to the side of the house to the hot tub, and found him. After spraying the remaining bees off with a garden hose, he covered his son with a towel.

Tears ran down his face, as he talked to the dispatcher on his radio, "Helen, this is Jim. Do you copy?"

"I copy, Jim." Her voice crackled back.

"I found my son, Cory—out by our hot tub. He's—he's dead—bee stings. The team is probably finishing up at the crash site of Tommy Wheeler. When they're done there—send them over here."

That night, Beatrix was at home by herself. She lived with her dad's brother, her Uncle Stewart, and his wife, Crystal. Her uncle had gone to an agricultural convention the Thursday before the deaths and was returning on Sunday. Her aunt was filling in on some extra shifts at the hospital.

Beatrix watched the breaking news on TV about the deaths of Kurt, Tommy, and Cory. She stared at the TV, mesmerized by the photos of each boy and the footage of each scene. Three times she stretched her bubble gum slowly out of her mouth, twirled it around her index finger, and then raked it off with her teeth back into her mouth. The fourth time she kept the gum wrapped around her finger. When the news coverage ended, she clicked off the TV, went into the kitchen, threw away the gum, and placed a piece of left over pizza in the microwave. At the ding, Beatrix took out the steamy pizza, then went to her bedroom, and shut the door. She sat on her bed, nibbling at her snack, entranced by a framed photograph propped up on her nightstand. The photo was taken last summer on a family vacation at Sea World. It was of her parents and her—all smiling—a month before their funeral.

After the deaths of her parents, Beatrix had moved from San Jose to live with her uncle and aunt. They lived in an old farmhouse on fifty acres of naval oranges in Terra Bella, a small farming community a few miles south of Porterville. Her parents had flown to Portland for their anniversary in her dad's small plane. Beatrix had stayed at a friend's house.

Landing in the middle of a downpour, their plane collided into another plane on the wrong runway. The fiery crash killed them instantly.

Uncle Stuart and Aunt Crystal were the only relatives who offered to take her in. They were childless. Beatrix didn't know why, and didn't ask. Her uncle was a good man, yet suffered flashbacks of Vietnam, and most weekends he'd lapse into a drunken stupor. When sober, he worked as a pollinator, assisting farmers with their nut and citrus trees. Aunt Crystal worked as a dietary technician at the Porterville Developmental Center, a hospital for the most severe cases of the physically and mentally disabled.

Beatrix had fit in at her previous school back in San Jose. She had belonged to a circle of friends that talked, dressed, and thought like her. She hated the farming community of Porterville. It was boring: lacking gigantic malls, cool restaurants, and the beach only thirty miles away. Most of the kids at Porterville High School had grown up together, seeing her as an alien and making sure she knew it. Only the A-Girls—feeling charitable—befriended her.

On a Friday night, after a home football game, and one week before the Porter Bowl and Kurt's death, Allison had invited Beatrix to a party at the home of one of the football players. The party was in the country, at a farmhouse surrounded by rows of almond trees. The boy's parents were out of town, had trusted him to watch the house, and had left explicit instructions, "No parties."

Although Beatrix didn't care much for hanging out with jocks and rah-rahs, she decided to go. It was her eighteenth birthday and she didn't want to spend it at home.

Before she left for the party, her uncle and aunt celebrated her birthday with her favorite dinner—corn dogs smothered in macaroni and cheese—and a present. Beatrix opened it, discovering to her delight a necklace with a silver setting of a honeybee, inlayed with opal birthstones. She put it on immediately and wore it to the party.

Most of the football team showed up at the party, as well as the pep girls. The players were elated. They had slaughtered the team that the week before had beaten the Marauders, making the Panthers the favorite for winning the Porter Bowl. Kurt, Tommy, and Cory—Triple-Trouble—felt confident, powerful, and celebrated by drinking too many beers. Their girlfriends, Ashley, Allison, and Amber, cheerleaders and best friends known as the A-Girls, partied with them.

Allison, bored with the bravado of Triple-Trouble, left the clique to talk to Beatrix standing alone in the kitchen.

"Hi Bea, glad you could make it. Ooh, hey, nice necklace." She reached out, held it in her fingertips, and admired it.

"Thanks, Allison, but I shouldn't of come tonight. I really don't fit in."

"Sure you do and don't worry about Triple-Trouble." The guys roared with laughter in the next room prompting her to add, "They're all talk, especially when its beer-babble. They'd never hurt anybody. Well, I'd better go get my A-Girls and get goin'. Cheer-coach Katie scheduled us at 7:00 am for the Porter Bowl pep routines."

"Ouch, no sleeping in. Bummer. By the way, thanks Allison, for inviting me and for the chat."

"Okay, see you in government."

Allison tugged her girlfriends away from Triple-Trouble, and headed for the door.

Their intoxicated boyfriends, Kurt, Tommy, and Cory, begged them to stay. The boys lost out and walked the girls out to Allison's car. Allison kissed and hugged Tommy goodnight and Amber did the same with Cory, then both girls got into the car, and waited for Ashley. The guys jumped into Tommy's Barracuda, started it up, and waited for Kurt. Kurt pinned

Ashley against the trunk of Allison's car squeezing her tight and kissing her hard, running his hands all over her.

In between kisses, she demanded, "Stop, Kurt. Pleeeease, stop. Not out here. Besides, I've got to go."

Kurt ignored her and kept groping, whispering in her ear, "Come on baby, stay for awhile. We'll take you home later."

"I can't Kurt. I'm sorry. They're waiting for me. I have to go!" She wrested her body from under his weight, popped open the car's backdoor, and scrambled in. She rolled down the window, and said in a huff, "Goodnight Kurt. I'll see you tomorrow."

Kurt, feeling rejected and angry, spat back, "Yeah, if your lucky, Ashley. All you care about is your girlfriends, and cheerleading. What about me?"

As the car backed out of the driveway, she hollered out the window, "I do care about you Kurt. You've had too many beers. Go home. I'll see you tomorrow after cheer practice."

Kurt popped into the passenger seat of Tommy's car. They pulled away from the house, but as soon as the girl's car was out of sight, Kurt ordered, "Tommy, flip a U-turn, and take us back to the party." Tommy followed the play, turning the car around.

Without the A-Girls at the party to keep an eye on them, Triple-Trouble got boisterous, telling stories about when they almost got into trouble and the times they did. It was all a joke to them. As Tommy told a story about pissing on the principle's car, Kurt looked over at Beatrix standing alone in the kitchen. He really hadn't noticed her before, but she looked wild—untamed—sexy. His senses ignored everyone and everything in the room as his eyes crawled over her body. Her tight, black jeans and top exhibited her erotic, curvy figure. Her gleaming black hair and funereal make-up were exotic, like he'd only seen in the magazines hid under his mattress. Her glossy lips bobbed sensuously as she chewed her gum. Her olive green eye shadow accentuated her emerald eyes—that had just noticed him gawking. He gave her a 'what's up' head nod.

Beatrix sheepishly smiled back at Kurt. She felt uncomfortable and decided to leave.

Kurt nudged Tommy and Cory to check her out. All three boys lusted after her as she walked from the kitchen, past them, to the restroom down the hall.

Kurt called a play: Tommy stepped outside, and disconnected the distributor cap on Beatrix's car.

Beatrix left the house, and got in her car, a black Omni that she had purchased with some of her parent's estate money. She cranked it. It wouldn't start. She tried repeatedly—nothing.

Triple-Trouble swaggered up along side her car.

"Can we help?" asked Kurt.

"The car won't start," she snapped in her frustration.

"Tommy, open the hood and check it out bro," ordered Kurt.

Tommy opened it, wiggled a few wires, and then tightened the oil and radiator caps. Since he had sabotaged it, he knew exactly what was wrong with it, yet did nothing about it.

"Try to start it again, Bea," said Kurt.

She tried again, but to no avail. After a few more attempts, Kurt said, "Don't worry, Bea, we'll give you a ride home. We're just leaving anyway. We got to get home and call our girlfriends."

She was reluctant, but didn't want to wake her Aunt and Uncle. Besides, the guys seemed sincere in wanting to help her. "Okay, as long as you take me straight home."

The guys glanced at each other and grinned. "Sure, not a problem," said Cory.

Before shutting the hood, Tommy reached over and snapped the distributor cap back on.

Triple-Trouble and Beatrix clamored into Tommy's Barracuda. Kurt rode shotgun, while Beatrix and Cory sat in the back seat. Tommy backed his car out of the driveway, shifted into first gear, punched the accelerator popping the clutch, and screeched the tires, inciting the partying teens on the front lawn to hoot and holler.

Barreling down the country roads toward Beatrix's house, Kurt demanded, "Hey Tommy, put the top down, so I can feel the cool air and see the stars."

Tommy slowed the vehicle down and lowered the top.

Feeling chilled, Beatrix whined, "Come on Tommy, put the top back up, pleeeease."

Tommy started to flip the toggle, but Kurt gruffed, "Oh, hell no! The air feels good, man. Leave it down!" He chugged down the rest of his beer, then hurled the bottle out of the car, smashing it dead center into a speed limit sign.

Tommy always obeyed Kurt. He wished he didn't, because over the years Kurt had gotten him into a lot of trouble. Kurt, always the "Quarterback," had a controlling way about him. Not only that, Kurt helped him to get the minimal passing grades needed to play football. He owed him.

"Hey guys," Cory hollered over the wind, "I don't know about you, but since my last piss, I've slammed down four beers and I've got to take a forty-eight-ounce leak.

Tommy yanked the car off the remote rural road, and drove it deep into an orange grove. He parked it between two rows of trees and turned off the engine, leaving the headlights on. All three inebriated boys stumbled out of the car, and stood shoulder to shoulder in the beams. Then, like the three Musketeers crossing swords, they peed, crisscrossing their streams of urine. In unison they yelled with a make-believe, fading echo, sounding like an announcer in a boxing ring, "Triple-triple-triple. Trouble-trouble-trouble!" The tradition had started when they were in second grade.

Beatrix, cold, tired and impatient snapped, "Come on guys, please stop acting gay, and take me home!"

Kurt zipped up his pants, turned, and glared at Beatrix. The bright headlights illuminated the scowl upon his face. No one assaulted his manhood.

"Oh, you think we're gay, do'ya?" he shot back. He strutted to the side of the car where she sat, and leaned on the car. "Well, my buds and I have been commenting on how sexy you look, Bea. Queers wouldn't talk about all the different ways, they'd like to have fun with a hot babe like you. You're not like the other stuck-up girls, saving themselves for marriage. I'd bet Tommy's car that you're not a virgin, and that in the sack, you're big-city nasty."

Beatrix had had boyfriends, but that was none of their business. "You're drunk, Kurt!" she blasted. "Just take me home!" She then crossed her arms and tried to ignore them.

Kurt opened the door, and crept into the back seat. She slid over against the opposite door and started to open it, but Tommy leaned on it. Cory stood next to him. Kurt pressed in beside her.

"Leave me alone!" Beatrix screamed. "If you touch me, I'll make sure you guys go to prison!"

"First of all, Bea," asserted Kirk with a smirk, "the town loves us, and you're somebody weird from San Jose. No one will believe you. Second, everybody is thinking about the Porter Bowl. No one will listen to you. Not only that, it's our word against yours, and don't forget that our dads control the city, the courts, and the law. So come on, Bea, show us how nasty a freaky, big city girl can be."

"No Kurt! If you try anything, I'll—I'll tell your girlfriends!"

"They won't believe you either, Triple-Trouble knows how to cover their asses. Besides if they get pissed, there're plenty of chicks waitin' for Kurt's big game."

She hung her head, knowing they spoke reality. She started to cry, begging, "Please guys—don't do this. Just please take me home."

Tommy reached in the car and shut off the headlights. Kurt grabbed her arms, pulling her in tight. Tommy and Cory walked a few trees down, and smoked a joint waiting their turn.

"This is going to be fun," cracked Cory in a comical high voice, holding in a deep inhale of pot smoke.

"And wild," added Tommy, releasing a thick, smoky exhale.

In her effort to wrest free of Kurt, her honeybee, birthday necklace broke and fell to the floorboard. The isolation and the thick foliage of the trees muffled her screams and struggle. In the dark, Kurt overpowered her.

As they drove her the few miles home, Beatrix cried softly in the back seat. Tommy had put the top up. Kurt nervously smoked a cigarette. Not one of the guys said a word. They had loitered in lots of trouble, but had never ventured this far into it. As the car stopped at the end of the dirt and gravel driveway, Beatrix jumped out, sobbing, and ran towards the house.

The next day, Beatrix sat mute, as her Uncle Stuart drove her to get her car. He and his wife wished they could talk with her about what was bothering her, but they had no clue. They had never had kids, especially a teenage girl who had just lost her parents. Arriving at her car, he climbed in it, put in the key, cranked it, and started it.

"It must have been flooded, Bea. If it happens again, give it a few minutes, and then try to start it. If you ever break down again, just call us. One of us will come and get you, no matter what time of day or night."

"Thank you, Uncle Stuart," she said softly.

"You're welcome Bea, we want to be there for you. Now, I've got to go and pick up some hives at a farm out east of Strathmore. I brought your bee suit in case you want to help again. I'll bring you back to your car later." Over the past few months, he had been teaching Beatrix the bee business.

"Not today, but thanks again for your help Uncle Stuart, I'm just gonna go back home."

"Okay, Bea, I'll be home for dinner."

The house was quiet. Aunt Crystal was at work. Beatrix thought about calling her friends in San Jose, but every time she did, they jabbered about the fun they were having with their new best friends. Beatrix lay on her bed and wept.

In a stupor, she stayed in her room for six days, missing school, and barely eating. On Friday morning, the day of the Porter Bowl, she stared intently out her bedroom window at the buzzing beehives loaded on her Uncle's flat bed truck. Her uncle was away for four days at a pollinator's convention and her aunt had left for work. She walked out to the shed that stored his bee keeping chemicals and supplies.

On Wednesday, after the deaths, entomologist Kelly Beebe pulled her white pick-up—with the State Department of Agriculture insignia on its door panels—into the parking lot of *The Chicken or the Egg* restaurant. In smaller letters, above the eatery's name, it asked, *Which came first?* It was famous locally for serving stuffed omelets and country-fried chicken, any time, day or night. She had driven five hours from Sacramento, to meet homicide detective Dwayne Ketcher, and assist him in the investigation of the bee stinging deaths of three teenage boys.

As she entered the place, she saw three elderly men in overalls sitting at the counter drinking coffee and debating politics. A few couples sat at tables. At the back, in a booth, she saw a man wearing a denim shirt, a navy blue tie, and jeans, shuffling through a stack of papers.

Kelly walked up to him, extended her hand, and said, "Hi, you must be Detective Ketcher. I'm Kelly, the bug lady. We talked on the phone."

"Nice to meet you, Kelly," he replied, standing up and

shaking her hand. "Glad you're here to help. Have a seat. Oh, and just call me Dwayne."

As they sat down in the booth, he thought it fortunate that he didn't know anyone in the restaurant, because rumors would fly if friends saw him—a paunchy, forty-five-year-old, balding married man—meeting with a blond haired, ponytailed, single girl, fifteen years younger than he. He cleared his throat, focused back on business, and said, "With the two of us working together, maybe we can determine if these incidents were a freak of nature, or the homicidal nature of some freak. You hungry?"

Since it was 10:50 a.m., and still morning, Kelly ordered an omelet. Thinking it was near to lunch, Dwayne ordered fried chicken.

Waiting for their food, the detective said, "Kelly, I want to bring you up on the situation here. I've spent the last couple of days reviewing reports and photographs of the scenes." He slid the file of information over to her. She perused the notes and photos as he continued, "I've interviewed each victim's family and wrote down the names of their friends for questioning. Over the next couple of days, while we wait for the forensic reports, we'll check out the scenes, and question some folks."

They discussed the case as they ate, agreeing to begin the investigation in chronological order, beginning with Kurt Sterling's death.

Leaving the restaurant, they headed to the football stadium. Both peered into the sky and then focused on the end zone and visualized the teen's death. They left the stadium and proceeded to the homes of some of the witnesses. They interviewed Coach Baier, several of the players from both teams, and the field's announcer, local DJ, Ricky Hammer. They found that all had been caught by surprise when the swarm descended into the stadium. They questioned Coach Baier about the anger he had displayed toward Kurt. They concluded he was riveted in his passions and pressures to win. With the tension and expectations of the Porter Bowl, the Marauders had a motive for taking out Kurt. In fact, once he was out of the game, they did win. They questioned Rudy Ramos of the Marauders, who, during the play of Kurt's death, had pointed a finger at him, and threatened, 'You're gonna' die dude!' They reasoned that he was simply trying to intimidate Kurt. Ricky Hammer just called it as he saw it. Kelly asked questions about the size of the swarm, the direction of its arrival and departure, and how it reacted to Kurt and the rescuers.

The next day, Dwayne, and Kelly, met at a small coffeehouse. He ordered a dark roast, black. She ordered a non-fat, mocha, caramel latte. They then drove out to the crash site of Tommy Wheeler. After taking a close look at the skid marks from the tires, and the smashed tree, they drove a few miles down the road, and questioned the farmer who had discovered the accident. He slowly shook his head and said, "Bees—lots of bees. The poor kid—lots of bees." From there, they went to the wrecking yard to see the wrecked car. They grabbed a burger on the way. Standing next to the smashed Barracuda, the detective ate French fries out of the bag as he watched Kelly examine the windshield plastered with bee guts. She stuck her head inside the vehicle. Something gleaming in the sunlight on the backseat floorboard caught her eye. She reached over the front seat and picked up a silver honeybee necklace with opal inlays. She placed it in a clear evidence bag, and then in her purse. They then drove out to Deputy Jim Lawson's place. Jim sobbed as he recounted the story. They stepped outside, looked at the hot tub, and walked the perimeter of orange trees.

On Friday, now one week after Kurt's death, Dwayne picked up Kelly at the Best Western hotel where she was staying. They grabbed some coffees and bagels from the hotel's continental breakfast. With word that the reports were in, they headed to his office.

Both grimaced as they studied the autopsy reports. There

were photographs of the boy's bodies displaying red and swollen skin, including numerous pictures of magnified bee stings. The reports summarized the number of bee stings, their location on the bodies, and the amount of bee venom sustained. There was an analysis on the grass and dirt of the football field, the game football, and swatches of Kurt's uniform. From Tommy's crash site: data on the samples of the soil, tree bark, the car's upholstery, and his clothes. From the scene of Cory's death: results on the hot tub water, and the towel. From all three sites: lab tests on the dead bees. They also studied phoned in reports from fans at the game whom recalled seeing a beekeeper working rather late in the orange trees near the stadium. A couple of ladies heading into town for shopping noticed a truck hauling beehives out on road 24. A passing farm-worker had seen a bee truck in the grove next to Cory's house. In conclusion, in all three cases—pulmonary-coronary arrest. The official cause of death—bee venom.

Kelly tossed the reports on Dwayne's desk, and said matter of factly, "I suspected it and now it's a fact. The analysis found that three of the samples tested—Kurt's football jersey, the upholstery of Tommy's Barracuda, and the water from Cory's hot tub—contained a foreign substance. All three showed extreme saturation of a chemical beekeepers use known as *swarm lure*: a powerful chemical developed from the *pheromones* of a queen bee. After the bees have pollinated a crop, beekeepers use it to lure the bees back to the hive, so they can transport them to another location.

"Does that stuff cause the bees to sting?" asked Dwayne.

"No, that's a different pheromone carried in the abdomen of each bee. The boys sustained so many bee stings because, once one bee's sting releases its pheromone, it signals the swarm to sting."

"That's weird," the detective replied wryly. He thought for a moment, and then said, "Also weird, is that all the beekeepers were out of town at a convention the weekend of the deaths. So, I wondered, who had a high schooler in the household? I discovered that only one beekeeper, Stuart Payne Pollination had a student attending Porterville high school. Her name—Beatrix Payne. Let's go and interview the girlfriends of the dead teens and then we'll go and pay a visit to Miss Payne.

They met Ashley, Allison, and Amber at Ashley's house. The A-Girls confirmed the rumors that something *'icky'* had happened after a victory party between Triple-Trouble and the new girl—Beatrix Payne.

Amber confirmed it, sharing with them the conversation she had with Cory just before he died.

As Dwayne and Kelly were leaving, Kelly held up the honeybee necklace that she had found in Tommy's Barracuda and asked, "Do you girls know whom this belongs to?"

"Beatrix Payne," answered Allison without hesitation.

Beatrix, at home in her bedroom, quickly packed her suitcase with clothes, make-up, the portrait of her mom and dad, and the cash from her parents' assets and life insurance. She had made a withdrawal from the bank that morning. The news had reported that the authorities had a suspect. She suspected that they suspected her. Anticipating the arrival of the police, she went out to the bee shed, then back into the house.

As Beatrix finished packing, Dwayne and Kelly rode in his sedan, turning onto the dirt and gravel driveway leading between the orange trees back to Stuart Payne's house. Bees zipped everywhere. There was a strong citrus smell. They passed by numerous white boxes swarming with bees, and a green flatbed truck loaded with buzzing hives. He parked his car next to a black Omni in the shade under a giant oak tree.

Above them, high up on a limb, hidden in the foliage dangled a huge cluster of bees.

Beatrix, ready to flee, heard a vehicle outside. She peeked between the closed curtains covering the window, and saw a man and a woman get out of the car.

Both Kelly and Dwayne noticed the curtains move. They approached the front door, all the while dodging bees. It was open, yet a locked screen door barred their entrance. He knocked on its frame, rattling its lock, and hollered, "Mr. Payne, Mrs. Payne, are you home?"

No answer. All was quiet except the humming sound of bees and a crow cawing off in the grove.

Assuming the Omni was Beatrix's, he shouted, "Beatrix, are you home?"

Silence, except a clacking ceiling fan inside.

Dwayne motioned Kelly to say something. He thought that maybe her feminine voice could coax the teenager to the door.

"Beatrix, are you here? Honey, we just need to talk to you a minute," beckoned Kelly.

"We saw the curtains move," barked the detective. "We know you're here!"

There was a moment of silence.

"I'm here," muttered Beatrix without showing herself.

"Beatrix, I'm Detective Ketcher, Porterville PD," Dwayne blurted out, "and this is Kelly Beebe, from the State Department of Agriculture. We need to talk to you about the deaths of Kurt Sterling, Tommy Wheeler, and Cory Lawson."

"Please, Beatrix, will you come outside," implored Kelly.

Through the mesh of the screen, they saw her girlish, obscure figure shift closer. The detective placed his hand on his gun holstered under his arm. Kelly took a step back.

Remaining behind the screen door without unlocking it, Beatrix spat, "Sorry, but no, I won't come outside, but I'll tell you what you want to know."

"Start talkin'," ordered the detective.

"I killed them," she said with disdain. "All three of them. After a party, those three morons, stupidly known as Triple-Trouble, tricked me into a ride home. They drove me to an isolated orange grove and..." she stopped as her mind began reliving the trauma.

"Tell us what they did Beatrix," urged Kelly.

"They raped me!" she yelled. "All three of them! I begged them not to, but Kurt, *Mr. Bigshot Quarterback* was callin' the play."

Kelly gasped with sympathy, as Dwayne continued questioning, "Then what did you do—as retaliation?"

"I'm tryin' to tell you detective. I felt ashamed, but more than that, I felt angry. I wanted to kill them," she said clenching her teeth. "Oh, and just in case you're wonderin,' Kelly, I started my period the next day, so I won't be birthin' a little Triple-Trouble bastard."

"Oh, okay Beatrix," responded Kelly with sympathy.

"Go on," demanded the detective.

"Since my uncle and aunt were gone, I took some chemicals and the truck loaded with hives."

"Weren't you afraid of the bees?" Kelly asked.

"No, my uncle has been teaching me about them, plus I have a bee suit. Anyway, I drove the truck to that idiotic Porter Bowl and parked it in the orange grove across the street. The smell of citrus made me remember that awful night, so I became more determined to hurt them."

"You said hurt them, not kill them?" Kelly inquired.

"I wanted them to feel pain, not die. I didn't really kill them; the bees killed them."

"Okay, then what happened?" snapped Dwayne.

"I filled up a large fountain drink cup with undiluted queen bee *pheromone*. I dribbled drops all along the way into the stadium. It was halftime, so I waited outside the Panther's locker room. As the marching band left the field, the players came rushing out of the locker room, including Kurt, who came face to face with me. His was shocked to see me. He probably thought I was going to cause a scene and embarrass him during the Porter Bowl. He yelled at me, 'What do *you* want, Bea?' I told him that I just wanted to wish him luck. He said, 'Whatever Bea, I got to go. I'm the hero.' Then I screamed, 'No Kurt, you're the zero!' Then I took the lid off the cup and splashed it into Kurt's face and helmet, drenching his jersey too. He got really mad and screamed, 'You bitch, you crazy freakin' bitch! I'll deal with you later, and it ain't gonna be as good as last time!' I told him, 'Oh, you think it was good, it was ten seconds of bad, Kurt!' He flipped me off in my face, then ran out on the field. I went back to the truck, released the bees, and then returned to the stadium. I watched the bees attack Kurt, and the ambulance take him away. I felt guilty about not feeling guilty about Kurt's suffering. Then I left the bleachers. The swarm had returned to their hives and I drove the truck home."

"What happened with Tommy Wheeler?" asked Kelly. "Come outside and tell us."

"No, Kelly," she snapped. "I'm confessing, so how about letting it rest until I'm ready to come outside."

"Okay, honey, please, just tell us what happened next."

Beatrix continued in a softer tone, "So, late that night, I drove my car to his house. The biggie-size jerk left the windows down in his car. I snuck up and pitched a large cup of the queen juice into his car, splashing it on the steering wheel, across the dash, and onto the driver's seat. I'd heard that all of dead Kurt's friends would be at Allison's the next morning, so I drove the truck out to an almond orchard on the way to her house. I dressed in my bee suit and waited. I saw Tommy's car racing toward me and released the bees. It's amazing how they got to him speeding in his car."

"Yeah, right, amazing. Now what about Cory?" questioned the detective.

"You sure are pushy detective. Is that how you get your wife to have sex with you?"

"Real cute, Beatrix. What about Cory?" he snarled.

"Well, that afternoon I drove over to Cory's and hid the truck in the grove next to his house. I thought about leaving until I smelled the oranges, and I got all pissed off again. I watched through the trees, waiting for them to come home. I had planned on dumping some *pheromone* into Cory's car when I saw his dad leave. Then I saw Cory walk outside and turn on the hot tub. When he went back into the house, I circled around, came up from the back, and dumped a bottle of *swarm lure* concentrate into the tub. Heading back to the truck, I trickled a trail of it on the ground. I waited until I saw him get into the tub. Then I released the bees. I couldn't watch though."

"Oh, honey, you need some help," Kelly said with compassion. "Come out, and we'll get you some trauma counseling, and under the circumstances, I'm certain the court will be lenient."

"I doubt that," snapped Beatrix. "Not after my bees killed the cherished heroes of this dumb little town. Everyone knows the monsters would've never been punished. Their dads would've seen to that."

"The jury will consider all that you've been through, with the death of your parents. Please come out before Detective Ketcher breaks down the door."

Beatrix became silent, contemplating what to do.

Dwayne stood impatiently, wanting to kick the screen in, and arrest her. He was relieved to hear her confess, but now he just needed to arrest her, and take her to the station to record her confession.

"Come on, Beatrix, open the door, and let us help you," said Kelly.

"Okay," replied Beatrix. She reached over to unlock the screen door.

Dwayne and Kelly breathed a sigh of relief.

Instead of unlocking the door, Beatrix reached down and picked up a spray wand attached to a pressurized plastic tank full of pure queen bee *pheromone*. She lifted up the spray gun and blasted the chemical through the screen door, drenching them both.

Ketcher drew his weapon. Kelly screamed.

A breeze scattered the scent. The bees in the oak tree and in the opened hives became agitated, unclustered, and took flight.

The detective, dripping with *swarm lure*, pointed his gun inside the house and yelled, "You little psycho, give yourself up!" Bees swarmed all about him. He swatted at them, as he continued pointing the gun.

"Stay calm, Dwayne! Lower your gun, and don't move!" yelled Kelly.

The detective froze in a stance and slowly lowered his gun. He tried to see through the dripping pheromone burning his eyes.

Beatrix set down the sprayer, strolled to her bedroom, and picked up her suitcase. She stepped out the back door, walked around to the front of the house, and stood, watching the bees massing on the bodies of Detective Ketcher and Kelly.

The detective radioed for help. As he did, he turned, and saw Beatrix. He cautiously raised his gun and pointed it at her.

"Don't move and they won't sting," Beatrix said wryly. "Don't fire the gun either. They don't like loud noises. It makes them angry. Remember, if *one* stings, they *all* sting."

"She's right." agreed Kelly. "Just stay calm. Help is on its way."

"Pretend you're a tree. Bees don't sting trees," quipped Beatrix. "Oh, and Kelly, thanks for wanting to help me—but I got to go."

The detective gradually lowered his gun. He and Kelly stood motionless. Thousands of excited bees engulfed their bodies crawling about them, seeking their queen.

Beatrix threw her suitcase in the car, got in, and drove away. She glanced into the rearview mirror through the driveway's clouding dust, and saw two dark, morphing statues of bees standing in front of the house. She turned out of the dirt drive onto two-lane highway 65. She headed south, and then west.

Arriving at the bus station in Delano, twenty miles away, she parked her car a block away from the terminal. In front of an old, run down bar, she left her car windows down and the keys in the ignition. At the bus station, she sat her suitcase down and called her insurance company, reporting her car stolen in Tulare, thirty miles north. The authorities would assume she was fleeing to San Jose. She bought a one way ticket to Los Angeles and hopped on the bus just as it released its airbrakes to leave. Once situated in her seat, she unwrapped two pieces of berry bubble gum and put them in her mouth. The bus headed south on highway 99. She chewed her gum, staring out the window at the lack of scenery.

As the bus climbed through the mountain pass on I-5, known as the Grapevine, Beatrix left her seat and made her way to the restroom at the back of the bus. She washed the gel out of her spiked hair, combing it straight back. She scrubbed off all of her churlish make-up, and after putting on a pink conservative top and blue jeans, she returned to her seat.

On the downhill side of the Grapevine, passing through Valencia, not far from LA, Beatrix peered out the window and saw countless beehives placed in an orange grove alongside the freeway. She thought about Los Angeles, a sprawling overpopulated people-hive and hoped she could vanish there amongst the drones of humanity. She smirked, stretched the purple gum out of her mouth, and then twirled it back in.

A Pirate's Fate

From the novel: A Pirate's Fate

"Eric! Eric!! Where is that boy? Sailor—find Eric, and tell him that the captain wants him at the deck rail—amidships, portside!"

"Aye, aye, Captain!" sounded off a nearby sailor cranking a rigging winch.

"Oh—and sailor, tell him not to dally. He must report to me immediately!

"Aye, sir!" hollered the sailor, dashing across the deck.

Captain Hartwell Steed peered again through his extended brass spyglass. For another arresting moment, the stately captain scrutinized the bizarre sight on the dock, dead ahead of his advancing ship.

His ship, the Angelica, a clipper with three masts, sailed into the emerald waters of the bay, propelled by a flight of square-rigged sails, each bellied stiff and gorging on the wind. With the wind jamming hard against the acres of sun-bleached ivory sailcloth, the spirited ship skimmed over the water like a seabird gliding on an ocean breeze.

The Angelica manifested a glimpse of glory! Her masts, spars, and upper hull glistened a pearlescent white above the lower hull sheathed in polished copper. The gleaming brass jib and bowsprit mast, rigged with triangular staysails, protruded from the bow like the horn on a mythical unicorn.

Affixed to her bow, the ship bore an ornate wooden figurehead of an angel, whose folded wings and long furrowed robe flowed around both sides of the bow. With arms extended and palms up, the magnificent carving peered toward the heavens, posed in a humble state of supplication. The angelic figurehead bestowed a sense of comfort to the sailors, who were far from their homes and families on an unpredictable voyage.

The ship had set sail from her homeport of San Francisco on January 15th, 1888. After six months at sea, she neared her last port of destination.

The lively island harbor bustled with ships of various sizes from numerous nations. Some sailed in or out of the tropical bay, while others, moored at the quay docks, loaded and unloaded cargo. A burgeoning town of mercantile shops and dwellings peeked out from beyond the wharf of sea scrubbed warehouses, shipyards, and saloons.

After two weeks of loading wares, provisions, and passengers, the Angelica would sail directly for her homeport.

The dignified captain raised his telescope to his right eye, and gawked once more at the striking scene. He then lowered it and muttered again, "Where is that boy?" as his eyes searched the decks from stem to stern.

He thought of young Eric, and the benefit to the boy of witnessing this sight. He thought of his pledge to Eric's father. The trustworthy Captain earnestly embraced his oath.

With a clack, he pressed the telescoping tubes back together, then stashed the spyglass into his right peacoat pocket. From his left pocket, he produced a scrimshaw pipe carved from whale ivory with a cherry wood bowl. He packed it with a plug of sweet tobacco, put a flame to it, then puffed it into a smoldering red glow. As he leaned his tall sea-worn frame comfortably against the deck rail, he raked back his wind swept gray hair, and stroked downward his mustache and beard. Waiting for Eric, he puffed contently at his pipe while gazing out at the scenery bordering the bay. The brilliant colors of the tropical flowers: red, pink, yellow, and white commingled with the dense green vegetation of the landscape.

"Captain, did you call for me?" asked the sprightly lad of twelve panting from his nimble dash starting at the orlop deck at the bottom of the ship, through the bulkheads, up the ladders, out the top hatch, across the quarterdeck and maindeck, to the portside rail.

"Yes, I did son! The way you monkey aloft in the masts and spars, I imagined that you had plummeted overboard unnoticed." He then asked calmly, "Where did you happen to be?" The Captain endeavored to be firm, not stern, with the boy.

"I was down in the orlop deck, sir, helping a mate make ready for the new stores coming aboard. Did you need me for something else, Captain?"

"Good spot to help Eric, as we will readily load the stores aboard. Also, you did a fine job polishing the brass on the spokes of the wheel and on the trim of the compass's binnacle box—they look splendid!"

"Thank you, sir!" Eric beamed with pride.

"Son—I hailed you on deck to behold an interesting sight, on the dock, dead ahead. I have already seen it through my spyglass. In a few minutes we'll be alongside of it, as the ship sails into her mooring berth."

The Captain placed two fingers over the bowl of his pipe, then drew in two short drags of air, stoking the embers. He looked at Eric and silently marveled at the resemblance between the boy and his father, Richard.

They looked akin for sure; the boy was unmistakably the youthful version of his father. Eric had camel color, shoulder length hair, combed straight back and parted down the middle, as well as fair skin with a few freckles across his blunt nose.

He had the same broad face and blue eyes, the chin with the small cleft, and the dimples accompanying the wide smile. The youngster even radiated with his father's same cheerful nature.

The Captain thought of Richard, a shipmate on many shared voyages, and a long time friend. For a moment, he reflected on the humble request that Richard had asked of him.

Just over four years ago, while in his homeport of San Francisco, the Captain eagerly accepted an invitation to Richard's house for supper. He was in need of good terra firma food, accompanied by earthy conversation with a solid-ground friend.

He walked briskly from his vessel moored at the waterfront, to Richard's house in the heart of the city. In rhythm with his stride, he whistled a lively sea chantey, then softly sang the chorus, "The sloshing sea I still adore, yet cheery to be on the steady shore!"

The starry night was chilly with a bothersome breeze. To keep warm, he buttoned up his wool greatcoat, flipped up the collar around his neck, and placed one of his hands snugly in the pocket. In the other hand, he carried a special package.

Upon arriving at his friend's modest home, he gave the door a lively rap. As the door swung open, he was shocked to see Richard so pale and gaunt. As they greeted one another, he noticed Richard's handshake was weak and clammy, and his movements feeble. Bouncing behind his father, eight-year-old Eric bubbled with excitement.

The Captain gave the boy a brisk rub on the head, then the package. Eric tore into the wrappings, as if it were Christmas morn, his eyes wide with anticipation.

Despite the alarming appearance of Richard, the Captain took great joy in the delight of young Eric over the exotic gifts from ports around the globe. The gleeful youngster sat on the floor, absorbed with his toys, while the two friends exchanged salutations and pleasantries.

As Richard prepared to serve a supper of bread and stew, Eric set the small round wooden table with plates, bowls, cups, and spoons.

As they dined, Richard talked about his shore job as a stevedore, and all the hearsay about their mutual friends and acquaintances. The Captain told of his rollicking adventures on his last sea voyage. The lad sat enthralled, seized by the Captain's regaling sea stories.

As the conversation drifted off into current events and activities of the city, Eric cleared off the table, then retreated to the kitchen to clean up. The Captain and Richard sipping brandy, serenely smoked their pipes, filling the room with redolent smoke.

As the chat between the two friends abated, Richard became somber.

Seeing Richard's pensive manner, the Captain asked, "Richard, I know there is something weighing heavily on your mind. Please tell me what it is, and how I can help."

The Captain took a prolonged puff on his pipe as Richard contemplated his reply.

After a few moments and a heavy sigh, Richard leaned toward the Captain and spoke softly, so that Eric, washing dishes, could not hear him. "When you arrived this evening, your face revealed that you perceived my condition. Steed—I am a very sick man. My disease is rapidly advancing. There is little hope. I will live but a few more months. As you know, my sweet wife died giving birth to Eric, and we have no other family. I gave up the sea to be here for my son. He is a good boy, conscientious, and obedient. I know my ailing health will get the best of me soon, and I am concerned about his well being." Richard paused as he gathered his thoughts.

Listening patiently, his eyes focused on Richard, Captain Steed took a sip of brandy and waited for him to continue.

"Steed, I would like to ask you—upon my death—if you will…" a grievous lump in Richard's throat stopped him mid sentence. He breathed a deep, calming breath, swallowed hard, then commenced, "Upon my death—will you care for Eric like a son—and teach him the craft of a sailor?"

The Captain felt honored that his friend would make this request. Sympathy and compassion welled up inside him.

"As you know Richard, living the life of a seaman, I have loved many a woman, but never married, even though one of my greatest desires was to have a family—especially a son."

"I've always known that Steed. My son thinks the world of you and desires whole heartedly to be a sailor, and I know and trust the depth of your goodness. My dearest friend, upon my death, with your consent—I wish for you to gain custody of Eric."

The Captain looked intently into the tear-filled, entreating eyes of Richard. He contemplated deeply for a moment, then responded in his Captain's firm voice of resolve.

"I will not deny your request, Richard—nor will I deny myself the innumerable blessings to be received, and I will definitely not deny your young lad a good life. I pledge to you Richard, my dearest friend, in case of your demise, that I will care for Eric, as if he were my own son. I will properly feed, clothe, and shelter him. I will protect him from harm. I will continue his schooling, and raise him to become a good man. I will be kind to the boy, and bequeath to him my legacy of the sea. Richard, I will live out this pledge. You have my solemn oath."

Finished with the cleaning, Eric entered the room, picked up one of his new toys, and sat at the table, between the two men. Richard took a prolonged look at his son. He smiled lovingly at his boy, reached out his left hand, ruffled the lad's hair, and gave him a reassuring wink. He then reached across the small, round table and placed his hand upon the forearm of the Captain, "Thank you, Steed. Peace fills my soul. My burden has been lifted."

The sailing master's hollers of, "Heave-to, tars—heave-to," and his crew's clamor to lag the ship brought Captain Steed's mind back to the approaching scene upon the dock and the lesson for Eric.

The mariners scurried about the decks and up on the yardarms; yanking on the sheets and halyards; furling in the mainsails, topsails, topgallants, royals, skysails, and moonrakers. The experienced crew knew exactly how to dock the ship. The coxswain steered the Angelica with precision through the channel, past the jetty, and into the harbor. Captain Steed had trained them well.

From the portside rail, the Captain pointed the ivory mouthpiece of his pipe, toward the churning wake waters of the ship. Eric glanced at the rippling water, seeing, to his delight, a playful porpoise leaping heartily alongside the ship.

"Eric," said the Captain, regaining the attention of the boy.

"Aye, Captain."

"Son, over the past four years, I have taught you much about the sea, and sailing this ship upon her."

In response to the Captain's serious demeanor, Eric's face instantly transformed from a beaming smile to an earnest regard for the Captain.

"You have learned to follow orders, work hard, and be an integral part of my crew. You are an enthusiastic pupil and quick to learn. You are willing to help anyone, anytime, anywhere without complaint. I am very proud of you; you are becoming a fine sailor.

"Thank you, sir!"

"What you are about to witness upon the dock ahead Eric, is a lesson about life. It is about the choices you make and the people you choose to befriend. There is an unscrupulous temptation that can befall a sailor. The lust for wealth can become irrepressible, causing a man to cut all his moral restraints, leading to the murder of his civility and the release of his savagery."

At "savagery," the bow of the ship reached the brink of the intriguing scene.

He raised his arm and pointed with his pipe, "Take a look son, take a long, hearty look!"

As the ship glided gracefully toward the sight, Eric fixed his attention on the peculiar scene posed at the end of the dock.

Upon the dock, he beheld a gallows. The builders had fastened a sizeable pedestal to the wooden dock with large bolts. An eight-foot tall iron post stretched up from the pedestal, with a wooden cross beam attached to the top.

A corpse hung from the gallows.

The attire of the dead man was elegant, though weathered. His chained hands hung at his sides; his shoe-clad feet were bound together.

A form-fitting cage of metal straps enveloped his head and body. The cage hung from a thick chain anchored to the crossbeam.

A glossy black raven perched on a strap on top of the head cage. The bird tipped down, poking its beak between the face rings, pecking at the pulpous eyes of the decomposing corpse. The bird cawed loudly, proclaiming its sovereignty at the head of the feast. Screeching seagulls, aroused by the fetid stench, flew in erratic patterns overhead, soaring and swooping about the scene. Three squawking gulls quarreled as they sat, wing to wing, on the crossbeam above the raven. Two more, routing about the dock, shrieked and flapped their wings as they scuffled over a shoestring dangling from one of the dead man's boots.

The pale, lifeless cadaver swayed in the breeze, back and forth like a pendulum in a grandfather clock. A hand painted sign nailed to the end of the crossbeam faced the sea, obvious to passing ships. It read;

Pirate
Jonathan Bastell Meen
June 18, 1888

Astonishment, mixed with intrigue, captured young Eric. As the noble ship glided by the ignoble scene, Eric scrambled aft toward the stern, positioning himself in front of the dangling remains.

The Captain stared at the corpse and the sign. His crew had once rescued this man from the intemperate ravages of the sea.

All of the sailors on deck paused in their duties to gawk at the passing spectacle. Sailors below deck peered curiously out of portholes. The ship entered total quietude, except for the sonance of her flapping sailcloth and the purling water of her wake. The silence of the men was not an expression of reverence for the dead. The harsh scene merely prompted in each sailor a stillness of inward reflection, reinforcing his soul with a resolution for the pursuit of righteousness nursed with an intense fear of justice.

Eric scampered over the maindeck and quarterdeck, up to the poopdeck, coming to a standstill at the taffrail of the stern. He gawked at the hanging man as the ship slid silently past the scene. He stared with wonder until the ghastly exhibition faded from view.

He raced back over the decks to amidships to find Captain Steed casually puffing his pipe.

"Captain—Captain Steed—why was that dead man hanging from a gallows, in a suit of metal straps? Was he really a pirate, as painted on the sign?"

Before answering, the Captain paused to puff his pipe, making certain that Eric was totally attentive. His abeyance added to Eric's suspense.

"Here is the lesson young Eric—hear me well! This punishment; this distinctive sort of spectacle—a dead man hanging from a gibbet, exhibited blatantly on a dock—is only exacted on a man for one crime. Simply put, Eric, this man, Jonathan Meen, was a pirate."

"I saw a pirate! A real pirate! Wow!" exclaimed Eric.

"Yes, you saw a pirate—a real dead pirate! As you have witnessed Eric, there is no wealth, no romance, nor prestige afforded a man without dignity, hanging dead from a gallows. His corpse will soon rot in this sweltering climate; then it will parch in the scorching sun. The torrential rains will lash at it, the bitter cold will pry at it, and the gluttonous birds will peck at it, until all that remains in the metal head straps and body harness, is the pirate's weathered skeleton. For years, his bare bones will hang from the gibbet, as a visual warning to all sailors who might entertain rambunctious thoughts of entering into the thievery and debauchery of piracy."

The wise Captain concluded his lesson with a strong admonition. "Son, the moral of this teaching is: Regardless of the circumstances of your life," Eric was wide-eyed, hanging on every word with curiosity and interest, "whether you are suffering from pain or grief; whether you wish for gain or recovery of loss; whether you are obsessed by hate and revenge; whether you are fleeing from iniquities, or craving excitement, whether you lust for fame and fortune; Eric, you must forego the life of a pirate, otherwise you will meet a pirate's fate, the same end as Jonathan Meen, the infamous pirate—Captain One Ear."

Eric furrowed his brow and looked confidently with resolve, straight into the soul-searching eyes of Captain Steed.

"Never Captain, never will I become a pirate!" promised the virtuous young lad.

"I trust and believe in your goodness, Eric. You will mature to be a good man like your father."

"I'll be like him, and like you too, Captain!"

Captain Steed smiled with pride.

As the ship slid slowly into its berth, the Captain said, "Well, we've got a ship to moor!"

"Aye, aye, Captain," said Eric cheerfully as he bolted off.

"Eric! Eric!!" hollered the Captain.

Eric slid to a stop, and looked back at the beaming Captain.

"I am proud of you, son!"

Eric grinned, then hustled off to help dock the ship.

THE CHUCKLING KITE

T HE AUTHOR SAT in a low, green folding chair on the beach, and proofread his soon to be published book of short stories. He swirled, sniffed, and sipped a glass of Edna Valley pinot noir. The shining sun and a cool breeze argued over whether or not he should wear his sweatshirt. After a ten-minute debate of hot air and cold remarks—the breeze won.

He looked up from his writings to see a whale grazing close to shore. He also noticed a father and his young son at the edge of the surf. The father had a red kite. His son, about seven years old, stood close by.

The father gripped the string tied to the kite, as his beaming son bounced and splashed in the shallow, surging tide; his hands poised to clap at all the fun. The reluctant kite lay lifeless in the sand, like the pile of seaweed next to it.

The man walked a short distance away from the kite until its string tightened. He then jerked and pulled on the string, hoping that the wind would snatch up the kite and introduce it to the sky. The wind could not convince it to socialize with anything but the sand.

He decided to add running to the jerking and pulling, which indeed created lift, but not much more than before. It shuttered, swooped left, then right, before it crashed upside down near several crabs scooting sideways to get away.

He stomped back to the kite, and flipped it over ready for take-off. He smiled sheepishly at his son, then bolted off running again. It did just as it had done before, but added a loop-de-loop before smashing into the sand. He tried again as a perfect formation of eleven pelicans flew over. He tried again as a surfer caught a wave and rode it all the way in. He tried again as a kid slid by on a skim board, and again as a lifeguard in a Jeep drove by.

Being a good father, he hoped to show his son the awesome thrill of holding onto a thrashing kite as the wind tries and tries to tug it out of your hand. The dad became exasperated and plopped down in the sand beyond the reach of the sea. The boy had long lost interest. He was playing with a little shovel and bucket in the surf that licked at his ankles like an excited puppy.

The kite was lying next to the dad, when a little breeze caused it to shutter. It looked as if it were chuckling at the father. The author thought if the chuckling kite could talk, it would teach the dad something very important about kites, and say, "I can't fly unless I have a tail. It's simple. You take a rag and cut it into strips. Then tie the strips together with knots, and tie it to my bottom. It will balance me out. No more shutter, swoop, or loop-de-loop. With a great enough ball of string, I will soar beyond the clouds."

"Thank you," the father would humbly reply, "I didn't know that. The next time my son and I are at the beach, you shall surely have a tail."

The father sat in the sand and marveled at the joy of his son playing in the surf.

The author put away his manuscript, the bottle of wine, and the wineglass in his beach-bag, and then gazed out at the horizon seducing the blushing sun to draw nearer. The sun peeped out from behind a cloud, then scooched in closer. The father, his son, and the kite were now silhouettes, as well as a couple holding hands walking their dog, and two guys tossing a Frisbee.

As the setting sun cast an avenue of glimmering gold upon

Faces in the Fog

the sea, the time came for the father and son to leave the beach. As they trudged across the sand toward the parking lot, the father held the kite in one hand and with his other, he held the small hand of his son. The son carried his bucket with the little shovel inside. The father looked at his son as the son looked up at his father. Both smiled.

Available at your local bookseller!

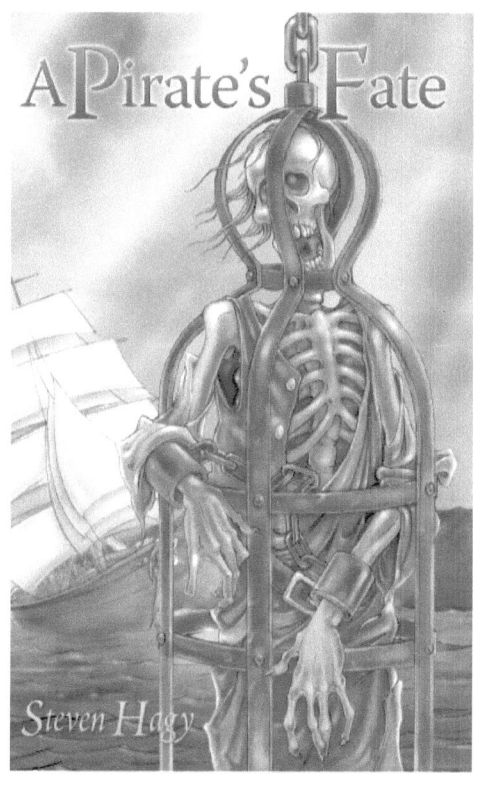

Pirates and clipper ships are the setting for this seafaring story about the turbulent life of sailor Jonathan Bastell Meen. Born the son of a wealthy shipping magnate, Meen sails to exotic ports around the world. When he's not at sea, he lives in an opulent chateau, until evil deeds and catastrophic events rob him of all that he loves. Overcome with debilitating grief, savage jealousy, and rage, he leads a brash mutiny and becomes the captain of the brawny Mendocino. He sinks further into the atrocities of piracy, pillaging ships of the Pacific with his band of cutthroats, until a string of disasters and fateful consequences force him to fight for his own survival.

www.ingramcontent.com/pod-product-compliance
Lightning Source LLC
Chambersburg PA
CBHW022009010726
47494CB00003B/964